BURDEN OF BLOOD

SHADOW OF THE SHIELD

ZACHARY STEINKE

THE VERIDIAN LUMINARY

PROLOGUE – THREE MOONS RISING

The three moons of Lunara hung in perfect alignment across the night sky, a celestial event not witnessed for generations. White Calanthir gleamed like polished bone, casting its pale light over the Thunder Plains. Green Harmony pulsed with life-giving radiance, while black Morvak loomed ominously, its shadow-kissed surface absorbing more light than it reflected.

At the Neutral Stones, seven towering monoliths arranged in a perfect circle, two groups approached from opposite directions. From the west came the Shieldbearers, their imposing forms silhouetted against the plains, their steel-reinforced leather armor adorned with their clan's distinctive shield emblem. From the east approached the Moongazers, their movements fluid and graceful, adorned with silver ornaments that caught the moonlight, their faces painted with sacred symbols.

Artak Stormshield stood tall at the center of the stone circle, his massive frame dwarfing most of his clansmen. Scars crisscrossed his weathered green skin, each with a story of battles survived and honor defended. His eyes, amber and piercing, fixed on the approaching human delegation.

Opposite him, Orion Skycaller of the Moongazers carried himself with quiet dignity. His silver-streaked dark hair was braided with trinkets representing each cycle he had served as chief. The traditional blue spirals of his people decorated his face, freshly painted for this momentous occasion.

The air between them crackled with centuries of distrust and bloodshed.

"Under the three moons, we meet as equals," Artak's voice rumbled like distant thunder. "For too long, our peoples have stained these plains with each other's blood."

Orion nodded solemnly. "Too many graves mark our shared history, Chief Artak."

Behind each leader, warriors and elders shifted uncomfortably. Generations of hatred could not be easily set aside, even for this night.

"Through this union between my son, Kargoth, and your daughter, Skye," Artak continued, raising a ceremonial cup carved from thunderwood, "we can end this feud between our clans and perhaps begin to heal the wounds between orcs and humans. Orion raised his own cup, carved from moonstone that seemed to capture and amplify the light of Calanthir. "May they bring peace to the Thunder Plains," he intoned. "Where armies have failed, perhaps a marriage can succeed."

The two leaders drank deeply, sealing their pact beneath the watching moons.

Not everyone present shared their optimism. Among the Shieldbearers, Grun Blackfist spat quietly into the grass. "Diluting our blood with humans," he muttered to those nearby. "Artak grows weak in his old age."

Across the circle, Lady Elara of the Moongazers kept her face carefully neutral, though her knuckles whitened around her staff. She had lost two brothers to orc raids. Now her niece would be given to them willingly.

Kargoth Stormshield stood a pace behind his father, his expression stoic despite the weight of destiny settling on his shoulders. His shoulders, broad and muscled beneath unadorned armor, spoke of many battles and rigorous training in the Shieldbearer traditions. He caught sight of Skye standing opposite him, slender, light-haired, with eyes that reflected the green light of Harmony. Their gazes locked across the circle of ancient stones.

"The Blackhands will never accept this peace," Kargoth said quietly to his father when the ceremonial words had ended. "Jalak Bloodhand would sooner die than break bread with humans."

Artak nodded grimly. "And the people of Riverstone may prove equally stubborn. Some wounds run too deep for a single union to heal." He clasped his son's shoulder. "But it is a beginning."

Orion approached with Skye at his side. She moved with the grace of her people, but there was steel in her spine and a healer's calculating assessment in her eyes as she studied her future husband.

"The moons align but once in a generation," Orion said. "Let us hope the alliance we forge tonight lasts longer than their conjunction."

Above them, the three moons watched impassively as orc and human cautiously began to mingle. Unnoticed by the gathering, a single shooting star streaked across the night sky, directly between white Calanthir and black Morvak.

CHAPTER ONE

A DIVIDED REFLECTION

Today is the day that I will show the entire clan I am a true orc and I belong here. The first light of dawn painted the eastern sky in hues of amber and gold, casting long shadows across the Shieldbearer encampment as the aroma of the first morning cooking fires began to mingle with with the cool air. Most of the clan still slept, their dreams undisturbed by the day's coming challenges. But not Decklan Stormshield.

He moved through the training grounds with deliberate precision, sweat dripping off his body, his breathing controlled despite the exertion. The wooden practice shield strapped to his left arm felt like an extension of himself as he pivoted, blocked an imaginary strike, and countered with a measured thrust of his training sword.

Step, block, strike. Step, block, strike.

The rhythm was familiar, comforting. Here, alone in the quiet of early morning, Decklan could focus solely on perfecting the form his mother taught him without the weight of expectations and sideways glances that followed him through the camp.

He paused mid-sequence, catching sight of his reflection in a still pool of water nearby. The face that stared back at him was neither fully orc nor fully human – a constant reminder of his divided heritage. His skin was a tanned bronze rather than the green-gray of full-blooded orcs, his features less pronounced. The slight tusks that protruded from his lower jaw were modest compared to those of his clanmates. Only his amber eyes and powerful build marked him clearly as his father's son.

Decklan's jaw tightened. Today was the annual Shieldbearer combat tournament, his opportunity to prove himself worthy of his father's name. To show the clan that despite his mixed blood, he was a true Shieldbearer.

"Your face ain't going to fight for you, want me to fetch a dress and a crown?"

Grom's voice broke through Decklan's thoughts. He turned to see his friend approaching with Krella Bloodfury close behind, both already dressed in training leathers.

"Some of us don't need beauty sleep," Decklan replied with a half-smile, grateful for the distraction from his own reflection.

Grom Wiseblood was as pure-blooded an orc as any in the clan, stocky and powerful, with prominent tusks and dark eyes that missed nothing. As the son of Gar'zul, the clan's respected shaman, he carried himself with the confidence that came from unquestioned belonging. He tossed a practice sword toward Decklan, who caught it one-handed.

"Thought you might want a moving target for once," Grom said, unsheathing his own training blade. "Tournaments tonight. Better make sure those human reflexes of yours can keep up."

Krella rolled her eyes, adjusting the leather bracers on her forearms. "Ignore him. He's just worried you'll embarrass him in front of the elders again." She was taller than most female orcs, with red hair braided tightly against her scalp and intricate tattoos marking her achievements in hunting and combat.

"That was one time," Grom protested, but his tusked grin betrayed his good humor.

Decklan settled into a ready stance; shield angled forward. "Then let's see if you've improved since last year."

They circled each other on the packed earth of the training grounds. Grom moved with the characteristic weight and power of an orc warrior, while Decklan's stance was lighter, more fluid, a blend of the techniques his father taught him and something uniquely his own.

Grom struck first, a powerful overhead blow that Decklan caught on his shield. The thump reverberated up his arm, but he held firm, twisting to the side and countering with a quick thrust that Grom barely parried.

"Not bad," Grom admitted, disengaging. "For someone with such skinny arms."

Something in his tone, or perhaps it was the pointed remark at Decklan's less orcish build, struck a nerve. Decklan felt a familiar heat rising in his chest, that mixture of insecurity and defiance that had been his constant companion since childhood.

Their practice bout intensified, the rhythmic clack of training weapons punctuating the morning air. Decklan found himself fighting with increasing aggression, pushing forward when he should have been patient, striking harder than necessary for a friendly spar.

When Grom made another quip about Decklan's "human features" giving him an unfair advantage in visibility without tusks to obstruct his view, something snapped. Decklan feinted left, then drove forward with his shield, slamming into Grom with more force than intended. The impact sent his friend stumbling backward, and Decklan pressed the advantage, sweeping Grom's legs with a vicious kick that dropped him heavily to the ground. Before Grom could recover, Decklan was on him, practice blade at his throat, shield pinning one arm.

"Yield," Decklan growled, breathing hard. The word came out harsher than he meant, revealing the frustration beneath.

Grom's eyes widened, not with fear but surprise at the sudden intensity. "I yield, by Gallant's shield," he muttered, then added more quietly, "Ease up, Decklan."

Grom accepted the help, rising to his feet with a grunt. "Remind me not to joke about your pretty face before the tournament," he replied, but the usual humor in his voice had flattened.

Krella stepped between them, her keen eyes assessing Decklan. "That was more Bloodfist than Shieldbearer," she said quietly, referring to the more aggressive orc clan known for their brutal combat style. "You alright?"

An uncomfortable silence settled over them, broken by the sound of approaching footsteps. Decklan turned to see his mother, Skye, walking toward them, a basket of herbs cradled in her arms. Her long, blond hair was braided intricately in the Moongazer style, small silver charms woven throughout that caught the morning light.

"So this is where you disappeared to," she said, her voice gentle but knowing. "Gallant's blessing on your training."

Decklan nodded stiffly, conscious of how quickly he distanced himself from his friends, as if caught doing something wrong. ""I brought some healing herbs," Skye continued, setting her basket down. "For after training." She surveyed the three warriors with a healer's practiced eye, lingering on Grom's reddened throat and Decklan's tense posture.

"We're fine," Decklan said too quickly. "Just finishing up."

Skye's expression revealed she understood more than he wanted her to. "There's no shame in needing healing, Decklan. Even your father accepts my remedies after council meetings."

Grom cleared his throat. "I wouldn't mind some of that throat-soothing tea you make, Lady Skye. Seems I've... strained my voice this morning."

Decklan shot him a grateful look as Skye smiled and began sorting through her herbs.

"You three should come to the central fire tonight," she said, handing Grom a small bundle of dried leaves. "The moons align in a special configuration, a powerful omen, according to my clan tradition."

"We have our own omens, Mother," Decklan said, returning his practice weapons to the rack with perhaps more force than necessary. "Shieldbearers look to Gallant for guidance, not to the moons."

A flicker of hurt crossed Skye's face, though she masked it quickly. "Of course. I only thought—"

"Sounds interesting to me," Krella interrupted, stepping forward. "I'd like to hear about these Moongazer traditions."

Skye's smile returned, warm and grateful. "You're always welcome, Krella. All of you are." Her eyes lingered on Decklan, who avoided her gaze.

The camp horn sounded across the grounds, signaling the morning meal. Grom's eyes brightened at the prospect of food. "We should go. Can't fight on an empty stomach!"

As they gathered their things, Decklan noticed a commotion near the eastern edge of the camp. A small group of younger orcs had surrounded a boy, a half-orc like himself, but younger, perhaps only twelve summers. The boy's human features were more prominent than Decklan's own, making him an easier target.

"Look at the puny human," one of the bullies taunted, pushing the boy roughly. "Think you belong with real Shieldbearers?"

The younger half-orc stumbled but remained standing, his hand instinctively forming a fist. "I'm as much Shieldbearer as you," he replied, voice quavering but defiant. "My father fought in the Battle of Broken Ridge."

"And your mother decided to lay with a soft skin," another tormentor sneered, shoving the boy again. "Half-breed weakling."

Decklan was moving before he realized it, his body cutting through the morning air with silent purpose. Behind him, he heard Grom swear softly and Krella's quickened footsteps following.

"Enough," Decklan said, his voice low but carrying the unmistakable weight of command. He placed himself between the boy and his tormentors, shield arm positioned subtly to guard the younger half-orc.

The bullies froze, recognition dawning on their faces. The largest among them, Gorrak, son of one of the clan's senior warriors recovered quickly, straightening to his full height.

"We were just teaching the half-breed his place," Gorrak said, though he took a small step back. "No concern of yours."

Decklan's gaze hardened. "His place? And where would that be?"

"With the soft skins," Gorrak muttered, glancing at his friends for support. "Not pretending to be a true Shieldbearer."

Decklan stepped closer, close enough that Gorrak could see the amber flecks in his eyes. "I am the son of Kargoth Stormshield, and I say his place is here." His voice remained measured, but the implied threat was clear.

"The chief's son," Gorrak sneered, emboldened by his friends' presence. "Half-chief, more like."

In a movement too fast to follow, Decklan's hand shot out, gripping Gorrak's tunic. He didn't strike—he didn't need to. The controlled threat of violence was enough.

"If you question his place," Decklan said softly, "you question mine. And if you question mine..."You question my father's." Decklan completed the thought, his voice a dangerous whisper. "And questioning the Chief is not something wise warriors do. Is that understood?"

Gorrak's bluster faltered under Decklan's unwavering gaze. His friends had already begun backing away, suddenly finding great interest in the distant treeline.

"Understood," Gorrak muttered, avoiding Decklan's eyes.

Decklan released him with a slight push. "Good. Now go find something useful to do with your strength. The clan doesn't need warriors who prey on their own."

As the bullies scattered, Decklan turned to the young half-orc, who stared up at him with a mixture of awe and apprehension. The boy had Decklan's same dual features, not quite orc, not quite human. A familiar shadow that Decklan recognized all too well.

"Thank you," the boy said quietly, straightening his shoulders in an attempt to appear stronger than he felt.

Decklan knelt to eye level with the young half-orc. "What's your name?"

"Thorne. Thorne Strongbranch."

"Listen carefully, Thorne Strongbranch," Decklan said, keeping his voice low so only the boy could hear. "They'll always look for weakness, so never show it—even when you feel it." He tapped the center of the boy's chest. "Your strength isn't just in your arms or how orcish you look. It's here. Remember that."

The boy nodded solemnly, his expression brightening with determination. Decklan stood, noticing Krella watching him with an approving smile.

"That was well handled," she said as they walked toward the central fire.

"Was it?" Decklan glanced back at the boy, who was now walking with renewed confidence. "Or did I just teach him to hide who he truly is?"

Before Krella could answer, a hunting horn sounded from the eastern watchtower. Three long blasts followed by two short ones, the signal for returning scouts with urgent news. The camp immediately shifted into organized motion, warriors moving toward the central gathering area, others securing the perimeter.

"What now?" Grom asked, already moving toward the gathering crowd.

"Something's wrong," Decklan said, quickening his pace. "Those weren't scheduled patrols."

They arrived at the central fire as the scouts entered the camp. Three warriors, bloodied and exhausted, supported a fourth between them. The injured scout's armor was torn and dark with dried blood. Behind them, Decklan's father emerged from the chieftain's lodge, his imposing figure drawing all eyes. Kargoth Stormshield moved with deliberate authority, his scarred face impassive as he surveyed the returning party.

"Report," Kargoth commanded, his deep voice carrying across the suddenly silent camp.

The lead scout stepped forward, fist to chest in salute. "Chieftain. We found tracks in the eastern borderlands, unfamiliar markings, deliberately disguised. We followed them to Ravenshadow Pass." He paused, swallowing hard. "Blackhand clan markers, sir. And Bloodfist. Many of them, moving together."

A murmur rippled through the gathered Shieldbearers. Decklan felt his muscles tense. The Blackhand clan was known for its cunning brutality, the Bloodfist for their savage battle prowess. If they were moving together...

"How many?" Kargoth's face remained stone, but Decklan recognized the subtle shift in his father's stance, preparation for unwelcome news.

"Too many for a hunting party," the scout answered grimly. "Enough for war."

The camp erupted in urgent whispers. Decklan exchanged a sharp glance with Grom, whose face had darkened at the mention of Blackhand. The clan had killed his mother years ago in a border raid, the wound still fresh even after a decade.

"And the fourth scout?" Kargoth asked, nodding toward the injured warrior.

"Ambushed. They weren't simple scouts, Chief. These were trained killers."

Kargoth studied the injured man, then looked to Skye, who had already begun preparing healing herbs. She nodded once, the man would live.

"Council members, to my lodge. Now," Kargoth ordered. His eyes swept the crowd until they found Decklan's. For a brief moment, father and son locked gazes, a silent communication passed between them that Decklan couldn't fully decipher. Pride? Concern? Expectation?

"Decklan," Kargoth said, his voice carrying the weight of command. "Come with us."

Murmurs rippled through the gathered clan. Decklan felt a rush of conflicting emotions, pride at being included, anxiety at what that inclusion meant. He nodded once, his face carefully composed in imitation of his father's stoicism.

"The rest of you," Kargoth addressed the clan, "prepare the defenses. Double the patrols. No one leaves camp without my direct order."

As Kargoth turned toward the council lodge, Decklan felt Krella's hand briefly squeeze his arm.

"Be strong," she whispered. "This is your moment."

Grom's expression was darker. "Blackhands," he muttered, his voice thick with old hatred. "If they've come for war, let's give them one they won't survive."

Decklan met his friend's gaze steadily. "We don't know what they want yet."

"What they've always wanted," Grom replied bitterly. "Our blood."

With a final nod to his friends, Decklan followed his father's retreating form. The council lodge was the largest structure in the encampment, its entrance adorned with the shields of fallen chieftains, a reminder of the price of leadership. As Decklan ducked through the entrance, the smell of cedar smoke and aged leather enveloped him.

Inside, the clan's elders and war chiefs had already taken their positions in the circle. Gar'zul Wiseblood, Grom's father and the clan's shaman, sat at Kargoth's right, his weathered face grave beneath intricate facial tattoos. At Kargoth's left was an empty seat – meant for Decklan, he realized with a jolt of surprise.

Kargoth gestured to the place. "Sit."

Decklan moved to the seat, aware of the evaluating gazes following him. He sat with deliberate control, back straight, face impassive—mirroring his father's demeanor. The council lodge fell into expectant silence as Kargoth took his place at the head of the circle.

"You've heard the reports," Kargoth began without preamble. "Blackhand and Bloodfist clans moving together through our eastern borders. This is unprecedented."

Gar'zul's voice rumbled from deep in his chest. "Not entirely unprecedented, Chief. The Ghost's raid a decade ago showed similar coordination."

A tense silence followed the mention of "The Ghost," the mysterious figure behind the devastating attack that had claimed many Shieldbearer lives, including Grom's mother. Decklan noticed his father's hand tightened almost imperceptibly on the armrest of his chair.

"This is different," Kargoth replied. "The Ghost's raid was a single strike. This appears to be a sustained movement of forces."

Elder Varkus, his age evident in the silver streaks through his braided beard, leaned forward. "What do we know of their numbers?"

"Scouts estimate at least three hundred warriors," Kargoth answered. "Possibly more concealed in the deeper passes."

Murmurs of concern rippled through the council. The Shieldbearer clan could muster perhaps two hundred fighters at most.

"Why now?" asked Thulsa, one of the younger war chiefs. "The winter truce still holds until the next full moon."

Decklan found himself speaking before he'd consciously decided to. "Unless they don't plan to honor the truce at all."

All eyes turned to him, and he felt a momentary flash of doubt, but he continued. "No clan moves in force without purpose, especially during the winter truce."

Kargoth's expression hardened, his gaze sliding past Decklan to address the council. "The scout reports indicate at least three war bands moving in coordinated patterns. Blackhand stealth tactics."

Decklan cleared his throat. "Father, the timing seems deliberate. With the tournament approaching—"

"The tournament preparations continue as planned," Kargoth interrupted, not acknowledging Decklan's input. "We cannot show weakness or disrupt tradition without provocation."

Decklan fell silent, the dismissal stinging more sharply than any rebuke. The elder council members nodded in agreement with Kargoth, while Gar'zul cast a brief, sympathetic glance toward Decklan.

"We should consider," Gar'zul suggested, stroking his gray-streaked beard, "that their movements may coincide with the tournament deliberately. Many clans will have observers present, an ideal opportunity for them to gather intelligence on our defenses."

Kargoth nodded. "A valid point, Shaman. The very observation I was considering."

Decklan stiffened, recognizing his own thought echoed almost exactly through Gar'zul's mouth, and immediately accepted when it came from the older orc. He kept his expression neutral, though his knuckles whitened where they gripped his armrest.

The council meeting continued as the elders debated strategy, Decklan's attention sharpening when his father's deep voice cut through the discussions.

"We will proceed with caution," Kargoth declared. "Triple the border patrols, but discreetly. I want eyes on their movements without revealing our awareness."

Elder Varkus stroked his silver-streaked beard. "And if they approach during the tournament?"

"Then we show them the strength of Shieldbearers through wisdom, not spectacle," Kargoth declared, his voice carrying the weight of difficult decisions. "The tournament is hereby suspended until we better understand this threat."

A murmur of surprise rippled through the council. Tournaments were sacred tradition, rarely postponed for any reason.

"Instead," Kargoth continued, rising to his full imposing height, "I will dispatch three specialized scouting parties to gather precise intelligence on their movements and numbers. Elder Varkus, assemble your best trackers. Thulsa, your stealth warriors will monitor the eastern passes. Gar'zul, we'll need your shamanic sight to detect any magical deceptions they might employ."

The elders nodded with grim determination, recognizing the gravity of Kargoth's decision. Tradition would yield to survival.

"We've defended our borders for generations," Kargoth concluded, his scarred hand resting on his shield's emblem, "but we've done so through foresight as much as strength. Prepare the clan for possible conflict, but quietly. Let our enemies believe we remain ignorant of their approach."

Decklan watched his father's face, noting the almost imperceptible tightness around his eyes, a sign of concern that few would recognize. There was something more troubling Kargoth than he was willing to share with the council.

As the meeting concluded, Kargoth assigned tasks to each elder and war chief. When the others had filed out, Decklan rose to follow, only to be stopped by his father's voice.

"Stay, Decklan."

The command was soft but unmistakable. Decklan resumed his seat, carefully controlling his expression as Kargoth studied him across the now-empty council circle. The silence stretched between them, heavy with unspoken words.

"You spoke out of turn," Kargoth finally said.

Decklan straightened. "I spoke what I observed."

"And it was the correct observation." Kargoth's admission surprised Decklan. "But timing and manner matter in council. You must learn this if you are to lead someday."

The rare acknowledgment of Decklan's potential future leadership sent a flush of pride through him, quickly tempered by his father's next words.

"Your observations were sound," Kargoth continued, his voice softening slightly as he moved to stand by the central fire. "But a leader must know when to speak and when to listen. The council respects wisdom delivered with patience."

Decklan watched his father carefully, sensing there was more to this private audience than a lesson in council etiquette. "You believe this movement is more than coincidence."

Kargoth nodded, a flicker of approval crossing his features. "The Ghost's attack ten years ago began with similar movements. Coordinated. Deliberate." His hand unconsciously moved to the long scar across his face—a memento from that bloody day. "But this time, the patterns are different. More calculated."

"What aren't you telling the council?" Decklan asked, emboldened by the rare moment of candor.

Kargoth studied his son, weighing something in his mind before speaking. "Three days ago, a messenger arrived from the human settlement at Riverstone. They've observed similar movements from the north, Blackhand scouts where they shouldn't be."

CHAPTER TWO

TRACKS IN THE BORDERLANDS

The three moons hung in perfect alignment above the Shieldbearer camp, Calanthir's white light, Harmony's green glow, and Morvak's black shadow forming a celestial triangle that the elders claimed appeared only in times of great change. Instead of celebration drums that should have marked the tournament's eve, only the soft crackle of watchfires and hushed conversations filled the night air.

Decklan sat at the edge of the central fire, whittling a stick in his calloused hands. The tournament's postponement, unprecedented in his lifetime, had cast a shadow over the camp that even the brightest flames couldn't dispel. Warriors who should have been boasting of coming victories now checked weapons with grim determination, voices low as they discussed the mysterious tracks and ritual sites.

"There you are." Krella dropped beside him on the log, her muscular frame moving with easy grace. "Hiding because the tournament is cancelled?"

"Not hiding. Thinking."

"Dangerous pastime." She nudged his shoulder with hers. "Your mother's been looking for you."

Decklan glanced toward the main fire where Skye stood conversing with the clan's elders, her healing satchel ever-present at her side. Even after fifteen years with the Shieldbearers, she remained distinctly human, her herbs and gentle ways as much a part of her as breath.

"She'll find me eventually. She always does." He tucked the twig into his vest. "Did you need me for something?"

Krella's amber eyes reflected firelight. "Always. Especially for tomorrow. Grom's planning a hunting trip. Borderlands. Says the scouts spotted unusual tracks during their patrol."

"What kind of unusual?"

"The kind that makes the shaman's son curious." She shrugged. "You in?"

Decklan considered his obligations, training younger warriors, helping repair the eastern palisade, checking traplines. All tasks that could wait.

"Dawn?" he asked.

"Before it." Krella stood, offering her hand. "Now come back to the fire. You've earned one night without brooding."

Decklan took her hand, noting how easily her fingers interlaced with his. "I don't brood."

Her laugh rang bright against the night. "Tell that to someone who hasn't known you since we were cubs."

The eastern sky barely hinted at dawn when Decklan met Grom and Krella at the camp's edge. Dew silvered the grass, and mist clung to the valley floor beyond the palisade. Decklan adjusted his hunting knife and checked the small shield strapped to his back, a habit more than necessity for a simple hunting expedition.

"The Chief's Son arrives," Grom said, his tusks gleaming in a half-smile. "Ready to track something more challenging than rabbits or tournament opponents?"

"Depends what we're tracking," Decklan replied. "Krella mentioned unusual signs."

Grom nodded, suddenly serious. "Three days ago, eastern patrol. Found tracks that shouldn't be there."

"Blackhand or Bloodfist scouts?" Decklan asked, instantly alert. The neighboring clan had maintained an uneasy peace with the Shieldbearers for nearly five years, but border incursions weren't uncommon.

"Maybe." Grom shouldered his pack. "But they took efforts to hide their numbers. Clever efforts."

Krella adjusted her bow. "Too clever for Bloodfists. They prefer intimidation to subtlety."

"Which is why we're going to look," Grom said, "instead of reporting unconfirmed suspicions to your father." This last part directed at Decklan.

Decklan understood the implication. His father valued evidence over conjecture, another trait that sometimes earned Kargoth criticism from more traditional orcs who preferred action to deliberation. Some whispered it came from his human wife's influence, usually when they thought Decklan couldn't hear.

"Let's move," Decklan said, pushing away the thought. "I want a clear trail before the day heats up."

They slipped through the eastern gate where the night guard, a grizzled veteran named Krog, merely nodded as they passed. The Shieldbearer's territorial border lay three hours east, a natural boundary marked by a shallow river and limestone.

The trio moved through the misty landscape with practiced silence. Decklan took point, his mixed heritage granting him sharper eyesight in the pre-dawn gloom than his full-blooded companions. The grasslands gradually gave way to scattered groups of silver-barked trees whose leaves shimmered even in the faint light.

"There," Grom whispered after their third hour of travel, pointing toward a limestone outcropping that marked the clan's eastern border. "The tracks start near the crossing stones."

Decklan crouched at the riverbank, examining the damp earth. The shallow water burbled quietly, barely knee-deep at its center. What he saw troubled him immediately. Footprints, partially obscured, showed where someone had carefully brushed over their tracks, but not completely.

"These are deliberate," he murmured. "Someone wanted to hide their numbers."

Krella knelt beside him, her hunter's eyes narrowing. "Look at the depth. Heavy warriors, carrying equipment."

"But spaced to appear like a small hunting party," Decklan added. "Three or four at most."

Grom scanned the opposite bank. "The real number?"

Decklan studied the subtle impressions, the bent grass, the pattern of disturbed stones in the riverbed. "At least fifteen. Maybe twenty."

"Blackhands don't hide their strength," Krella said, voicing what they were all thinking. "They flaunt it."

"Bloodfists, then?" Grom suggested. The Bloodfist clan, known for their berserker warriors, occasionally probed Shieldbearer territory, though they typically approached from the north.

Decklan shook his head. "Bloodfists leave a mess. This is... calculated."

They crossed the shallow river, following the disguised trail. The rising sun burned away the morning mist, revealing a landscape of scattered trees and rocky outcroppings. Decklan's unease grew with each careful step. Whoever had passed this way knew how to move through hostile territory.

Two hours past the border, Grom raised his hand for halt. The trail had led them into a small clearing surrounded by twisted, ancient trees. Their gnarled branches created a natural canopy that dappled the ground with shadows.

"There," he whispered, pointing to a circular arrangement of stones at the clearing's center.

Decklan approached cautiously, hand resting on his knife. The stones had been deliberately placed, seven outer stones surrounding a larger central one. Dark stains marked the center stone's surface.

"Blood," Krella confirmed, crouching to examine it. "Not animal. Painted in patterns."

Decklan studied the markings, curved lines intercepted by sharp angles, forming symbols he didn't recognize. "Some kind of ritual site."

Grom's face had grown serious, his shaman father's influence evident in how he carefully circled the stones without touching them. "These aren't Shield-bearer markings. Not Blackhand or Bloodfist either."

"Could be human," Krella suggested, though her tone indicated doubt.

"No." Decklan shook his head. "I've seen my mother's prayer circles. Human settlements use different patterns." He didn't add that his occasional visits to human trading posts with Skye had exposed him to many of their customs.

A subtle shift in the air made Decklan look up. Among the twisted branches above, small objects dangled, bones and feathers strung together with dark sinew. They twisted slightly in the breeze, creating almost imperceptible movements.

"We should go back," Grom said suddenly, his voice uncharacteristically tense. "My father needs to see this."

"Agreed," Decklan replied, still studying the hanging tokens. "This isn't a scouting party. This is something else."

As they turned to leave, a rasping voice called from the tree line. "You three! What business in the borderlands?"

An elderly orc emerged from the shadows, leaning heavily on a gnarled staff. Nar'gul, one of the clan's oldest hunters, his face weathered by decades of borderland patrols. His rheumy eyes narrowed as he recognized them.

"The chieftain's son," he growled, "and the shaman's boy. Bloodfury's daughter too. Far from camp without a patrol."

"Elder Nar'gul," Decklan acknowledged with appropriate respect. "We're tracking unusual signs along the border."

The old warrior hobbled closer, his gaze shifting to the stone circle. He stopped abruptly, raising his staff defensively.

"Moon's curse," he muttered. "You found one of them."

Krella stepped forward. "You know what this is?"

"Found three such circles this past month. Reported to your father." He nodded at Decklan. "He sent the shaman to investigate."

Grom's posture stiffened. "My father examined these sites and didn't tell me?"

"Not for young ears." Nar'gul tapped his staff against the earth. "Dark workings here. The moons speak through blood, but not all listeners have good intentions."

Decklan approached the elder. "What did my father conclude about these sites?"

The old orc's expression darkened. "That we should strengthen our borders and watch for strangers. That something stirs beyond our lands that doesn't walk in daylight's honor."

A cold sensation settled in Decklan's stomach. His father wasn't prone to superstition or unnecessary caution.

"We should return to camp," he decided. "Report what we've found."

"Wise choice, half-blood," Nar'gul said, using the term without the malice it often carried. "But first, we should hide our tracks. Whatever made these circles may still be watching."

As if summoned by his words, a sound cut through the clearing, a low, rhythmic drumbeat from somewhere deep in the borderlands. All four froze, listening as the pulsing grew louder, then suddenly stopped.

"Now," Nar'gul whispered urgently. "We leave now."

The group retreated from the clearing with practiced stealth, Nar'gul leading despite his age, moving with the quiet efficiency of one who had spent decades in these borderlands. Once they reached the river crossing, Decklan paused to obscure their tracks, a technique his mother had taught him from her Moongazer days.

"The old hunter speaks true about these markings," Grom murmured as they crossed the shallow water. "During my father's teachings, he mentioned ancient symbols used to commune with darker aspects of the moons."

"Morvok's influence?" Krella asked, her voice low.

Grom nodded grimly. "The Black Moon's worshippers exist among all peoples, though few practice openly."

Decklan listened while scanning the treeline behind them. The distant drumming had not returned, but the silence felt weighted, as if the forest itself held its breath.

"Your father should have shared this information with the clan," he said finally.

"Information or speculation?" Nar'gul countered. "Better to understand a threat before alarming warriors eager for combat."

The implication was clear, Kargoth's cautious approach, so often criticized, was perhaps justified. Decklan felt the familiar tension between pride in his father's wisdom and frustration at being kept ignorant of potential dangers.

They traveled in silence until the Shieldbearer camp appeared on the horizon. The noon sun cast harsh light over the palisade walls, where guards paced with watchful eyes. Something had changed while they were gone, more sentries posted, warriors checking weapons by the main gate.

"Something's happened," Krella observed.

Inside the camp, they found unusual activity. Warriors gathered in small groups, speaking in hushed tones. Several nodded respectfully toward Decklan, Grom, and Krella as they passed, but their expressions carried tension.

Gar'zul Wiseblood, Grom's father and clan shaman, stood near the central fire pit speaking intently with two senior warriors. His elaborate bone necklace clinked softly as he gestured toward the eastern border. When he spotted their approach, his eyes narrowed, gaze fixing particularly on his son.

"Found them at the border, Shaman," Nar'gul announced. "Investigating what you already knew was there."

Gar'zul dismissed the warriors with a curt nod before turning to the returning group. "My son should know better than to cross clan boundaries without authorization."

"We stayed within our patrol range," Grom replied, a hint of defiance in his voice. "And found a ritual circle you never mentioned in your teachings."

"Some knowledge comes with proper timing," Gar'zul said coldly. His gaze shifted to Decklan. "Your father wishes to speak with you. Immediately."

"What's happening here?" Decklan asked, gesturing to the unusual camp activity.

"That is for the chieftain to explain." The shaman's expression softened slightly. "Go. He waits in the council lodge."

Decklan exchanged glances with Krella and Grom before heading toward the large structure at the camp's center.

Inside, Kargoth Stormshield stood studying a crude map spread across the central table. Several clan elders seated around him fell silent as Decklan entered. Kargoth looked up, his weathered face betraying unusual fatigue.

"You crossed the border," his father said without preamble.

"We tracked suspicious signs," Decklan replied, standing straight. "Found a ritual site with blood markings."

Kargoth's expression remained impassive, but his eyes, so similar to Decklan's own, revealed concern. "And did you disturb anything at this site?"

"No. Elder Nar'gul found us there and advised caution."

The chieftain nodded slightly, then dismissed the elders with a gesture. When they had filed out, leaving father and son alone, Kargoth's rigid posture softened almost imperceptibly.

"Show me on the map where you found it," he said, his deep voice quieter now.

Decklan approached the table, scanning the roughly drawn landscape until he found the limestone outcropping that marked the river crossing. He pointed to a spot beyond it.

"Here. A clearing with twisted trees. Seven stones in a circle around a larger one. Blood symbols I didn't recognize."

Kargoth placed a worn stone marker on the spot. Three similar markers already dotted the map in a rough arc along their eastern border.

"The fourth we've found," he confirmed. "Each discovered during the waning of Harmony's light."

Decklan studied the pattern. "They're surrounding our territory."

"Perhaps." Kargoth's calloused finger traced the arc. "Or marking something else entirely."

"What do the symbols mean?"

His father's expression darkened. "Gar'zul believes they're invocations to Morvok. Old magic, summoning the Black Moon's influence."

The chill Decklan had felt at the clearing returned. Morvok's worshippers were rare among the clans, who typically followed Ravakhhor the Wrathful Sovereign, or like the Shieldbearers, Gallant the Eternal Vanguard. His mother prayed to Viviana the Life Weaver, but even that was accepted, if sometimes grudgingly, by the clan.

"Blackhand work?" Decklan asked.

"Uncertain." Kargoth straightened, crossing his arms across his broad chest. "Which is why I've called a council with neighboring settlements, including the human outpost at Riverstone."

"Riverstone?" Decklan couldn't keep the surprise from his voice. Contact with human settlements was rare, and formal councils with them rarer still. "You believe they're threatened as well?"

"They've reported similar findings on their borders." Kargoth's voice remained steady, but Decklan caught the underlying concern. "Whatever this is, it doesn't discriminate between orc and human territory."

Decklan considered this. His father had always maintained more diplomatic relations with human settlements than most orc chieftains, another policy that earned him criticism from traditionalists. Some attributed it to Skye's influence; others recognized the practical value of information exchange and occasional trade.

"When is this council?" he asked.

"Three days hence. At the Neutral Stones." Kargoth turned back to the map, studying it with the intensity that had made him a formidable chieftain for over fifteen years. "You will accompany me."

This wasn't phrased as a request. Still, it surprised Decklan. Such meetings typically included only the chieftain, the shaman, and perhaps one or two senior warriors.

"Why me?" The question escaped before he could consider its wisdom.

Kargoth's gaze remained fixed on the map. "The humans will be... more comfortable with your presence."

The statement hung between them, acknowledging what was usually left unspoken, that Decklan's mixed blood might serve a diplomatic purpose. He wasn't sure whether to feel pride at the recognition or resentment at being used for his human heritage.

"Gar'zul will attend as well?" Decklan asked, changing the subject.

"No." Something in his father's tone suggested this decision hadn't been without conflict. "He believes meeting with humans shows weakness. I've asked him to investigate these ritual sites more thoroughly instead."

This explained the tension he'd witnessed between Grom and his father. If Gar'zul opposed the council, he would see Grom's borderland expedition as potentially undermining his position.

"Prepare yourself," Kargoth continued. "We leave at dawn, two days from now," Kargoth continued. "The journey to the Neutral Stones takes a full day."

"I'll be ready," Decklan promised, then hesitated before adding, "Thank you for including me."

Kargoth finally turned from the map, his amber eyes studying his son with an unreadable expression. "Your tracking skills today were impressive. You found what seasoned warriors missed, showing both strength and wisdom, even without the tournament to prove yourself."

The unexpected praise caught Decklan off-guard. Compliments from his father were as rare as summer snowfall.

"I learned from the best," he replied carefully.

A ghost of a smile touched Kargoth's face. "From both your mother and me, I think." The smile faded as quickly as it had appeared. "Now go. Tell no one of the council except your mother. Some in the clan would misunderstand our purpose."

Decklan found Krella and Grom waiting near the training grounds, both looking expectantly at his approach. The afternoon sun cast long shadows across the packed earth where warriors still practiced despite the camp's unusual tension.

"Well?" Grom asked as soon as Decklan was within earshot. "What did your father say about the ritual site?"

"It's the fourth they've found," Decklan replied quietly, leading them toward a more secluded spot near the palisade. "They form a pattern along our border."

Krella's eyes narrowed. "An encirclement?"

"Maybe." Decklan glanced around to ensure they wouldn't be overheard. "There's more, but I can't speak of it yet."

Grom's expression darkened. "More secrets? Like the ones my father keeps?"

"It's not like that—"

"Isn't it?" Grom interrupted, unusually sharp. "The elders decide what we should know, what dangers we should prepare for. They treat us like cubs while expecting us to defend the clan."

Krella put a restraining hand on Grom's arm. "Your father has his reasons for caution, as does the chieftain."

"Caution?" Grom pulled away. "Or fear that we might act where they hesitate?" He turned to Decklan. "You saw the symbols. Whatever left them isn't cautious, it's preparing."

"For what?" Krella challenged.

"That's what we should be discovering instead of waiting for the next ritual site to appear," Grom insisted.

Decklan understood his friend's frustration. The desire to act, to confront threats directly, ran strong in their blood. But he'd also witnessed how his father's deliberate approach had kept the clan safe through difficult seasons.

"Give me two days," Decklan said quietly. "Then I'll tell you everything."

Grom studied him, conflict evident in his expression. Finally, he nodded curtly. "Two days. But if more circles appear before then, I'm going to investigate, with or without clan approval."

As Grom stalked away, Krella sighed. "His father's secretive nature doesn't help. Gar'zul treats shamanic knowledge like jealously guarded treasure."

"He believes some knowledge is dangerous in unprepared hands," Decklan replied, though he understood Grom's position.

"And what do you believe?" Krella asked, her amber eyes searching his.

The question caught him off-guard. What did he believe? His life had always been a balancing act between two heritages, two ways of seeing the world.

"I believe..." he began slowly, "that secrets kept for pride or fear only grow more dangerous. But knowledge shared without wisdom can be equally harmful."

A smile touched Krella's lips. "There you go again, trying to find the middle path."

"Is that a criticism?"

"An observation." She bumped her shoulder against his, the casual contact sending an unexpected warmth through him. "But middle paths don't always exist. Sometimes you must choose a side."

"I know." Decklan gazed across the camp toward his mother's healing lodge, where Skye would be preparing remedies as she did each afternoon. "But sometimes the strongest position stands between two worlds, not firmly in either."

"Your tracking today proved that," Krella said softly. "I've never seen anyone with such skill."

Decklan felt a moment of pride at her words, different from the satisfaction of his father's rare approval. Before he could respond, a commotion near the main gate drew their attention. Warriors were gathering, voices raised in surprise or alarm.

Without speaking, they moved quickly toward the disturbance. As they approached, the crowd parted, revealing three Shieldbearer scouts supporting a fourth between them. The injured warrior's leg was wrapped in bloodied cloth, his face pale beneath its greenish hue.

"Morg's patrol," Krella whispered. "They weren't due back until tomorrow."

Gar'zul pushed through the gathering, immediately examining the wounded scout. Decklan recognized Torven, one of their most experienced trackers.

"What happened?" Gar'zul demanded as he probed the injury.

Torven winced but remained stoic. "Ambush... northwest boundary. Something hit me from the shadows, wasn't natural."

"Animal attack?" someone suggested.

Torven shook his head firmly. "No tracks. No scent. Just... darkness that moved."

A murmur ran through the gathered Shieldbearers. Decklan caught fragments, "black moon magic," "border spirits," "omen of war," superstitious whispers that would normally be dismissed with contempt by hardened warriors.

"Get him to the healing lodge," Gar'zul ordered, his expression grim. As the scouts carried Torven away, the shaman's gaze swept the crowd, lingering briefly on Decklan before finding Grom near the edge of the gathering. Whatever silent message passed between father and son caused Grom's posture to stiffen.

The crowd dispersed slowly, warriors clustering in small groups, voices low but urgent. Krella remained at Decklan's side, her presence steady.

"Northwest," she noted. "Opposite from where we found the ritual site."

"Coordinated?" Decklan wondered aloud.

"Or coincidental." She didn't sound convinced. "Either way, the borderlands don't feel as familiar as they once did," Krella finished, her voice low.

The camp remained restless into evening. Decklan sought out his mother in her healing lodge, where she tended to Torven with her customary calm efficiency. The scout lay on a pallet, his wound cleaned and wrapped in fresh bandages infused with herbs that filled the lodge with a pungent yet soothing aroma.

"Will he recover?" Decklan asked after Torven had drifted into an herb-induced sleep.

Skye nodded, wiping her hands on a cloth. "The wound itself isn't severe. But there's something unusual about it." She lowered her voice. "It resists my usual treatments. As if something... lingers in the tissues."

"Poison?"

"Perhaps." She tucked a strand of hair behind her ear, a habit Decklan had observed countless times during his childhood. "Or something else entirely."

Decklan described the ritual site they'd discovered, watching his mother's expression shift from concern to something deeper, a knowing fear he rarely saw in her calm features.

"Your father mentioned similar findings," she said carefully set out more bandages at Torven's bedside. "The symbols you describe... they have meaning to those who worship Nyxthera."

"You recognize them?" This surprised him. His mother followed Viviana the Life Weaver, whose teachings seemed opposite to Nyxthera's dark influence.

"Recognition doesn't require belief," she replied, meeting his gaze steadily. "The Moongazer tribe taught their healers about all divine influences, including those that harm rather than heal."

Decklan hesitated before asking his next question. "Father has called a council with the human settlement at Riverstone."

Skye's hands stilled in their work of organizing herbs. "Yes. He consulted me before deciding."

"He's asked me to accompany him."

Something like pride flickered across her features. "Good. You possess insights from both worlds that others lack."

Decklan wasn't sure how to articulate his discomfort. "Some will see it as him using my human blood for advantage."

"And is that wrong?" she challenged gently. "Your heritage is not a burden to be hidden, Decklan, but a gift that grants you perspectives others cannot share."

Decklan shifted uncomfortably. "Easier said than believed when you've spent your life being called 'half-blood' like it's a curse."

His mother's expression softened. She approached, placing her hands on his shoulders, she had to reach up now, though he remembered a time when she seemed tall to him.

"Your father sees your value," she said quietly. "He wouldn't include you in this council otherwise."

"And if I'm only invited to make humans more comfortable?" The question emerged more bitter than he'd intended.

"Then you serve your clan by using every advantage you possess." Her grip tightened slightly. "Just as your father uses his strength, Gar'zul his knowledge, and I my healing. We all have different gifts to contribute."

Decklan nodded, not entirely convinced but unwilling to argue. His mother had always viewed his mixed heritage as a blessing. Growing up among orcs who prized purity of bloodline, he'd struggled to share her perspective.

"Rest tonight," Skye advised, releasing him. "The journey to the Neutral Stones is not difficult, but the conversations there will require all your attention."

As Decklan left the healing lodge, the evening fires were being lit throughout the camp. Warriors gathered around them, sharing meals and quieter conversations than usual. The injured scout's return had cast a shadow over the camp that even firelight couldn't fully dispel.

He found Krella near the training grounds, methodically sharpening her hunting knives. The repetitive scrape of stone against metal had always seemed meditative to her, and he hesitated to interrupt.

She looked up as he approached, somehow sensing his presence despite his quiet footsteps. "Your mother's assessment of Torven?"

"He'll heal," Decklan replied, sitting beside her on the log. "But the wound is... unusual."

Krella nodded as if this confirmed something. "The patrols have been doubled. Your father's orders."

"Sensible precaution."

"Is it just precaution?" Krella set her knife aside, giving Decklan her full attention. "Or does he know more than he's telling the clan?"

Decklan hesitated, caught between loyalty to his father's instructions and trust in Krella. "There's... concern that whatever created those ritual sites may have larger plans."

"Hence the council with Riverstone." It wasn't a question.

Decklan looked at her sharply. "How did you know about that?"

"My father serves on the war council," she reminded him. "He mentioned preparations for a journey to the Neutral Stones. Wasn't difficult to connect it to our findings today."

Of course. Despite her youth, Krella possessed a keen mind for clan politics, perhaps sharper than his own. While he'd spent years trying to prove his physical prowess to compensate for his mixed heritage, she'd been observing the subtler currents of power within the clan.

"I'm to accompany my father to this council," he admitted.

Something flashed in her eyes—surprise, perhaps respect. "A significant responsibility."

"Or a convenient tool," he muttered. "The half-blood makes jumpy humans feel safer."

Krella's expression hardened. "Is that what you think of yourself? A tool?"

"It's what some think."

"Some are fools." She picked up her knife again, testing its edge with her thumb. "Your father is many things, Decklan, but he doesn't use people carelessly—especially not his son."

The conviction in her voice gave him pause. Krella had always seen him clearly, sometimes more clearly than he saw himself.

"You sound certain."

"When we returned from the scouting trip. The pride he showed when he heard you found the ritual site told me so."

Decklan absorbed her words, wanting to believe them. Yet today's discoveries, ritual circles, injured scouts, talk of councils, had already overshadowed that moment of triumph.

"Something's coming, isn't it?" Krella's voice had dropped to barely above a whisper. "Something that has even your father concerned."

Decklan nodded slowly. "I think so. These ritual sites, the attack on Torven, they're connected somehow."

The camp fell quieter as night deepened. Around them, warriors retired to their lodges while sentries took up positions along the palisade, more numerous than usual. The three moons hung in the sky, their light casting multiple shadows behind each object, a phenomenon unique to Lunara that the clan's elders often said represented the different paths each soul might walk.

"You should prepare for the journey," Krella said finally, rising from the log. "The Neutral Stones are a day's travel, and if I know your father, he'll want to depart before dawn."

"Will you be here when I return?" Decklan found himself asking.

She paused, looking down at him with an expression he couldn't quite read. "I'll be waiting. Why?"

"I'd like to tell you what happens at the council. Your perspective... it matters to me."

Something softened in her amber eyes. She reached out, placing her calloused fingers briefly on his chest.

"This is what I've always felt was true about you, Decklan. You possess a strength that doesn't blind you, and a wisdom that doesn't make you hesitate. Remember that at the council."

Before he could respond, she turned and walked away toward the warriors' lodges, her silhouette merging with the shadows between fires.

CHAPTER THREE

SHADOWS AT THE COUNCIL

The journey to Neutral Stones took a full day across the rolling plains that separated Shieldbearer territory from the human settlement of Riverstone. Decklan rode beside his father, stealing occasional glances at the chieftain's stoic profile. Kargoth had barely spoken ten words since they departed, focused on the horizon with unwavering determination.

Their escort consisted of six warriors, veterans who had proven themselves both in battle and restraint. Each had been hand-selected by Kargoth for their ability to maintain composure in potential provocations from other delegates. So as not to frighten the humans by their approach, Kargoth chose to have the entire party ride horses instead of the giant war wolves the orcs typically used.

"You're quiet," Kargoth finally said as they crested a hill overlooking the ancient meeting grounds. The Neutral Stones rose from the earth like broken teeth, a circle of weathered monoliths that had served as meeting grounds between clans and settlements for generations.

Decklan adjusted the shield strapped to his back. "I'm listening to the land, as you taught me."

A hint of approval flickered across Kargoth's face. "Good. What does it tell you?"

"That we're being watched," Decklan replied, nodding toward a distant ridge where the sunlight had briefly caught something metallic. "Human scouts. They've been tracking us since midday."

"And what else?"

"The birds aren't singing where they should be. Something else passed through recently."

Kargoth nodded. "You see with both eyes now. Remember that during the council."

As they approached the Neutral Stones, Decklan saw delegations already gathering. Human representatives from Riverstone stood in a tight cluster, their weapons peace-bound with ceremonial cords. To their left, a small group of Moongazers, including a silver-haired woman who raised her hand in subtle greeting toward Kargoth. Decklan recognized his mother's cousin, Lyara, head priestess of their wandering clan.

"Unexpected guests," Kargoth muttered, nodding toward the eastern entrance where a contingent of Blackhand orcs entered the circle, their black war paint visible beneath ceremonial cloaks. They moved with practiced precision, forming a perfect crescent at their designated position.

Decklan tensed. The Blackhands were known for their cunning and ruthlessness, traits his father had often warned against. Their presence at a peace council between Shieldbearers and human settlements was unusual, to say the least.

"Stay alert," Kargoth murmured as they dismounted. "But remember why we're here."

The Shieldbearer delegation took their place within the ancient circle. Decklan stood slightly behind his father, acutely aware of the scrutiny from all sides. He could feel the human delegates examining his features—too human for an orc, too orcish for a human, their expressions a familiar mixture of curiosity and wariness.

Lord Aldric of Riverstone stepped forward, a gray-bearded man with calculating eyes. "Chieftain Kargoth. You honor us with your presence." His voice carried the practiced neutrality of a seasoned diplomat.

"The Shieldbearers honor their commitments," Kargoth replied, clasping his arm in the human custom rather than the traditional orc greeting of grasped forearms. It was a small gesture that spoke volumes.

Decklan watched the Blackhand delegation from the corner of his eye. Their leader, a broad-shouldered orc with intricate scarification across his face, observed the exchange with unnerving intensity. Unlike the other delegations, the Blackhands had brought more warriors than was customary.

The council began with traditional invocations to the three moons, followed by formal statements from each delegation. Lord Aldric spoke of recent territorial disputes, missing livestock, and concerns about hunting rights in the contested valleys. His tone remained respectful but firm.

When Kargoth's turn came, Decklan felt a surge of pride at his father's measured words.

"The Shieldbearers seek no conflict with Riverstone. Our traditions speak of balance, not bloodshed. The valleys have sustained both our peoples for generations. There is game enough for all if hunting is conducted with respect for the land's rhythms."

As Kargoth continued, Decklan noticed a subtle movement among the standing stones. A shadow where no shadow should be. His pulse quickened.

"Father," he whispered, but the warning died on his lips as the first arrow whistled through the air.

Instinct took over. Decklan lunged forward, the shield from his back already in his hand as he pulled his father down. The arrow meant for Kargoth's heart grazed his shoulder instead, tearing through leather and flesh.

"Treachery!" roared the Blackhand leader, drawing his weapon as chaos erupted.

More arrows rained from hidden positions among the stones. Two River-stone delegates fell instantly. A Moongazer priest collapsed with a shaft protruding from his chest.

"Defensive circle!" Kargoth commanded, blood seeping from his wounded shoulder. The Shieldbearer warriors responded immediately, forming a protective formation with shields outward.

Attackers emerged from behind the monoliths, figures in dark clothing with faces obscured by cloth masks. They moved with deadly precision, targeting delegates from all factions.

Decklan found himself fighting back-to-back with his father, their movements synchronized like a well-rehearsed dance. His blade found purchase in an attacker's side, while his shield deflected a thrust meant for Kargoth's back.

"The stones offer no cover!" Decklan shouted above the din of battle. "We need to reach the horses!"

A female assassin with twin daggers leapt toward them, her blades weaving a deadly pattern. Decklan parried with his shield while Kargoth's axe forced her back. For an instant, the woman's eyes locked with Decklan's, amber irises filled with cold calculation. She hesitated, almost imperceptibly, before disengaging and vanishing into the chaos.

Working together, the Shieldbearers created a path toward the edge of the stone circle, protecting delegates from all factions who had been caught in the ambush. Decklan noticed with surprise that the Blackhand warriors fought alongside them, their earlier suspicion replaced by battlefield alliance.

As they reached the horses, Decklan glanced back at the Neutral Stones, now stained with blood. The mysterious assassins were retreating, disappearing into the surrounding landscape as quickly as they had appeared.

Lord Aldric's voice rang out above the chaos. "Regroup! To me!" His command was firm despite the arrow lodged in his thigh, which he'd snapped at the shaft to continue moving.

The surviving delegates rallied, mounting horses or supporting wounded comrades. A Moongazer healer was already working on the most critically injured, her hands glowing faintly with silver light as she whispered prayers to Viviana.

"This was no random attack," Kargoth said grimly, examining the arrow he'd pulled from his shoulder. "These markings, they're made to look like Bloodfist clan work, but the fletching is wrong."

Decklan scanned the tree line, searching for any sign of the amber-eyed assassin. "Someone wanted this council to fail. Someone who could benefit from conflict between all our peoples."

The Blackhand leader approached, blood streaming from a cut above his eye. "Chieftain Kargoth, it seems we have a common enemy." His voice was surprisingly melodious for such an imposing figure. "I am Brugh, emissary of Reyn Nightshade."

Kargoth stiffened slightly at the name. "I was unaware the Blackhands had business at this council."

"Our business," Brugh replied, "was to observe. Now it seems we share a more pressing concern." He gestured to the bodies being gathered. "These assassins knew of this meeting. They came prepared."

Lord Aldric limped over, supported by one of his guards. "This attack targeted all of us equally. I lost two good men today."

"And I a treasured advisor," added Lyara, the Moongazer priestess, her silver robes now stained crimson. "The question remains, who benefits from chaos between our peoples?"

"These tracks," he said, pointing to barely visible depressions in the soil. "They're deliberately misleading. Some head west toward human lands, others east toward orc territories. They want us blaming each other."

The revelation hung in the air, heavy with implication. Decklan stooped to examine the tracks more closely. His training with the Moongazers gave him insights others might miss.

"The weight distribution is wrong," he murmured. "These weren't made by fleeing attackers. They must have been here before we arrived." He looked up, meeting the surprised gazes of the delegates. "Someone knew exactly where we would be."

Brugh exchanged glances with his warriors. "The Blackhands recognize such tactics," he admitted reluctantly. "This bears the mark of the Ghost."

A murmur rippled through the gathering. The Ghost, a name whispered with dread across the territories. An unseen hand behind numerous conflicts, leaving no trace but bodies and blame.

"We should move," Kargoth announced, his voice cutting through the tension. "These grounds are no longer safe."

The wounded were secured on horses, and the various delegations prepared to depart. Decklan noticed Lord Aldric and Kargoth exchanging quiet words, their former suspicion replaced by grim alliance.

As they rode from the blood-stained stones, Lyara fell in beside Decklan.

"Your father lives because of you," she said softly. "Your instincts saw what his senses missed."

Decklan shifted uncomfortably. "I just reacted."

"Do not diminish what happened here today," she replied. "Your unique traits are not a weakness, Decklan Stormshield. Remember that in the days to come."

He looked ahead to where his father rode, straight-backed despite his wound. For the first time in his memory, Kargoth had publicly acknowledged the value of Decklan's human heritage.

As they crested the hill, Decklan glanced back one final time. A lone figure stood among the distant stones, too far to discern features, but something about the silhouette sent a chill down his spine. He blinked, and the figure was gone, like a shadow dispelled by sudden light.

A day later, they returned to the Shieldbearer encampment. Word of the attack had preceded them, and the clan gathered to welcome the returning party.

The Shieldbearer camp erupted in a flurry of activity as the returning party crested the final hill. Decklan could see warriors gathering, their faces etched with concern as they counted the riders. Six had left with the chieftain; only five returned. Grim reality settled over the camp like a shroud.

Decklan rode slightly behind his father, watching Kargoth's straight-backed silhouette against the setting sun. Despite his bandaged shoulder and the dried blood staining his leather armor, the chieftain showed no signs of weakness. The Shieldbearers expected nothing less from their leader.

Skye was among the first to meet them, her healer's bag already slung over her shoulder. Her eyes found Decklan first—a mother's instinct—then moved to Kargoth's bandaged wound. Relief and concern battled across her face.

"The council?" she asked quietly as Kargoth dismounted.

"Bloodshed," he replied simply. "Targon fell defending our retreat."

A murmur passed through the gathered clan members. Targon had been a respected warrior, an elder who had served three generations of chieftains.

"His shield protected us to his last breath," Decklan added, meeting the eyes of Targon's kin in the crowd. "He died with honor and is worthy to be honored with the Mourning Shield Ritual."

Kargoth nodded in solemn agreement before turning to address the clan. "The Neutral Stones run red with the blood of all peoples today. Shieldbearers, Riverstone humans, Moongazers, and even Blackhands fell to hidden blades and arrows."

Concerned whispers rippled through the gathering. The mention of Blackhands raised many eyebrows.

"Who is responsible?" called Gar'zul Wiseblood, his lined face grim beneath his ceremonial headdress.

"The attackers wore no colors and left false trails," Kargoth replied. "But their arrows bore markings meant to implicate the Bloodfists."

"Then let us march against the Bloodfists!" shouted a young warrior, brandishing his axe. Several others roared in agreement.

Kargoth's raised hand cut through the war cries like a blade, silencing the eager warriors. His expression remained stone-carved and resolute.

"We will not be manipulated into war based on false evidence," the chieftain declared, his voice carrying across the hushed gathering. "The arrows were crafted to deceive, the fletching betrays a different hand than Bloodfist."

Decklan stood at his father's side, noticing how Kargoth subtly shifted his weight to minimize strain on his wounded shoulder. Few would notice such a minute gesture, but Decklan had grown attuned to his father's subtle movements.

"If not Bloodfists, then who?" demanded Korrash, a roughshod warrior. "Who dares shed Shieldbearer blood?"

Kargoth's eyes scanned the crowd. "The delegates spoke of a name, the Ghost."

"A myth," Gar'zul scoffed, his ceremonial staff thudding against the earth. "A convenient name for unnamed fears."

"I witnessed their work firsthand," Decklan countered, stepping forward. "Their attack targeted all delegations equally. They wanted us fighting amongst ourselves."

Skye moved closer to examine Kargoth's wound. "You need proper treatment," she murmured, already unwrapping the hasty battlefield dressing.

"Later," Kargoth replied, though he did not stop her ministrations. "The clan must understand the threat we face."

As Skye worked on Kargoth's shoulder, Grom pushed his way through the crowd, his expression tense. "Friend or foe?" he asked Decklan, nodding toward the camp's eastern boundary where dust clouds rose.

Decklan squinted against the setting sun. "Riders approaching. Blackhand colors."

The clan erupted in fresh alarm. Warriors rushed to collect weapons while families gathered children toward the center of the encampment.

"Hold!" Kargoth commanded. "They come under banner of parley."

Indeed, the approaching riders carried a staff wrapped with white cloth, the universal signal for peaceful intent.

CHAPTER FOUR

TANGLED WEB

Night had fallen over the Shieldbearer camp, but sleep eluded Decklan. The events at the Neutral Stones continued to play in his mind like restless spirits, the sudden attack, the amber-eyed assassin, the way she had looked at him with recognition. And now Blackhand riders approached their camp under a banner of parley.

He stood outside his dwelling, watching as Kargoth and the clan elders gathered to receive the Blackhand delegation. Torches illuminated the central clearing, casting long shadows that danced across weathered faces. His father's shoulder was bound with Skye's healing herbs, but he stood tall, betraying no weakness before potential rivals.

Six Blackhand warriors entered the circle, led by a towering figure in elaborate armor adorned with raven feathers and bone. Unlike most orcs, she wore her black hair in intricate braids threaded with silver ornaments that clinked softly as she moved.

"Reyn Nightshade," Grom whispered, appearing at Decklan's side. "Chieftain of the Blackhand Clan."

Decklan studied her with narrowed eyes. "She doesn't look like any Blackhand I've ever seen."

"That's because she's different. My father says she took control of the clan through cunning rather than strength. Some whisper she practices blood magic."

Kargoth stepped forward, his voice carrying across the clearing. "The Shield-bearer Clan acknowledges your banner of parley, Reyn Nightshade."

The Blackhand chieftain removed her gauntlets, revealing hands covered in intricate black tattoos. "I come seeking alliance, not conflict, Kargoth Stormshield. We face a common enemy."

Murmurs rippled through the gathered Shieldbearers. Alliance with the Blackhand was unprecedented.

"The attack at the Neutral Stones targeted all clans equally," Reyn continued. "This is not the first such incident. For months, my scouts have found evidence of a force working to pit our peoples against each other. They call themselves 'the Ghosts,' mercenaries and assassins who profit from chaos."

Decklan felt a chill travel down his spine as he watched Reyn speak. Something about her was mesmerizing yet deeply unsettling, like the beauty of a predatory cat before it strikes.

"I've tracked their movements across three territories," Reyn continued, producing a worn leather map. "They strike, leave false evidence implicating other clans, then vanish like morning mist. But they've made mistakes. My shaman, Vexxa Darkseer, has identified patterns in their movements."

A slender figure stepped forward from behind Reyn. Vexxa's face was partially concealed by a hood adorned with small bones and feathers, but Decklan could see her eyes, sharp, calculating, and entirely too aware. She surveyed the gathering until her gaze landed on Decklan. Her lips curved in a subtle smile that made his skin crawl.

"The Ghosts seek something," Vexxa said, her voice unexpectedly melodic. "Something they believe lies within our combined territories. Their recent activities suggest they're closing in on their target."

Kargoth studied the map Reyn had unrolled. "These ritual sites match those we've found within our borders."

"Precisely," Reyn nodded. "They're establishing a perimeter, preparing for something significant."

Gar'zul Wiseblood stepped forward, his ceremonial staff clacking against the hard ground. "What evidence do we have that you aren't behind these attacks yourself? The Blackhand Clan has never sought peace with the Shieldbearers before."

"A fair question, Shaman," Reyn replied smoothly. "I would be suspicious too. But consider this, if I wished to attack your clan, why would I create such elaborate deceptions? Why not simply mass my warriors and strike? No, I come because survival demands cooperation."

Decklan observed the interaction carefully, noting how Reyn's words seemed to flow like honey, sweet and enticing. Yet her eyes remained cold and calculating. Beside him, Grom shifted uncomfortably.

"My father doesn't trust her," Grom whispered. "And neither do I."

Krella joined them, her expression guarded. "Blackhands speaking of alliance? The world truly has turned upside down. Look at how she studies us, like a wolf deciding which sheep to take first."

Decklan nodded slightly. "She's hiding something. And that shaman keeps looking this way."

Indeed, Vexxa Darkseer's gaze repeatedly drifted toward their position. Each time her eyes found Decklan, that same unsettling smile played across her lips.

"We will consider your proposal," Kargoth was saying. "Until then, you may camp at the eastern ridge under our observation."

"A sensible precaution," Reyn agreed, bowing slightly. "I would expect nothing less from the legendary Kargoth Stormshield. Before we depart, might I ask—have you noticed anything... unusual about the moons lately?"

The question seemed innocent, but Decklan noticed how Vexxa tensed slightly, her attention fully on Kargoth now.

"The moons are as they have always been," Gar'zul answered instead. "What concern are they to the Blackhand?"

"Merely an observation," Reyn replied. "The priests in human settlements speak of an approaching alignment, a convergence of all three moons that happens once in many lifetimes. Such events often herald... change."

With that cryptic statement, the Blackhand delegation withdrew. As they passed, Vexxa slowed near Decklan.

"The divided blood runs strong in you, young Stormshield," she murmured, her voice too low for others to hear. "We will speak again soon."

Before Decklan could respond, she was gone, following her chieftain into the darkness.

The next morning, Decklan found his father alone by the river, methodically sharpening his blade.

"You should be resting that shoulder," Decklan said, sitting beside him.

Kargoth grunted. "A leader shows no weakness, especially when surrounded by wolves."

"You mean the Blackhands?"

"Them. And others." Kargoth tested his blade's edge with his thumb. "There are those in our own clan who believe my caution is weakness. They would have us march to war at the first provocation."

Decklan watched his father's practiced movements, the blade singing softly against the whetstone.

"You don't trust Reyn Nightshade," he said. It wasn't a question.

"I trust the sunrise and sunset. I trust your mother's healing hands." Kargoth paused, his weathered face solemn. "Everything else must be earned."

"But you're considering her proposal."

Kargoth sighed, setting down his blade. "A wise leader examines all paths before choosing one. The Blackhand Clan has always been our adversary, but enemies can become allies when faced with a greater threat." He looked directly at Decklan. "What did you observe last night?"

Decklan considered his answer carefully. "Reyn speaks well, too well. Her words flow like water over stone, smooth and practiced. But her eyes remain cold, calculating."

"And what of the shaman?"

"Vexxa..." Decklan hesitated. "She watched me throughout the meeting. She called me 'divided blood' when they left."

Kargoth's expression darkened. "That troubles me. The Blackhands have always despised mixed heritage. For their shaman to take such interest in you..."

"Father, what did Reyn mean about the moons aligning?"

"Ancient superstition," Kargoth replied, though Decklan noted a flicker of concern cross his features. "The three moons align completely once every century. Legends speak of increased magical power, prophecies fulfilled." He shrugged. "Tales to frighten children."

A horn sounded from the perimeter, three short blasts, visitors approaching.

"We're becoming popular," Kargoth muttered, rising stiffly.

They returned to find the camp in a flurry of activity. Warriors were donning armor, mothers ushering children to safety.

"Bloodfist riders approaching from the west," Grom reported, meeting them at the edge of the clearing. "A large party, at least twenty."

Kargoth's expression remained impassive. "Under what banner?"

"That's the strange part," Grom replied. "They fly no banner at all."

Decklan exchanged concerned glances with his father. Bannerless riders meant one of two things: raiders or exiles. Neither boded well.

"Form a defensive line," Kargoth ordered, his voice calm but firm. "No aggressive posture, but be prepared."

Warriors moved into position at the western approach, shields interlocking in the traditional Shieldbearer formation Decklan had practiced countless times. He took his place beside his father, trying to emulate Kargoth's stoic composure while his heart thundered in his chest.

The riders appeared at the edge of the clearing, massive orcs with crimson armor and weapons adorned with crude spikes. Their mounts, thick-necked, war wolves from the northern plains—snorted and pawed at the earth. At their lead rode the largest orc Decklan had ever seen, his scarred face partially hidden behind a mask made from a giant wolf's skull.

"Snarlgar Zoggorn," Krella whispered from nearby. "Bloodfist Chieftain."

The riders halted just outside bow range. Snarlgar removed his skull helmet, revealing a face mapped with ritual scars and yellow eyes that gleamed with predatory intelligence.

"Kargoth Stormshield!" he bellowed. "I come to speak of treachery and war!"

Kargoth stepped forward, keeping his stance relaxed but ready. "The Shieldbearer camp hears you, Snarlgar Zoggorn. Speak your piece."

"Your new friends, the Blackhands maggots, attacked three of my hunting parties yesterday," Snarlgar spat. "Slaughtered to the last warrior, with shields left beside the bodies." He reached behind him and threw something that landed with a wet thud before the defensive line, a Shieldbearer emblem, crusted with dried blood.

Murmurs of disbelief rippled through the ranks. Kargoth's expression darkened as he examined the emblem.

"This is not ours," he stated firmly. "The markings are similar, but the craftsmanship is wrong. This is a deception."

Snarlgar laughed, a harsh bark without humor. "How convenient! I followed the tracks from the massacre strait here to your guests camped on the eastern ridge."

"We formed no alliance with the Blackhand Clan," Kargoth replied evenly. "They came under parley to discuss a common threat, these 'Ghosts' who leave false evidence to incite conflict between our peoples. It seems their strategy continues."

Snarlgar's yellow eyes narrowed. "Pretty words, Stormshield. But while you talk of 'common threats,' my warriors lie dead. The Bloodfist Clan demands blood payment."

Decklan studied the Bloodfist warriors behind Snarlgar. Their faces were masks of barely contained rage, hands gripping weapons. This was a powder keg waiting for a spark.

Kargoth remained unfazed. "We had no part in these attacks. If you seek the true killers, join us in uncovering this deception rather than falling prey to it."

A lean orc in elaborate shamanic garb urged his mount forward to Snarlgar's side. His calculating gaze swept over the Shieldbearers, lingering momentarily on Decklan before returning to Kargoth.

"Wise Kargoth speaks of deception," the shaman said, his voice silky and measured. "Yet the Blackhand camp lies just beyond your eastern ridge. How convenient that you offer them sanctuary while denying responsibility for their actions."

"And who might you be?" Gar'zul demanded, stepping forward.

"Morgul Vorgath, voice of the ancestors to the Bloodfist Clan." The shaman smiled, revealing filed teeth. "The spirits speak clearly of betrayal and bloodshed to come."

Decklan felt the tension thickening like storm clouds. One wrong move would unleash violence that would engulf all three clans. He glanced at his father, seeing the calculations behind Kargoth's impassive expression.

"I propose a council," Kargoth said finally. "Representatives from all three clans, meeting at the Neutral Stones. We will investigate these killings together and uncover the truth."

Snarlgar's massive hand tightened around his axe. "While we talk, more of my warriors may die."

"And if you attack us now, more death."

The tension at the perimeter lingered like a storm cloud waiting to break. Snarlgar Zoggorn's massive form seemed to swell with barely contained rage as he considered Kargoth's words.

"Your proposal for council means nothing," Snarlgar growled. "Bloodfists do not settle matters with talk."

Morgul Vorgath leaned closer to his chieftain, whispering something that made Snarlgar's yellow eyes narrow thoughtfully. After a moment, the Bloodfist leader grunted.

"Three days," he declared. "You have three days to produce those responsible for attacking my warriors. After that, we settle this the old way." He pulled his mount around sharply. "And keep your Blackhand friends close, Stormshield. When we return, we'll take their heads along with yours."

The Bloodfist party departed in a whirlwind of fur and dust, leaving the Shieldbearers in uneasy silence. Kargoth watched them go, his face impassive but his shoulders tight with tension.

"Three days," Gar'zul muttered. "Three days to solve a mystery that's been plaguing us for months."

Kargoth turned to address the assembled warriors. "Double the patrols. I want eyes on both Blackhand and Bloodfist movements." He beckoned to Decklan and Gar'zul. "You two, with me."

As the defensive line disbanded, Krella caught Decklan's eye, her expression concerned. He gave her a reassuring nod before following his father toward the council tent.

Inside, Kargoth paced like a caged predator. "This is precisely what our enemy wants, to turn us against each other while they work from the shadows."

"The question is why," Gar'zul said, settling onto a worn cushion. "What purpose does this chaos serve?"

"And who benefits?" Decklan added.

Kargoth stopped pacing. "We need more information. Decklan, take Grom and Krella to where those Bloodfist warriors were killed. Find what Snarlgar's people missed."

CHAPTER FIVE

VISIONS IN THE MIST

Decklan crouched beside the trampled undergrowth, examining the scattered remains of what had once been a Bloodfist hunting party. The morning mist clung to the forest floor, wrapping around the trunks of ancient oaks like spectral fingers and the smell of dead leaves lingered in the air. Three days had passed since Snarlgar's ultimatum, and time was running dangerously short.

"This doesn't make sense," he muttered, studying the blood patterns that had dried to a rusty brown on the leaves. "Look at the footprints. The attackers came from multiple directions, yet there's no sign of scouts or sentries being taken out first."

Krella knelt beside him, her brow furrowed. "Bloodfists always post sentries, especially this close to our territories."

"Which means they were expecting someone," Grom added, circling the clearing's perimeter. "But not an attack."

Decklan nodded, piecing together the evidence. "They were meeting someone. Willingly."

He moved to the center of the carnage where the earth was scorched in a perfect circle. Small stone markers had been placed equidistant around the circumference, each bearing the same symbol, three crescent moons aligned vertically.

"This wasn't just an ambush," Decklan said, kneeling to inspect one of the markers. "It was a ritual. And these symbols..."

"The three moons," Grom finished, his voice dropping to a whisper. "Like Reyn mentioned."

Krella drew her knife, suddenly alert. "We're not alone."

The mist thickened unnaturally around them, swirling into tendrils that reached toward the trio. Decklan drew his sword, backing toward his companions until they stood back-to-back in the center of the circle.

"This isn't natural fog," Grom warned, reaching for a protective talisman his father had given him. "There's magic in it."

The mist condensed, forming wispy figures that flickered at the edge of perception. Decklan felt a chill emanate from the ground beneath his feet. The stone markers began to glow with a faint blue light.

"We need to leave. Now," Decklan commanded, his voice cutting through the unnatural silence that had fallen over the clearing.

But as they moved toward the edge of the circle, the mist solidified like a wall before them. The blue glow from the stone markers intensified, sending ripples of light through the fog. Decklan's skin tingled with arcane energy.

"It's a containment spell," Grom said, voice tight with tension. "Someone's activated the ritual site."

The mist figures danced closer, taking more defined shapes, orc warriors with hollow eyes and gaping wounds. Decklan recognized the Bloodfist markings on their spectral armor.

"The dead," Krella whispered, her knife trembling slightly in her grip. "They're showing us how they died."

One phantom warrior reached toward Decklan, its misty hand passing through his chest. Cold gripped his heart as visions flooded his mind—betrayal, a meeting gone wrong, knives in the dark. Not random violence, but calculated execution.

"They were betrayed," Decklan gasped, struggling to maintain his footing as the vision threatened to overwhelm him. "Lured here with promises of alliance against... against us."

The largest spirit, clearly the hunting party's leader, drifted to the center of the circle. It knelt, placing ghostly hands on the scorched earth. The ground beneath rippled like water, revealing a hidden compartment. Inside lay a carved stone tablet, untouched by the violence that had occurred above it.

Grom moved cautiously toward it, the protective talisman held before him. "It's an ancient warding stone. My father spoke of these, they're used to seal magical boundaries."

As Decklan approached the tablet, the mist swirled violently around him. A new figure formed—taller, more defined, wearing elaborate shamanic garb he didn't recognize.

"You stand at the crossroads, divided blood," the apparition spoke with a voice like wind through dead leaves. "Three moons will align, and you must choose which path to walk."

"Who are you?" Decklan demanded, sword raised. "What do you want from me?"

The figure merely gestured to the tablet. "Read what is written," the spectral figure commanded, its form wavering in the mist. "The tablet speaks to those of divided blood."

Decklan hesitated, feeling the weight of ancient power emanating from the stone. Carefully, he knelt beside it, conscious of Krella and Grom flanking him protectively. Strange symbols covered the surface, flowing and shifting beneath his gaze like living things.

"I can't read this," he admitted, then gasped as the markings suddenly resolved into words he could understand. "Wait... it's changing."

The engraved text glowed with an inner light as Decklan began to read aloud: "When the three moons align, the veil thins between worlds. The one of divided blood shall stand as bridge or breaker." He looked up at the apparition. "What does this mean?"

"It means you are marked by fate," the spirit replied, its hollow eyes fixed on Decklan. "The Blackhand and Bloodfist seek to use you. The shamans have seen your coming."

Grom stepped forward, protective talisman clutched tightly. "My father never spoke of this prophecy."

"Because he fears it," the apparition replied. "As do all who cling to the old ways."

The mist thickened around them, and Decklan felt a sudden pressure against his temples. Images flashed through his mind, his father's shield shattered, his mother kneeling in a circle of moonlight, himself standing between two armies with blood on his hands.

"Stop this!" Krella shouted, slashing at the mist with her blade. The spirit flickered but didn't disperse.

"Three nights hence, the moons align," it continued, voice growing fainter. "The blood price will be demanded. Treachery has occurred. The shield will fall."

Decklan struggled to his feet, fighting against the visions. "What blood price? Speak plainly!"

But the apparition was already fading, its final words barely audible: "Return to your father while you can, son of two worlds. The shadow falls tonight."

With a sudden rush of wind, the mist dissipated. The stone markers stopped glowing, and the forest clearing returned to normal, save for the tablet now visible in its hidden compartment.

Silence hung heavy in the clearing as the three companions stared at the exposed tablet. Decklan's heart hammered against his ribs, the spirit's warning echoing in his mind.

"We need to take this to my father," Grom said finally, reaching for the stone.

"No," Decklan said, placing a restraining hand on Grom's arm. "If your father feared this prophecy enough to hide it, we can't be sure how he'll react."

Krella nodded grimly. "The spirit warned of treachery within our own ranks."

"But it could be lying," Grom argued, his loyalty to his father evident in his strained voice. "These spirits, they could be manifestations created by our enemies."

Decklan's gaze swept the clearing one last time, taking in the evidence of betrayal and ritual. The spectral warning had struck too close to his own fears to dismiss.

"We take this directly to my father," he decided, carefully lifting the tablet. Its weight seemed to shift in his hands, heavier than stone should be. "Tonight. The shadow falls tonight."

As they prepared to depart, Krella suddenly froze, her keen hunter's senses alert. "Someone's coming."

They melted into the undergrowth just as a small party of Bloodfist scouts entered the clearing. The leader, a battle-scarred warrior with ritual markings of Morgul Vorgath painted across his face, examined the disturbed earth where the tablet had been hidden.

"The ward is broken," he snarled. "The half-blood has found it."

"What do we tell Morgul?" another scout asked, nervously fingering his weapon.

"That we failed. And that Nightshade's pet shaman was right, the prophecy is in motion." The leader kicked at the empty compartment in frustration. "Snarlgar will have our hides for this."

"And the attack? It proceeds tonight?"

The leader nodded grimly. "Nothing changes. The Chieftain falls when the feast begins."

The three companions exchanged alarmed glances from their hiding place. When the Bloodfists finally departed, Decklan signaled for silence until they were well away from the clearing.

CHAPTER SIX

THE SHADOW FALLS

T he celebration fires burned bright against the night sky, casting long shadows across the Shieldbearer camp. Warriors passed cups of fermented honey mead, their laughter and the scent of cooked meat carrying on the wind as they celebrated the recent peace negotiations. Despite the looming threat from the Bloodfist clan, Kargoth had insisted the feast proceed, a show of strength and normalcy in uncertain times.

Decklan stood at the edge of the gathering, the stone tablet from the ritual site concealed beneath his cloak. They had raced back to camp, but arrived too late to speak privately with Kargoth before the feast began. Now his father sat at the head table, surrounded by clan elders and honored warriors.

"We should tell him now," Krella whispered, her eyes scanning the perimeter of the camp.

Grom shook his head. "Not in front of everyone. The warning could be a trick."

Decklan's gaze fixed on his father, who raised a hand to silence the crowd. The prophecy's words echoed in his mind: *The shield will fall*. He took a step forward.

"Brothers and sisters of the Shieldbearer clan," Kargoth began, his voice carrying across the camp. "We face uncertain days, but tonight we celebrate our strength—"

"Father," Decklan called out, pushing through the gathered warriors. "I need to speak with you."

Kargoth's expression hardened at the interruption, but something in Decklan's face made him pause. He nodded slightly.

"After the traditional words," he said, then raised the ceremonial cup carved from ancient oak. "To those who came before us, who taught us to stand as one—"

The words died in his throat. Kargoth's hand trembled, the cup slipping from his grasp. It bounced against the stone table, dark liquid spattering like blood.

"Father?" Decklan rushed forward as Kargoth clutched at his chest, his face contorting in pain.

The chieftain collapsed, toppling from his seat. Decklan caught him before he hit the ground. Chaos erupted around them as warriors surged forward, voices raised in alarm.

"Make way!" Skye's voice cut through the chaos as she pushed through the crowd. "Give him air!"

Decklan cradled his father's head, watching in horror as dark veins spread beneath Kargoth's skin, radiating outward from his neck where the ceremonial cup had touched his lips. Kargoth's eyes locked with his son's, filled with pain and desperate urgency.

"Poison," Gar'zul Wiseblood pronounced, kneeling beside them. The shaman's weathered face was grim as he examined the spilled liquid. "A powerful one."

Skye's hands moved with practiced precision, checking Kargoth's pulse and pupils. "Help me carry him to our dwelling," she commanded. Four warriors stepped forward immediately, lifting their fallen chief with reverent care.

Decklan reached for the shattered remains of the cup but Gar'zul stopped him. "Don't touch it. The poison could still harm you."

As they moved Kargoth to the healer's tent, the celebration dissolved into fearful whispers. Warriors gripped weapon hilts, scanning the darkness beyond the firelight. Elders huddled in urgent conference.

Inside the dwelling, Skye worked frantically, grinding herbs and mixing potions as Decklan held his father's hand. Kargoth's breathing grew increasingly labored, his powerful frame wracked with spasms.

"Fight, Father," Decklan whispered, his voice breaking. "You must fight this."

Kargoth's eyes flickered open, recognition dawning through the pain. With tremendous effort, he raised a trembling hand to grasp Decklan's forearm.

"My son," he gasped, each word a struggle. "Listen carefully."

Decklan leaned closer as Gar'zul and Skye exchanged grave looks over their preparations.

"Trust... your whole self," Kargoth managed, his voice barely audible. "Bew are... the shield's shadow."

Confusion crossed Decklan's face. "What do you mean? What shadow?"

Kargoth's grip tightened painfully. "The divided blood... prophecy is"...real." Kargoth's voice faltered as his body seized with another wave of pain. Blood trickled from the corner of his mouth as he struggled for one last breath. "You must... unite..."

His final word dissolved into a rattling exhale. The mighty hand gripping Decklan's arm went slack, falling away. Kargoth Stormshield, Chieftain of the Shieldbearer Clan, was dead.

"No!" Decklan's anguished cry pierced the night. "Father!"

Skye dropped her mortar and rushed to her husband's side, pressing her hands to his chest as if she could will life back into him. Her healing chants grew more frantic, more desperate, until they broke into sobs.

Gar'zul placed a weathered hand on Kargoth's forehead, murmuring the ancient rites to guide a warrior's spirit to the ancestors. Outside, the news spread like wildfire through the camp, wails of grief rising into the night sky.

Decklan remained frozen, his father's final words echoing in his mind. The prophecy. The divided blood. The shield's shadow. What had Kargoth been trying to tell him?

"The cup," he said suddenly, rising to his feet. "I need to see the cup."

He strode from the dwelling, Grom and Krella following close behind. Warriors parted before him, their faces etched with shock and grief. At the feast table, Decklan found two elders examining the shattered remains of the ceremonial cup.

"Let me see it," he demanded, his voice raw with emotion.

The elders exchanged glances before stepping aside. Decklan knelt, examining the fragments without touching them. The ancient oak cup had been used in clan ceremonies for generations, but now he noticed something he'd never seen before, tiny markings carved around the rim, nearly invisible to the casual observer.

"These aren't Shieldbearer markings," he said, pointing to the strange symbols.

Grom leaned closer. "They look like... ritual marks. Similar to what we found at the stone circle."

"Look at the inside," Krella said, her voice tight with anger. "The stain pattern is wrong. It's not from normal use, this was recently hollowed deeper and treated with something."

Decklan nodded grimly. "This wasn't just poison. It was a ritual killing." He stood, scanning the gathered faces. "Who handled the ceremonial cup today? Who prepared it?"

An uncomfortable silence fell over the crowd until an elder stepped forward. "I retrieved it from the sacred chest this morning, as is tradition. But I gave it to Gar'zul for the blessing ritual before the feast."

All eyes turned to Gar'zul, who had just emerged from the chieftain's dwelling. The shaman's expression darkened.

"I performed the blessing as always," he said, his voice steady. "Then I placed it on the table myself. Anyone could have approached it afterward."

"Or before," muttered someone in the crowd.

Decklan felt a cold certainty settling in his gut. This was not a random attack. The mysterious spirit's warning, the prophecy, his father's final words, all pointed to something larger, more calculated than a simple assassination.

"The markings match the ritual circle we found," he announced, looking from the cup to the faces around him. "The same ones where Bloodfist warriors were killed. This was done by the same hand."

Grom stepped forward, his expression troubled. "We found something else today." He looked to Decklan, who nodded and produced the stone tablet from beneath his cloak.

"A prophecy," Decklan said, holding up the tablet so all could see. "About the three moons aligning and someone of 'divided blood' who will stand as bridge or breaker." His voice caught. "My father's last words confirmed it was real."

Murmurs spread through the crowd. Gar'zul's eyes widened almost imperceptibly before his expression hardened.

"Dangerous talk," the shaman warned. "This is not the time for mysterious prophecies. Our chief lies dead. We must prepare for what comes next."

An elder warrior stepped forward, his scarred face twisted with grief and rage. "What comes next? Vengeance! Our chief was murdered by treachery. We must answer blood with blood!"

Shouts of agreement rose from the gathered warriors, weapons rattling as they were raised in anger. The grief of the clan was transforming rapidly into bloodlust.

"The Bloodfists threatened us," another warrior called out. "They gave us three days, but struck in one! This was their doing!"

"Or the Blackhands," someone else shouted. "Their timing was too convenient!"

Decklan raised his hands, trying to quiet the growing chaos. "We don't know who did this yet. The cup was tampered with, but we need—"

"We need war!" The crowd's voice swelled, drowning out his words. "For Kargoth!"

Gar'zul stepped forward, his weathered face solemn in the firelight. "The spirits call for justice," he intoned, his deep voice carrying authority that silenced even the angriest warriors. "I will commune with the ancestors tonight. They will guide us to Kargoth's murderers."

The shaman turned to Decklan, eyes unreadable in the shadows. "Until then, we must prepare the fallen chief for his journey to the ancestors. And..." he paused, "we must consider who shall lead us now."

All eyes turned to Decklan, standing with his father's blood still on his hands, the prophecy tablet clutched in his grip. The weight of expectation settled over him like a suffocating cloak.

"The son of the chief," an elder woman said, "has first claim by tradition."

"But he is half-human," came a muttered response. "In these dangerous times, can we afford—"

"Enough!" Krella's voice cut through the whispers. "Kargoth's body isn't yet cold, and you debate succession? Have you no respect?"

Her words brought shameful silence. Decklan looked around at the faces of his clan, some grief-stricken, others calculating, many simply lost. His gaze finally settled on his mother, who stood in the doorway of their dwelling, her face a mask of anguish as she watched the clan's reaction unfold. She held his gaze for a long moment, her eyes reflecting a mix of profound grief and growing concern for what was to come.

"Krella is right," Decklan said, his voice gaining strength despite his grief. "Tonight, we mourn. Tomorrow, we will seek answers." He straightened, shoulders squared against the weight now pressing upon them. "And I swear by my father's blood that those responsible will pay."

The declaration hung in the night air as warriors nodded grimly. Decklan turned back toward his family's dwelling, where his father's body lay. As the crowd parted to let him pass, he caught Gar'zul watching him with an inscrutable expression.

Inside the dwelling, Skye had begun the ritual preparation of Kargoth's body. Silent tears tracked down her face as she worked, her hands steady despite her grief. Decklan knelt beside his father's body, placing his hand over Kargoth's heart.

"I will find who did this," he whispered. "And I will honor your final words, though I don't yet understand them."

Skye looked up, her eyes red-rimmed but clear. "Your father believed in you completely," she said softly. "Not despite your dual heritage, but because of it." She touched the stone tablet that Decklan had set aside. "This prophecy, you believe it speaks of you?"

"The spirit in the mist said as much," Decklan replied. "And Father confirmed it with his dying breath."

Skye was silent for a long moment, her fingers tracing the ancient symbols. "The Moongazers have stories of such prophecies," she finally said. "When the three moons align, the veil between worlds thins. Old magic stirs."

"What does it mean to be 'bridge or breaker'?" Decklan asked.

"I don't know," Skye admitted. "But your father's last words... 'unite.' Perhaps that's your answer."

Before Decklan could respond, Grom and Krella entered the dwelling, their faces grim.

"The camp is in chaos," Grom reported. "Some warriors are already preparing for war, convinced the Bloodfists are responsible."

CHAPTER SEVEN

ASHES OF LEADERSHIP

T he funeral pyre burned high against the night sky, orange flames licking upward as if trying to reach the three moons that hung ominously overhead. Kargoth Stormshield's body lay wrapped in ceremonial hides atop the wooden structure. His prized shield, now painted black in mourning and placed beside the pyre for the journey to Gallant's Halls, would soon pass to Decklan

Decklan stood nearest the pyre, his face illuminated by the dancing flames. The heat seared his skin, but he welcomed it, anything to distract from the hollow ache in his chest. Around him, the entire Shieldbearer clan had gathered, their faces solemn masks of grief and anger. Many wept openly. Others stood with clenched jaws and fists, already thirsting for vengeance.

Behind him, Decklan could feel their eyes, judging, questioning, wondering. The son of Kargoth: half-human, half-orc, fully trusted by neither.

Gar'zul stepped forward, his massive frame silhouetted against the flames. The shaman raised his arms, his voice carrying across the gathering.

"Kargoth Stormshield walks now to Gallant's Halls, where the brave never truly die!" he proclaimed. "The Vanguard welcomes a warrior whose shield protected us all. But his shield is broken, and our clan bleeds!"

Murmurs rippled through the crowd. Decklan glanced sideways at Grom, who stood rigid, eyes focused on his father with an intensity that bordered on suspicion.

"The spirits demand justice," Gar'zul continued, his voice dropping to a growl. "They demand blood for blood!"

The murmurs grew louder, angrier. Warriors pounded spear butts against the ground in agreement.

"I have performed the divination ritual," Gar'zul said. "The signs are clear, our enemies conspire against us. The Blackhand and Bloodfist clans have brought this darkness upon us!"

Decklan's gaze snapped to the shaman. Something felt wrong. The markings on the poisoned cup had been distinctive—unlike anything he'd seen from either clan.

"We must strike before they can further weaken us!" a voice shouted from the crowd.

"Blood for blood!" another warrior bellowed.

Decklan watched as the clan's grief transformed into rage before his eyes. He looked to his mother, who stood apart from the others, her face showing concern rather than bloodlust. Beside her, Krella observed with narrowed eyes, her hand resting on her weapon's hilt.

"Wait," Decklan said, his voice barely carrying over the growing chants for war. He cleared his throat and tried again. "WAIT!"

The crowd fell silent, surprised by his command.

"My father—" Decklan's voice caught. He swallowed hard and continued. "My father would not rush to war without certainty. The markings on the cup match neither Blackhand nor Bloodfist traditions."

Gar'zul's eyes flashed. "You question the spirits' guidance, boy?"

"I question hasty conclusions," Decklan replied, meeting the shaman's gaze steadily. "Someone wants us at each other's throats. The attack at the Neutral Stones, the ritual sites, the prophecy, they're all connected."

Before Gar'zul could respond, a commotion arose at the edge of the gathering. Two scouts pushed their way through the crowd, their expressions grave.

"Messengers approach from both the Blackhand and Bloodfist clans!" one announced. "They demand audience."

Murmurs of suspicion rippled through the assembly. Gar'zul stepped forward.

"I will speak for the clan in our chief's absence."

"No," Decklan said firmly. "I am Kargoth's son. I will hear what they have to say."

The crowd parted as two figures were escorted forward. The first, a tall Blackhand warrior bearing Reyn Nightshade's insignia, bowed his head slightly in acknowledgment of the funeral proceedings. The second, a heavyset Bloodfist with ritual scars covering his face, merely scowled.

"The Blackhand clan offers condolences for your loss," the first messenger said. "Chieftain Reyn Nightshade sends word that she had no part in this treachery and seeks continued alliance against our common enemy."

"Lies," the Bloodfist messenger spat. "The Blackhands orchestrated this to blame us. Chieftain Snarlgar demands the Shieldbearers honor our territorial boundaries or face war. He will not be held responsible for another clan's treachery."

The gathering erupted in angry shouts. Decklan raised his hand, and to his surprise, the crowd quieted.

"You bring threats to a funeral pyre?" Decklan's voice remained steady despite the rage building inside him. "My father's body isn't yet ash, and you speak of boundaries and war?"

The Bloodfist messenger sneered. "The weak mourn. The strong prepare."

Decklan stepped closer, his amber eyes reflecting the funeral flames. "Tell your chieftain that the Shieldbearers are neither weak nor foolish. We know when we're being manipulated."

"Your father was weak," the messenger growled. "He chose words over strength. The strong rule—"

Before he could finish, Decklan's fist connected with his jaw. The Bloodfist staggered backward, spitting blood onto the sacred ground.

"You dishonor this ceremony," Decklan said quietly, his controlled voice more frightening than any shout. "Leave now with your lives, and tell your masters that the Shieldbearers will not be pawns in their game."

As the messengers were escorted away, Gar'zul approached Decklan, his expression unreadable.

"The clan needs leadership, not diplomatic words," the shaman said. "With Kargoth gone, the elders must determine succession."

"There is no question of succession," growled a battle-scarred elder named Varkus. "Kargoth's son stands before us."

"A half-human son," another elder countered. "Our traditions speak clearly, only pure blood may lead."

The words struck Decklan like physical blows, but he kept his expression neutral. He'd heard them all his life, yet they never lost their sting. Silence fell over the gathering as the clan watched, waiting for his response.

"My blood may be mixed," Decklan said, his voice carrying in the stillness, "but my heart belongs to this clan. My father taught me that the Shieldbearer's strength lies not in purity but in protection—of our people, our traditions, our future."

He turned to face the entire assembly, standing tall beside his father's pyre.

"I do not demand leadership by birthright. I offer my service because it is needed. The threat we face targets all clans. If my mixed blood allows me to see what others cannot, then it is an asset, not a weakness."

Murmurs spread through the crowd, some approving, others doubtful. Skye stepped forward, her human features illuminated by the flames.

"The Moongazer tribe has prophecies about times when the three moons align," she said. "They speak of old magics stirring, of veils thinning between worlds. Whatever forces are at work here transcend clan rivalries."

"Human superstitions," scoffed an elder.

"Wisdom our enemies might also possess," countered Varkus. "I fought beside Kargoth for thirty winters. He valued his son's perspective. So should we."

Gar'zul raised his staff for attention. "The spirits must be consulted. I will perform the ritual of succession tonight, as the moons align. Until then, we should prepare our defenses."

As the gathering began to disperse, Grom approached Decklan, his expression troubled.

"My father's eagerness for war concerns me," he whispered. "The ritual sites, the prophecy... something isn't right."

Krella joined them, her eyes alert for eavesdroppers. "The poison cup bore markings unlike any clan totems. Someone wants us fighting each other when we should be standing together."

"The divided blood prophecy," Decklan murmured. "Bridge or breaker... My father's final words told me to unite, not divide."

Skye approached, laying a gentle hand on her son's arm. "Your father believed in you, all of you. Remember that in the days ahead."

Decklan nodded solemnly, his gaze returning to the funeral pyre where flames continued to consume what remained of Kargoth Stormshield. The firelight cast long shadows across the gathering, and for a moment, Decklan thought he saw his father's silhouette among them.

As the clan dispersed to prepare defenses, Decklan remained by the pyre. Varkus approached, the old warrior's face deeply lined with grief and concern.

"They question your blood," the elder said gruffly, "but I watched you grow. Kargoth saw strength in your differences. Leadership isn't about who you are born as, it's about who you choose to become."

"And if I'm not ready?" Decklan asked quietly.

Varkus gestured toward the three moons hanging ominously in the night sky. "None of us are ready for what comes. But the burden falls to you nonetheless."

Later that night, as the funeral pyre burned down to embers, Decklan sat alone in his father's dwelling. Kargoth's belongings surrounded him, weapons, ceremonial items, and the clan's ancient records inscribed on hide scrolls. The weight of legacy pressed down upon him like a physical force.

A soft sound at the entrance made him look up. Krella stood there, her silhouette backlit by moonlight.

"The camp is secure," she reported, stepping inside. "But rumors spread among the warriors. Many prepare for war regardless of tomorrow's decision."

"And what do you think?" Decklan asked.

Krella sat beside him, her face solemn in the dim light. "I feel like your father was murdered by someone who understands us too well, someone who knows exactly how to manipulate our anger."

She paused, then added more quietly, "I also feel you're stronger than you believe. Your human blood is not weakness, it's perspective. We need that now more than ever."

A gust of wind rattled the dwelling's entrance covering. Outside, the three moons had begun their rare alignment, casting an eerie multicolored glow across the camp.

"Tomorrow," Decklan said, his voice firming with resolve, "I'll face the succession ritual. Whether they accept me or not, I know what my father wanted, unity, not division."

Krella leaned forward, her eyes reflecting the dim firelight. "The warriors respect strength, but they also respect wisdom. You've shown both today."

"Some see only my human blood," Decklan replied, running his fingers over his father's shield emblem.

"Those who matter see all of you," Krella said softly. Her hand briefly touched his before withdrawing. "Get some rest. Dawn brings challenges enough."

After she left, Decklan stepped outside. The three moons hung in perfect alignment overhead, bathing the camp in an otherworldly glow. Warriors stood at their posts, their silhouettes sharp against the night sky. The air felt charged, as though the world itself held its breath.

Near the healer's tent, Decklan spotted an unfamiliar figure, a woman he hadn't seen before. She stood motionless, observing the moons, her face tilted upward. Something about her stillness seemed unnatural, almost ethereal in the strange light.

When she turned, sensing his gaze, her eyes caught the moonlight in a way that made them appear to glow. She nodded once in acknowledgment before disappearing between the dwellings.

Decklan moved to follow but stopped at the sound of raised voices from the shaman's tent. He recognized Grom's voice, then Gar'zul's deeper tones, their argument heated though the words indistinct.

"—cannot be trusted!" Grom's voice became suddenly clear.

"You question too much," came Gar'zul's growled response. "The spirits have spoken. The clan must follow tradition."

"Even if tradition leads us to destruction?"

Silence followed, then the sound of something heavy being thrown. When Grom emerged, his face was flushed with anger. He nearly collided with Decklan before recognizing him in the moonlight.

"My father prepares for his succession ritual," Grom said bitterly. "He's determined that only a 'pure-blood' should lead."

"And you disagree?" Decklan asked, studying his friend's troubled expression.

Grom looked over his shoulder toward his father's tent, then pulled Decklan further into the shadows between dwellings.

"My father speaks of tradition and purity," Grom whispered, "but I've seen the texts he keeps hidden, ancient prophecies about times when the moons align. They speak of 'divided blood' as a bridge between worlds." He paused, his eyes searching Decklan's face. "He fears you, Decklan. Or rather, he fears what you represent."

Decklan absorbed this, the pieces slowly connecting. "The prophecy mentioned at the ritual site... bridge or breaker."

"My father believes the prophecy threatens the old ways. He thinks 'divided blood' will end orc dominance." Grom gripped Decklan's shoulder. "But I think it means something else entirely. Maybe 'bridge' means uniting our peoples, finding strength through alliance rather than conflict."

Their conversation was interrupted by the sound of approaching footsteps. Both turned to see the strange woman Decklan had noticed earlier. Up close, her features were striking—neither fully human nor orc, with eyes that seemed to shift colors in the moonlight.

"The divided blood stands at the crossroads," she said, her voice melodic yet somehow ancient. "Two paths lie before you, Decklan Stormshield."

"Who are you?" Decklan demanded. "How do you know my name?"

"I am Kyra," she replied simply. "I arrived with healers from the western settlements. Your mother welcomed me." She glanced skyward at the aligned moons. "What matters is not who I am, but what approaches. The veil thins. Old powers awaken. And you must choose."

"Choose what?" Grom asked suspiciously.

"Whether to be bridge or breaker," Kyra answered. "Whether to unite or divide." She fixed her gaze on Decklan. "Your father knew. That is why he died."

Before either could respond, drums began to sound from the center of camp. The succession ritual was beginning.

"Go," Kyra said. "But remember, the shield's strength is not in the metal itself, but in the arm that wields it and the purpose that guides it."

Decklan and Grom exchanged troubled glances before hurrying toward the clan's central gathering space. The rhythmic pounding of ritual drums grew louder, their primal beat resonating through the ground beneath their feet.

CHAPTER EIGHT

STRANGER'S ARRIVAL

The entire clan had assembled around the sacred circle where generations of Shieldbearer chieftains had been chosen. Elders formed an inner ring, their weathered faces grave in the multicolored moonlight. Warriors created a protective outer circle, weapons at the ready as though expecting the very night to attack.

Gar'zul stood at the circle's center, his massive frame adorned with ceremonial totems and painted symbols. He raised his staff, and the drums fell silent.

"The three moons align," the shaman intoned, his deep voice carrying across the hushed gathering. "The ancestors watch. The spirits speak." He gestured toward the night sky. "In times of greatest peril, the Shieldbearer clan must have its strongest leader."

Decklan stepped forward, entering the circle. The clan's collective gaze weighed upon him, hope from some, doubt from others, and from a few, open hostility. At the circle's edge, he spotted his mother standing with Krella and, surprisingly, the stranger Kyra.

"I am Decklan, son of Kargoth," he declared, his voice steady despite the turmoil within. "I claim the right of succession."

A murmur ran through the assembly. Gar'zul's expression remained impassive as he gestured toward three stone markers at the circle's center.

"Three trials determine worthiness," the shaman announced. "Strength of arm, wisdom of mind, vision of heart." He pointed to each stone in turn. "Fail any, and leadership passes elsewhere."

Decklan nodded. These were the traditional trials his father had described years ago.

"Who challenges this claim?" Gar'zul asked the gathering.

A hulking warrior named Drogath stepped forward, tribal scars covering his muscled frame. His eyes narrowed as he regarded Decklan with barely concealed contempt.

"I challenge," Drogath growled. "The son of Kargoth only by blood, not by spirit." His gaze swept dismissively over Decklan. "Half-human, half-strength, half-worthy."

Several warriors grunted in agreement. Decklan felt the familiar anger rising within him but forced it down, remembering Kyra's words about choice.

"Anyone else?" Gar'zul inquired, scanning the crowd.

To Decklan's surprise, a second figure stepped forward, Varkus, the elder who had supported him earlier.

"I too challenge," the clan elder announced. His eyes met Decklan's with unexpected warmth. "Not to lead, but to test properly. Our future demands no less."

Understanding dawned on Decklan. Varkus wasn't opposing him but ensuring the trials would be conducted fairly. The old warrior was offering himself as counterbalance to Drogath's clear prejudice.

Gar'zul nodded solemnly. "It is decided. The first trial begins at dawn's first light, strength of arm." He struck his staff against the ground. "Until then, the challenger and challenged must prepare in isolation."

As the gathering began to disperse, Decklan found himself ushered toward a small preparation tent at the edge of camp. Tradition dictated he spend the night in meditation before the trials. Two guards took position outside.

Inside, he found a simple pallet, a water skin, and his father's shield leaning against the center pole, the only possession of Kargoth's he was permitted during the succession rituals.

Alone with his thoughts, Decklan traced the worn edge of the shield, feeling the notches and dents that told the story of his father's countless battles. The emblem of the Shieldbearer clan, a mountain with a shield before it, had been polished to a soft gleam.

"What am I supposed to do, father?" he whispered to the empty tent. "How can I unite what's been divided for generations?"

The tent flap rustled, and Decklan spun, reaching for his dagger. But it was Kyra who slipped inside like a shadow, her unusual eyes catching the lamplight.

"The guards—" Decklan began.

"Are temporarily distracted," she replied with a hint of amusement. "We don't have long."

She moved to the center of the tent, her gaze falling on Kargoth's shield. With reverent fingers, she traced the clan emblem.

"Do you know why your clan is called the Shieldbearers?" she asked.

"Of course," Decklan answered. "We're known for our defensive prowess in battle."

Kyra shook her head slightly. "That's what most believe. The true meaning is older." She met his eyes. "In the ancient tongue, 'shield' and 'bridge' share the same word. Your ancestors were not just protectors in war, but bridges between peoples in peace."

Decklan frowned. "That's not what I was taught."

"Many truths have been forgotten, or deliberately buried." Kyra's voice lowered. "Your father was beginning to understand this when he died."

"Who are you really?" Decklan demanded, studying her strange, almost luminous features. "You're no ordinary wanderer."

A small smile played at the corners of her mouth. "I am what I claimed to be, a healer. Though perhaps I heal more than just bodies."

She reached into her robes and withdrew a small bundle wrapped in cloth. "You face three trials tomorrow. The first, strength of arm, will be as you expect. Drogath will try to humiliate you with pure orcish might."

"I can handle him," Decklan said, though uncertainty crept into his voice.

"Perhaps." Kyra unwrapped the bundle, revealing a collection of dried herbs. "But the other trials will test more than your physical strength. Gar'zul has altered the traditional tests. He fears the prophecy."

"Why would he fear it?"

"Because he cannot control it." She crushed the herbs between her fingers. "And because he doesn't understand that a divided bloodline means twice the strength, not half."

She produced a small clay bowl from her robes and mixed the crushed herbs with water from Decklan's skin. "This will help clear your mind. The second trial, wisdom of mind, will involve a riddle or puzzle, but Gar'zul will likely choose one with no solution to ensure your failure."

Decklan watched as she stirred the mixture with practiced motions. "And the third trial?"

"Vision of heart is the most dangerous." Her eyes took on a distant quality. "Gar'zul will use sacred herbs to induce a vision-trance. He'll attempt to guide your spirit toward scenes that will break your resolve."

"How do you know all this?"

Kyra's smile was enigmatic. "I've witnessed many succession rituals across many clans. The patterns repeat, especially when fear guides the test-givers."

She offered him the bowl. "Drink this before you sleep. It will protect your mind during the vision trial."

Decklan hesitated, studying the strange woman's face. There was something familiar about her, though he couldn't place it, something in the way she moved, in the cadence of her speech.

"Why help me?" he asked. "You owe no allegiance to the Shieldbearers."

"I serve something greater than any single clan," she answered softly. "As did your mother's people. As your father was beginning to understand."

A shout outside indicated the guards had returned to their posts. Kyra pressed the bowl into Decklan's hands.

"Remember, Decklan Stormshield, you stand at the crossroads of two worlds, but that makes you a bridge, not a half-measure of either." She moved toward the tent flap. "In each trial, look beyond the obvious challenge. What seems like weakness can become strength when viewed differently."

As silently as she had arrived, she slipped out into the night.

Left alone, Decklan stared at the herbal mixture, the liquid catching the moonlight filtering through the tent's seams. After a moment's hesitation, he drank it down in one swallow. The taste was surprisingly sweet, with undertones of something ancient and earthy.

He lay back on the pallet, his father's shield beside him, and closed his eyes. As sleep began to claim him, questions swirled in his mind. Who was Kyra really? What was Gar'zul hiding? And most importantly, could he truly be a bridge between worlds when he had spent his entire life trying to belong to just one?

Sleep claimed him gradually, and with it came dreams unlike any he'd experienced before. He saw himself standing on an actual bridge spanning a great chasm. On one side stood the Shieldbearer clan, on the other, his mother's Moongazer people. Below the bridge, shadows gathered like hungry mist, reaching upward with tendrils of darkness.

The figure of his father appeared beside him, silent but nodding toward the center of the bridge where Decklan stood. His father's shield gleamed not with reflected light but with an inner luminescence.

When Decklan awoke at the first light of dawn, the dream lingered with unusual clarity. The guards called from outside, announcing it was time. As he rose and took up his father's shield, he felt something different, not the usual desperation to prove himself, but a quieter, deeper resolve.

The first trial awaited, and with it, the chance to redefine what strength truly meant.

CHAPTER NINE

TRIAL OF STRENGTH

T he rising sun cast long shadows across the training grounds as Decklan approached the circle marked for the first trial. Warriors and elders gathered in concentric rings, their faces a mixture of anticipation, skepticism, and in some cases, thinly veiled hostility. His mother Skye stood at the edge, her face a mask of concern beneath her composed exterior.

At the center of the circle stood Drogath, his massive frame adorned with battle trophies and ritual scars. The warrior's lips curled into a sneer as Decklan approached.

"The first trial is the Test of Strength," Gar'zul announced, his voice carrying across the assembled clan. "Not merely the strength of muscle, but the strength to endure, to overcome, to continue when flesh fails."

Gar'zul raised a ceremonial spear decorated with feathers and bone talismans. "The challenger who holds this spear aloft the longest shall prevail. Should the spear touch ground, the warrior fails."

Decklan studied the spear as Gar'zul placed it in the center of the circle. It appeared ordinary enough, though the shaft gleamed with some kind of oil.

"Begin!" Gar'zul's staff struck the ground.

Drogath lunged for the spear, but Decklan, anticipating this, moved with the quickness he'd inherited from his mother's people. His fingers closed around the shaft a breath before Drogath's.

The moment Decklan grasped the spear, a searing pain shot through his palm. The shaft wasn't merely oiled, it had been treated with some caustic substance. He nearly dropped it from the shock but gritted his teeth and maintained his grip. Kyra's warning echoed in his mind: "Look beyond the obvious challenge."

Drogath grabbed the opposite end, and their eyes met. The warrior's lips twisted into a knowing smile, revealing he'd been forewarned about the spear's treatment.

"Let us see how long half-breed hands can bear what true orc strength endures," Drogath taunted.

The spear became increasingly heavy as they held it aloft, the acidic substance burning into Decklan's palms. He could feel blisters forming, the skin cracking as the caustic oil seeped deeper. The pain was extraordinary, but he refused to show it on his face.

"Your human weakness shows," Drogath growled, his own hands displaying angry red welts. "Soon your soft skin will give way."

Decklan didn't respond, focusing instead on his breathing. He recalled his mother's teachings about enduring pain, not fighting against it, but acknowledging it, letting it flow through without surrendering to it. The Moongazer way.

An hour passed. Sweat poured down both competitors' faces. The crowd had grown silent, many shocked by their endurance. Grom stood near the edge of the circle, his eyes darting between Decklan and his father Gar'zul, suspicion evident in his gaze.

"Impressive," Drogath admitted grudgingly as the second hour approached. "But endurance alone will not make you chieftain."

"I don't seek to impress you," Decklan finally spoke, his voice steady despite the trembling in his arms. "I seek to serve the clan."

Drogath snorted. "Noble words runt."

Another hour passed. Decklan's vision began to blur, but he found something unexpected happening. As his physical strength waned, a different kind of strength emerged, one born from enduring sideways glances and whispered doubts.

"You've spent your life being tested," Kyra had told him. "Every day has been a trial."

Drogath was struggling now, his breathing labored. The toxic substance had eaten away at both their palms, blood mingling with the caustic oil. When their eyes met again, Decklan saw something new in Drogath's gaze, a reluctant respect.

As the sun reached its zenith, Drogath's arms began to tremble violently. With a roar of frustration, he released the spear and fell to one knee.

"I"I yield," Drogath growled, the words clearly painful to utter.

Decklan remained standing, the spear still held aloft in his bleeding hands. The crowd fell silent, many unable to believe what they had witnessed. Even those who had doubted him looked on with newfound respect.

"The first trial is complete," Gar'zul announced, unable to fully mask his surprise. "Decklan Stormshield has proven his strength."

As Decklan finally lowered the spear, Krella rushed forward with clean cloths and a water skin. She gently took his hands, wincing at the sight of his ravaged palms.

"I've never seen anything like that," she whispered, carefully cleaning the wounds. "You shouldn't have been able to hold on for so long."

Elder Varkus approached, nodding approvingly. "Your father would be proud," he said, his gruff voice softened with genuine respect. "He always said your greatest strength wasn't in your arms, but here." The elder tapped his chest over his heart.

As Skye approached with healing herbs, Decklan caught Gar'zul watching him with narrowed eyes. The shaman quickly looked away, conferring with his acolytes in hushed tones.

"The second trial begins at dusk," Gar'zul announced. "The Test of Wisdom awaits."

Grom helped Decklan back to his tent, while Krella walked protectively at his side.

"My father didn't expect you to pass that test," Grom admitted once they were alone. "The spear was treated with stonebite extract. I've seen it burn through leather."

"Then how did he hold it?" Krella asked, applying Skye's salve to Decklan's blistered hands.

Decklan remained silent, remembering Kyra's herbs and her words: "Your divided blood is not weakness but strength, able to endure what others cannot."

As they bandaged his hands, he gazed at his father's shield leaning against the tent wall. For the first time, he truly understood what it meant to bear the Stormshield name.

CHAPTER TEN

THE CHALLENGE

T he shadows lengthened across the Shieldbearer camp as dusk approached. Decklan sat in his tent, meditating as his mother applied a final layer of healing salve to his burned hands. Though Skye's remedies had worked remarkably well, his palms remained raw and tender.

"The Test of Wisdom is often more dangerous than the Test of Strength," Skye warned, wrapping fresh bandages around his hands. "Your father once told me it reveals the mind's deepest fears and doubts."

"I have plenty of those," Decklan admitted with a wry smile.

Skye placed her hand gently on his cheek. "That's why you'll succeed. The wisest know their limitations." Her eyes searched his. "Gar'zul has altered the traditional tests. Be cautious."

A horn sounded three times, calling everyone to gather. Decklan rose, flexing his bandaged fingers.

"Whatever happens," Skye said, "remember who you are."

The clan had assembled around a large circle marked with stones. At its center stood three pedestals, each bearing a covered object. Gar'zul waited beside them, his expression unreadable in the fading light. Torches blazed around the perimeter, casting dancing shadows.

Elder Varkus approached from the opposite side, looking calm and composed. Decklan noted no sign of Drogath.

"The Test of Wisdom challenges not your knowledge, but your judgment," Gar'zul announced. "Three choices lie before you. You must select one, explaining your reasoning. Choose poorly, and you prove yourself unworthy to lead."

Decklan scanned the crowd, finding Grom's concerned face and Krella's encouraging nod. There was no sign of Kyra.

"Approach the pedestals," Gar'zul commanded.

The torchlight flickered across the three pedestals as Decklan studied the symbols carved into each. The first bore the hammer and shield of Gallant the Vanguard, patron deity of the Shieldbearers. The second displayed the flowing leaves and healing hands of Viviana the Life Weaver, revered by his mother's Moongazer tribe. The third pedestal was marked with the cracked skull and bone dagger of Ravakhor, the Wrathful Sovereign, a deity often worshipped by orc clans to the east, such as the Bloodfists.

"These symbols represent different paths," Gar'zul explained, his staff tapping each pedestal in turn. "Choose one, reveal what lies beneath its cover, and explain why your choice best serves the clan."

Elder Varkus went first, approaching the pedestals with measured steps. After careful consideration, he selected Gallant's pedestal, lifting the cover to reveal an ornate war axe.

"I choose the path of Gallant," Varkus announced, his voice strong despite his years. "The Vanguard teaches us to stand firm, to protect what is ours through strength and vigilance. A chieftain must be the shield of his people."

Murmurs of approval rippled through the crowd as Varkus stepped back. It was a traditional choice, one that would resonate with most of the clan.

Now it was Decklan's turn. He approached the pedestals, acutely aware of every eye upon him. His bandaged hands throbbed as he considered his options. The obvious choice was to follow Varkus's example and select Gallant's path, the safe choice, the expected choice for a Shieldbearer.

But something about the test felt wrong. If Gar'zul had tampered with the first trial, what awaited beneath these covers?

Kyra's voice echoed in his memory: "Look beyond the obvious challenge."

Decklan's heart pounded as he circled the pedestals, feigning contemplation while studying the binding runes etched into their bases. His mother had shown him similar markings in the Moongazer texts—symbols meant to contain or manipulate spirits. This wasn't merely a test of choice; it was a trap.

The crowd grew restless at his deliberation. Murmurs rippled through the assembled warriors. From the corner of his eye, Decklan caught Gar'zul's impatient shift, the shaman's knuckles whitening around his staff.

"Choose, son of Kargoth," Gar'zul prompted, his voice carrying an edge. "A chieftain must be decisive."

Decklan nodded, moving to stand equidistant from all three pedestals. The bandages on his hands gleamed white in the torchlight as he raised his voice to address the clan.

"Before I choose," he said, "I would know what each path truly offers."

Confusion spread across many faces. Elder Varkus frowned, clearly puzzled by Decklan's approach.

"The test is to choose without knowing," Gar'zul countered. "That is wisdom, judging what lies beneath the surface."

"True wisdom," Decklan announced, his voice carrying across the gathered clan, "is not making blind choices, but recognizing when the choices themselves are flawed."

A ripple of whispers moved through the crowd. Gar'zul's eyes narrowed dangerously.

"This test," Decklan continued, "asks me to choose between Gallant, Viviana, or Ravakhor, between protection, healing, or vengeance. But a chieftain cannot limit himself to just one path."

He stepped forward, examining the runes more carefully. They pulsed faintly in the torchlight, not just binding marks, but something more sinister.

"My father taught me that a leader must know when to fight, when to heal, and yes, sometimes when to seek justice," Decklan said. "To choose just one is to abandon the others."

Gar'zul's knuckles whitened around his staff. "You delay, half-blood. Choose now or forfeit the trial."

Decklan looked directly at Gar'zul. "I choose none of these."

Gasps erupted from the crowd. Gar'zul's face twisted with anger, but before he could speak, Decklan continued.

"These pedestals are marked with binding runes," he declared, pointing to the almost invisible markings. "This isn't a test of wisdom, it's a trap."

Grom pushed forward through the crowd, peering at the markings. "He's right," he called out. "Those are containment sigils!"

"Ridiculous!" Gar'zul thundered. "The traditions demand a choice!"

Elder Varkus moved closer, his weathered face concerned. "Let me see these markings."

"Enough!" Gar'zul slammed his staff into the ground. "Make your choice or be declared unworthy!"

Decklan saw genuine fear flash across the shaman's face. Whatever lay beneath those covers, Gar'zul desperately wanted him to choose one. Taking a deep breath, Decklan stepped toward the center pedestal, the one marked with Viviana's symbol.

"If I must choose," Decklan announced, his voice carrying across the hushed gathering, "I choose Viviana's path, the middle way between strength and vengeance."

Gar'zul's expression flickered between alarm and satisfaction as Decklan reached for the cover. Skye stepped forward instinctively, sensing danger.

"Decklan, wait—" she called.

But his bandaged hand had already lifted the cover. A blinding flash of green light erupted from beneath, accompanied by a high-pitched wail that seemed to pierce directly into the mind. The crowd recoiled as a swirling apparition rose from the pedestal, not the expected symbolic object, but a bound spirit, twisted and writhing in obvious agony.

The entity's form coalesced into something vaguely feminine, with elongated limbs and eyes that burned with ethereal fire. It released another piercing shriek as it broke free from the binding circle, flinging itself toward the nearest living beings.

"Spirit breach!" Gar'zul shouted, raising his staff defensively. "The bindings were compromised!"

Decklan reacted instinctively, lunging for his father's shield that he had brought to the ceremony. As the entity swept toward a group of onlookers, he positioned himself between them and the spirit, raising the shield.

The apparition collided with the shield's surface, causing it to vibrate violently and emit a deep resonant tone. The spirit recoiled momentarily, then circled around, seeking another target.

"Stay back!" Decklan shouted to the clan members, who were scattering in panic.

Before anyone could react, the spirit dove toward a young warrior named Torkal who stood frozen in shock. Decklan threw himself forward, shield extended, but the spirit was faster. It passed partially through Torkal before Decklan's shield forced it away.

Torkal screamed and collapsed, his left side suddenly withered as though years of life had been drained from him in an instant.

Gar'zul began chanting furiously, his staff tracing complex patterns in the air. "The binding was faulty," he called out. "Someone has tampered with the sacred pedestals!"

The spirit hovered above the chaos of the gathering, its ethereal form twisting and contorting as it surveyed the panicked clan members below. Decklan stood with his father's shield raised, his eyes tracking the entity's erratic movements.

"Everyone stay together!" he shouted above the commotion. "Form circles, backs to the center!"

To his surprise, the warriors responded immediately, organizing themselves into defensive formations as they'd been trained. Even in their fear, the discipline of the Shieldbearers held.

Gar'zul continued his chanting, but Decklan noticed something disturbing, the shaman's incantations seemed to agitate the spirit rather than contain it. Each verse caused the entity to pulse brighter, its keening wail intensifying.

"Stop your chanting!" Skye called out to Gar'zul. "You're feeding it power!"

Gar'zul ignored her, his voice rising in volume. The spirit suddenly plunged toward him, drawn by his magic. At the last moment, it veered away, circling back toward Decklan with unnerving speed.

Without thinking, Decklan raised the shield between himself and the approaching entity. As before, when the spirit collided with the shield's surface, a deep resonant tone echoed across the gathering place. This time, however, Decklan noticed glowing sigils flickering to life across the shield's face, ancient markings he'd never seen before.

The spirit recoiled, its form becoming more unstable. It seemed... afraid of the shield.

"It knows this shield," Skye said, appearing suddenly at Decklan's side. "Kargoth used it to protect the clan from such entities before."

"What is this thing?" Decklan asked, keeping the shield between them and the hovering spirit.

"A bound lunar guardian," she replied. "Twisted and corrupted by improper binding."

The spirit circled them warily, unable to approach while the shield's sigils glowed. Decklan realized it was deliberately trying to separate him from the rest of the clan.

"The third trial has begun," came Kyra's voice from behind him. She had appeared as silently as a shadow," Decklan thought as he turned to see Kyra standing near him, her eyes fixed on the hovering spirit.

"This is the Vision of Heart," Kyra continued quietly. "Not as Gar'zul intended, but as the fates have decreed."

The spirit suddenly let out another piercing wail and dove toward a group of children huddled behind their parents. Decklan sprinted forward, his muscles burning with effort as he threw himself between the spirit and its targets, shield raised high.

When the entity struck the shield this time, the impact sent Decklan sliding backward several paces, his boots digging furrows in the dirt. The sigils on the shield blazed with blinding intensity, and the spirit's form seemed to shred at the edges, wisps of ethereal essence dissipating into the night air.

"The shield weakens it!" Grom shouted. "Keep it at bay, Decklan!"

Gar'zul's face contorted with a mixture of fear and rage. "This spirit should have been bound to the pedestal! Someone has interfered with the sacred trial!"

Instead of raising the shield, Decklan did something unexpected. He lowered it slightly, meeting the spirit's gaze directly. In its writhing, tormented form, he saw something familiar, a reflection of his own inner struggle, torn between worlds and identities.

"I see you," he said softly as the entity approached.

The spirit halted mere inches from his face, its ethereal features rippling with confusion. The crowd gasped, anticipating Decklan's destruction, but he remained steady.

"You're caught between worlds," Decklan continued, his voice gentle yet firm. "Bound improperly, forced to serve purposes not your own."

The spirit pulsed, its keening softening to a low hum.

"I understand division," Decklan continued, his voice steady despite the spectral face hovering inches from his own. "Being pulled between realms, belonging fully to neither."

The spirit's wailing subsided to a low, mournful tone. Its form rippled, becoming less chaotic, more defined. The ethereal features resembled a female face, twisted by pain but increasingly focused on Decklan's words.

"This spirit is no enemy," Decklan announced to the stunned onlookers. "It's a guardian, bound against its will and corrupted by improper rituals."

Gar'zul stepped forward, staff raised threateningly. "The spirit breached containment! It must be banished before it drains more life!"

"No." Decklan's voice carried surprising authority. "It was improperly bound, twisting its purpose."

The spirit drifted closer to Decklan, its form continuing to stabilize. When it spoke, the sound was like wind through hollow reeds.

"Divided blood... shield-bearer... bridge-walker..."

Skye approached cautiously, her healer's instinct overcoming fear. "It recognizes you, Decklan. The guardian spirits were meant to test worthiness, not attack."

Decklan lowered his shield completely, facing the entity without protection. "I am Decklan Stormshield, son of Kargoth and Skye. I stand between worlds as you do."

The spirit hovered before him, its ethereal eyes studying him intently. Slowly, it extended a translucent hand toward his chest.

"The third trial," it whispered. "Vision of Heart."

As the spirit's hand pressed against Decklan's chest, visions flashed through his mind, glimpses of truth that no deception could hide. He saw Gar'zul meeting with shadowy figures in a moonlit clearing, heard fragments of whispered conspiracies, felt the weight of betrayal.

"Enough!" Gar'zul's staff came down with a thunderous crack. The shaman's face was ashen, his eyes wide with something Decklan had never seen there before, fear.

The spirit withdrew its hand, drifting backward as Gar'zul unleashed a barrage of binding spells. Unlike his previous attempts, these incantations were desperate, powerful, and effective. The entity's form began to dissolve, pulled back toward the pedestal.

"The trials are suspended!" Gar'zul shouted, his voice cracking with strain. "This ceremony has been corrupted by outside forces!"

The spirit, nearly rebound, locked eyes with Decklan one final time. Its voice, barely audible, whispered: "Beware the shield's shadow..." before collapsing into a swirl of ethereal energy that Gar'zul quickly contained within a hastily drawn circle.

Elder Varkus stepped forward, his weathered face grave. "What is the meaning of this, Gar'zul? The trials have never been suspended before."

Before the shaman could answer, a horn sounded from the edge of camp, three short blasts followed by one long call. The signal for approaching enemies.

"Bloodfist scouts!" A breathless warrior sprinted into the gathering. "A large force, moving quickly toward our northern boundary!"

Gar'zul seized the interruption. "The council must gather immediately! The trials can wait, our borders cannot!"

The clan erupted into controlled chaos as warriors rushed to retrieve weapons and armor. Mothers gathered children, elders secured supplies, and scouts departed to assess the approaching threat.

In the council lodge, elders and senior warriors gathered around the central fire. Decklan stood somewhat apart, still processing the visions granted by the spirit's touch.

"The Bloodfist forces are larger than mere scouting parties," reported Tharak, their chief scout. "At least fifty warriors, moving in formation. This is no raid, it's an invasion force."

"We should strike first!" Drogath pounded his fist on the council table. "Before they reach our outer settlements."

Elder Varkus raised a weathered hand. "We must first determine if this is truly a Bloodfist force. After what we've seen tonight, deception seems to surround us."

All eyes turned to Gar'zul, who had been uncharacteristically silent since containing the spirit. The shaman's face was tight with concealed emotion.

"The trials cannot be completed tonight," he declared finally. "But the clan needs leadership. I propose we name Decklan as war chief until the succession can be properly determined."

Murmurs of surprise rippled through the council. Decklan himself was stunned by Gar'zul's suggestion.

"Decklan has demonstrated strength and courage tonight," Elder Varkus agreed cautiously. "But not all three trials were completed."

"Which is why I suggest war chief, not chieftain," Gar'zul replied smoothly. "A temporary measure until we can resolve the... irregularities... in tonight's ceremony."

Decklan recognized the strategy. By naming him war chief rather than chieftain, Gar'zul maintained ultimate authority while giving Decklan responsibility for the coming battle, a battle where he might conveniently fall.

"I accept," Decklan said before the council could debate further. "But I will need full authority to organize our defenses."

After a tense silence, the elders nodded their agreement. Gar'zul's expression revealed nothing, but Decklan caught the slight tightening of his grip on his staff.

"So be it," Elder Varkus announced. "Decklan Stormshield will lead our warriors as war chief until the succession is resolved."

Decklan stood alone in his father's tent, now his by right of succession, temporary though it might be. Moonlight filtered through the smoke hole above, casting pale silver light across the war table where maps and clan tokens lay scattered. His mind raced with preparations for the coming conflict, weighing strategies against the limited time before the Bloodfist forces would reach their borders.

A soft rustling at the tent flap pulled his attention from the maps. He expected Krella or Grom, but found only emptiness when he turned. A folded piece of parchment lay on the ground just inside the entrance.

His bandaged hands stung as he bent to retrieve it. The parchment was delicate, inscribed with his mother's flowing script:

Decklan,

I've gone to the Moongazer settlement. Their seers may have knowledge about the prophecy and the binding ritual that released the guardian spirit. The alignment of the three moons concerns more than just our clan.

What you saw tonight was only a shadow of the danger approaching. Re-member what your father said: "Trust your whole self." Your divided blood may be our salvation.

I will return with help if I can. Until then, be cautious of the shield's shadow. The oath remains.

—Skye

Decklan crumpled the note in his fist, a surge of conflicting emotions wash-ing through him. His mother had left at the most critical moment, when the clan faced imminent attack. Yet he understood her reasoning, if supernatural forces were at work, the Moongazers' knowledge might prove more valuable than a single healer in battle.

"She's gone, isn't she?"

Decklan turned to find Grom standing in the entrance, his expression somber.

"To her people," Decklan confirmed, gesturing with the crumpled note.

"At least we know where she is," Grom said. "Unlike Kyra, who vanished the moment the spirit was contained."

Decklan hadn't noticed Kyra's disappearance amid the chaos. Her absence now seemed significant, especially after her warnings about the trials.

"We have more pressing concerns," Decklan said.

Chapter Eleven

INTO THE STORM

Decklan stood at the edge of the Shieldbearer camp, his father's shield, now his, strapped firmly to his back. Shadows stretched long across the ground as warriors gathered in small groups, checking weapons and exchanging quiet oaths of vengeance. Decklan felt their eyes upon him, some questioning, others expectant.

The weight of leadership pressed down on his shoulders like a physical burden. Just days ago, he'd been fighting for acceptance. Now he led warriors into battle, warriors whose complete trust he wasn't sure he had earned.

"The scouts report Bloodfist movement to the north and the Blackhands left the eastern ridge some time during the night," Krella said, materializing beside him. She'd tied her dark hair back tightly, her face painted with the traditional Shieldbearer war markings. "We should encounter their outer patrols by midday if we push hard."

Decklan nodded, grateful for her steadfast presence. "And you're certain of the route?"

"As certain as the stars," she replied, her eyes meeting his with unwavering confidence. "The eastern path keeps us in the shadow of the ridge. They won't expect us from that direction."

Grom approached, axe already in hand, his expression eager. "The warriors are ready. Let's spill Bloodfist blood before nightfall."

Decklan studied his friend's face, noting the hunger for battle that hadn't been there before his father's death. The loss had changed them all.

"We move with purpose, not haste," Decklan said, loud enough for nearby warriors to hear. "This isn't a raid for glory. It's revenge for my father."

He turned to address the gathered Shieldbearers, forty strong. Many bore the scars of previous battles, though none had fought in a conflict like this, clan against clan in open warfare.

"We cross the border today not as raiders," Decklan called out, finding strength in his voice that surprised even himself. "We march as judges, executioners of those who murdered our chieftain through cowardice and poison. Kargoth Stormshield's blood demands vengeance!"

The warriors raised their weapons, a low rumble of approval spreading through their ranks. Decklan raised his hand for silence.

"My father taught us that a Shieldbearer's first duty is protection. Today, we protect our clan's future by eliminating those who would destroy us through treachery. Remember his words: 'The oath remains.'"

"The oath remains!" the warriors echoed, thumping weapons against shields.

As they moved out in formation, Decklan took point with Krella and Grom flanking him. The eastern sky began to lighten, painting the clouds in shades of amber and gold. They crossed the border markers, stone monoliths carved with ancient symbols, and entered the disputed territories between clan lands.

The terrain grew rougher as they advanced, following game trails that wound through dense forest and rocky outcroppings. Decklan set a demanding pace, yet deliberately held them back from exhaustion. He caught Krella watching him with approval.

"You're finding your stride as a leader," she said quietly as they paused at a stream crossing.

"I'm doing what needs to be done," Decklan replied, unsure if her assessment was accurate. Every decision felt like a gamble.

By midday, as Krella had predicted, their scouts returned with news of Bloodfist movement.

"War party," whispered Tharak, their lead scout. "At least twenty, moving south along the old trade route. They're painting themselves for battle."

Decklan crouched, sketching a quick map in the dirt. "Show me."

As Tharak indicated the Bloodfist position, Decklan felt a chill. "They're positioning themselves between us and home."

"A trap," Grom growled. "They knew we were coming."

Decklan studied the makeshift map, his mind racing. Something didn't feel right. "No... they're not waiting for us specifically. Look at their position, they're setting up to ambush anyone coming from the Neutral Stones."

"Another diplomatic party?" Krella asked, eyes widening.

"Or returning travelers," Decklan replied. "Either way, we have an opportunity."

He quickly outlined a plan to circle behind the Bloodfist position. Several warriors objected, preferring a direct assault, but Decklan stood firm.

"We're not here for a glorious last stand. We're here for revenge, and that means surviving to deliver it."

His tone left no room for argument. The warriors reluctantly accepted his decision, though Decklan noted the lingering doubt in some eyes. They moved out, taking a narrow deer trail that wound through a dense thicket of thornbushes.

An hour later, they encountered their first Bloodfist scouts, a pair of warriors moving carelessly through the underbrush, clearly not expecting enemies from this direction. Without hesitation, Decklan signaled for silence, then led Krella and Grom in a swift flanking maneuver.

The fight was brief but decisive. Decklan moved with a fluidity that surprised even himself, his body remembering the countless drills with his father. He feinted with his shield, drawing the scout's attention, then struck with precision, a technique his mother had taught him while hunting. The scout fell without raising an alarm.

Beside him, Grom dispatched the second scout with brutal efficiency, then looked at Decklan with newfound respect. "You fight differently now," he observed, wiping his blade.

"I fight as myself," Decklan replied simply.

They continued forward, more cautious now. From a ridge overlooking the old trade route, they observed the main Bloodfist force, thirty warriors at least, more than Torven had estimated.

"Too many for a direct confrontation," Krella whispered.

Decklan studied their formations, noticing how they positioned themselves in the narrow pass. "They're waiting for something specific," he murmured. "See how they've arranged their archers?"

The Bloodfists had positioned their forces to funnel travelers into a killing zone. It was a sophisticated ambush, not a random patrol.

Decklan made his first truly confident decision as leader. "We change course," he announced. "The main Bloodfist force is too entrenched. We'll move northeast, toward their encampment instead."

Grumbles rose from several warriors, but Krella backed him immediately. "The war chief has spoken. The target isn't random warriors, it's their leadership."

As they adjusted their route, the day turned to dusk. The war party made camp in a sheltered valley, keeping fires small and hidden beneath the canopy. Sentries were posted with extra vigilance, and Decklan made sure to visit each post, offering quiet words of encouragement.

As night deepened, Decklan sat alone on a fallen log at the camp's edge, studying the stars. The familiar constellations offered little comfort tonight. He traced his finger along the edge of his father's shield, feeling each dent and scrape, a history of battles fought and survived.

"You should rest," Krella said, approaching quietly. She sat beside him, her presence somehow both comforting and unsettling.

"A war chief doesn't rest until all threats are accounted for," Decklan replied, echoing his father's words.

"And if the war chief exhausts himself, who leads the warriors?" Krella countered with gentle firmness. "You've made good decisions today. Trust them. Trust yourself."

Decklan looked at her, seeing not just his childhood friend but a capable warrior whose confidence in him never wavered. "I keep wondering if I'm leading them to death rather than justice."

"Such thoughts plague all good leaders," she said. "The bad ones never question themselves."

Their conversation was interrupted by a startled cry from a sentry. Decklan leapt to his feet, weapon drawn, as warriors throughout the camp stirred to alertness.

"The sky," the sentry called out, pointing upward. "Look at the moons!"

Decklan tilted his head back and felt his breath catch. All three moons, Calanthir, Harmony, and Morvok, had aligned in a perfect triangle, directly overhead. Their combined light bathed the valley in an eerie silver-green glow, turning familiar shapes strange and otherworldly.

"The three-fold crossing," Grom whispered, appearing at Decklan's side. "My father spoke of this. It happens once in a generation."

Warriors gathered, weapons half-drawn, staring skyward with a mixture of awe and unease. The air itself seemed charged with potential, the normal night sounds of the forest fallen silent.

"What does it mean?" Krella asked, her usual confidence wavering.

Decklan stared at the three moons, their light washing over him like cold water. The hairs on his arms stood erect, and he felt a strange resonance within, as if the aligned moons pulled at something deep in his blood.

"I don't know," Decklan answered honestly, unable to tear his gaze from the celestial alignment. "But I feel it... here." He pressed his fist against his chest.

"An omen," muttered Tharak. "The three moons watch our vengeance march."

Grom nodded solemnly. "My father would say this means our cause is blessed by the gods themselves."

Decklan wasn't so certain. The alignment felt more like a warning than a blessing, but he kept this thought to himself. The warriors needed confidence, not doubt.

"Whatever its meaning," he said firmly, "our path remains unchanged. Get some rest. Dawn comes early, and with it, our advance continues."

The warriors dispersed slowly, many casting final glances at the aligned moons before returning to their bedrolls. Decklan remained standing, studying the phenomenon until Krella gently touched his arm.

"You too, War Chief," she said, a hint of warmth beneath her formal address. "Even vengeance requires clear heads."

Decklan nodded, but sleep proved elusive. He lay awake, the light of three moons seeping through the canopy, casting strange shadows that seemed to dance with purpose. His thoughts turned to his father, what would Kargoth have made of this alignment? Would he have seen it as blessing or warning?

The answer eluded him, much like sleep, until exhaustion finally claimed him just before dawn. His dreams were vivid, running through forests with the moons chasing him, his father's broken shield in his hands, and a voice that seemed to come from everywhere and nowhere: "Bridge or breaker. The choice remains yours."

CHAPTER TWELVE

DIVIDED CAMP

D ecklan stood atop a flat boulder, surveying the warriors as they prepared for the day's march with practiced efficiency. The tension was palpable, not just anticipation of coming battle, but an undercurrent of doubt directed at him. The warriors moved in distinct groups; younger ones who had trained alongside Decklan worked eagerly, while the veterans clustered together, their sideways glances speaking volumes.

"They'll follow your orders," Krella said, climbing up beside him. "But some need convincing you deserve to give them."

Decklan nodded. "My father earned their loyalty over decades. I have days."

"Then use them wisely," she replied, her amber eyes reflecting the morning light. "Start by assigning duties that play to strengths. Show you understand who they are."

Taking a deep breath, Decklan raised his voice. "Gather round!"

The warriors assembled, forming a loose semicircle before the boulder. The division was clear, veterans to one side, younger warriors to the other, with a conspicuous gap between them.

"We establish three perimeters," Decklan began. "Tharak, your scouts take the outer watch, silent signals only." The grizzled veteran nodded appreciatively, his specialty acknowledged. "Vorka, your shield-sisters hold the middle line." The female warriors straightened proudly. "Grom, organize the inner camp, fires small and shielded."

As he continued assigning duties, Decklan noticed the subtle shift in posture among the veterans. Not acceptance yet, but recognition that he understood their capabilities.

"We are not here for glory," Decklan concluded. "We are here for vengeance. Remember that when blood runs hot."

The warriors dispersed to their tasks, the gap between factions slightly narrowed. Grom approached, his expression troubled.

"You sound like a war chief," he said. "Almost like your father."

"Almost isn't enough for them," Decklan replied, gesturing toward the veterans. "They want a pure-blooded leader, not half-measures."

Grom frowned. "You stood the trials. What more do they want?"

Before Decklan could answer, a commotion erupted at the edge of camp. A scout stumbled through the brush, blood seeping from a gash across his shoulder. Decklan leaped from the boulder and rushed to meet him.

"Bloodfist... patrol," the scout gasped, collapsing to one knee. "Five warrior s... tracked me until the stream."

Krella was already examining the wound. "Axe cut. Not deep, but needs binding."

Decklan's mind raced. "Tharak, double the outer watch. Grom, prepare to move camp if needed." He turned to the wounded scout. "Did they follow you here?"

"No," the scout winced as Krella applied pressure to the wound. "Lost them in the rapids. But there's more, they weren't alone. Blackhand warriors moved with them."

A murmur rippled through the gathered warriors. Cooperation between the Bloodfist and Blackhand clans was unprecedented.

"Sentries, fall back closer to camp," Decklan ordered. "No one hunts alone now."

As the warriors dispersed with renewed urgency, Vorka, approached. "If the clans have united against us, we're outnumbered ten to one. We should return to defend the Shieldbearer camp."

Several older warriors nodded in agreement.

"We continue as planned," Decklan stated firmly. "But we need information. Tharak, organize a capture party. I want a prisoner by nightfall."

The evening brought success in the form of a bound Bloodfist warrior, dragged into camp by Tharak's scouts. The prisoner's face was bruised but defiant as he was forced to kneel before Decklan.

"He was separated from his patrol," Tharak reported. "Tracking something to the east."

Decklan studied the captive, noting the ritualistic scarring that marked higher-ranking warriors. "Your name?"

The prisoner spat at Decklan's feet. "I am Gorthar of the Bloodfist. I will tell you nothing, half-breed."

Murmurs rippled through the gathered warriors. Some hands moved instinctively to weapons, such disrespect to their war chief demanded blood. Decklan raised a hand for silence, his amber eyes fixed on the prisoner.

"Gorthar of the Bloodfist," Decklan said evenly. "You're far from your territory. Why do your warriors move with Blackhand?"

"Kill me and be done with it," Gorthar growled. "I won't betray my clan to a human's spawn."

Decklan circled the kneeling warrior slowly. "You think I'll kill you for that insult? That would be... human of me." He crouched before the prisoner, meeting his gaze. "Orcs honor courage, even in enemies. You've shown yours."

The prisoner's expression flickered with confusion.

"Bring water," Decklan ordered. When a waterskin arrived, he held it to Gorthar's lips, allowing him to drink deeply. Several of the older warriors exchanged glances at this unexpected mercy.

"The alliance with Blackhand," Decklan continued. "It's new, isn't it? Your clan marks are still separate."

Gorthar remained silent, but his eyes betrayed uncertainty.

"Your chieftain Snarlgar," Decklan pressed, "would never bow to another clan's lead. Unless the reward was great."

"We bow to no one," Gorthar snapped, then immediately regretted speaking.

Decklan nodded. "So Reyn Nightshade promised something valuable. Territorial gains? Ancient weapons?"

The prisoner's eyes widened slightly at Reyn's name.

"Ah," Decklan said softly. "So it is Reyn who orchestrated this alliance."

Grom stepped forward, his face dark with anger. "Stop toying with him. He insulted you before the clan. Traditional punishment is—"

"I know the traditions," Decklan cut him off. "But we need information." He turned back to the prisoner. "Your clans massacre each other one season, then hunt together the next. Why?"

Gorthar's jaw clenched stubbornly, but his eyes darted between the warriors surrounding him.

"The Blackhand shaman," Decklan continued. "Vexxa Darkseer. She's performing rituals, isn't she? Something to do with the moon alignment."

A flicker of surprise crossed the prisoner's face before he mastered it.

"Put him under guard," Decklan ordered. "Feed him, treat his wounds. He's worth more alive than dead."

As warriors led Gorthar away, Tharak approached Decklan, his expression troubled. "The clan would not have shown such mercy."

"My father would have," Decklan replied.

Tharak shook his head. "Not to one who dishonored him publicly."

"Perhaps that's why we're here," Decklan said quietly. "Because someone manipulated us into blood feud when cooler heads might have prevailed."

The veteran warrior considered this, then offered a grudging nod before walking away.

Krella joined Decklan as the gathering dispersed. "That was unexpected. The veterans didn't approve."

"Let them disapprove," Decklan replied. "We need to understand our enemy before we can defeat them."

"Some would call that human thinking," she said, but her tone held no criticism.

Decklan adjusted his father's shield on his back. "Then perhaps human thinking is what we need right now."

Dawn brought new complications. The sentry's blew three short bird calls. Not the alarm, but a signal for caution.

Decklan reached the northern perimeter to find two unfamiliar figures being held at spearpoint, humans dressed in leather hunting garb, their hands raised in surrender.

"Found them tracking deer," the sentry reported. "They tried to flee when they spotted us."

The humans, a middle-aged man and a younger woman, stood rigid with fear. Even unarmed, humans were rarely seen this far into contested territory.

I am Decklan Stormshield, War Chief of the Shieldbearers," he said, first in orcish, then switched to the common tongue of the western settlements. "Why do you hunt in disputed lands?"

The humans exchanged surprised glances at his fluent speech. The man swallowed hard before answering.

"We're from Oakridge," he said, his voice steadier than his trembling hands. "Game's been scarce since the Blackhand patrols increased. We needed meat."

The younger woman added, "We didn't know Shieldbearers had moved so close to the border. We would have gone elsewhere."

Decklan studied them, noting their worn but well-maintained gear. "Oakridge is three days east of here."

"We've been following the herds westward for a week," the man explained. "The Blackhand have been driving game from their territory toward the neutral lands."

This caught Decklan's attention. "Deliberately?"

"Seems so," the man nodded cautiously. "They've been burning sections of forest in patterns. Unnatural patterns. Driving both game and people toward the west."

Several of the Shieldbearer warriors muttered darkly, hands tightening on weapons. Burning forest was considered sacrilege among the clans.

"Have you seen their numbers?" Decklan asked. "How many warriors?"

The woman spoke up. "More than we've ever seen gathered. And not just Blackhand, Bloodfist too. They're camped near Thunder Ridge, maybe five hundred warriors in all."

Decklan felt the weight of every warrior's eyes upon him. Five hundred against their forty was suicide.

"Let them go," he ordered, much to the surprise of his warriors. "They've done nothing wrong."

"War Chief," Tharak protested, "they'll reveal our position."

"To whom?" Decklan countered. "These are hunters, not warriors. And they have valuable information." He turned back to the humans. "Return to your settlement. Avoid the main paths, Bloodfist scouts are thick on the ground."

Relief flooded the humans' faces, but the man hesitated. "There's something else," he said. "We passed through Silverbrook three days ago. The village was abandoned, but not destroyed. Everyone just... left."

The younger woman nodded. "We found other human settlements the same way. It's like everyone's being herded somewhere."

Decklan exchanged a troubled glance with Krella. "Where are they going?"

"West," the man replied. "All west, toward the mountain passes. There are rumors of safe haven beyond the peaks."

After the humans departed, the camp divided into heated debate. The veterans argued for immediate return to the Shieldbearer camp to prepare defenses, while younger warriors still hungered for direct confrontation with those responsible for Kargoth's death.

"Five hundred warriors," Vorka emphasized. "Even your father wouldn't face those odds."

"My father would want to understand what drives this alliance before acting," Decklan countered. "Something larger is happening, humans fleeing, clans uniting. This isn't just about us."

As night fell and the camp settled into uneasy quiet, Tharak approached Decklan at his solitary fire.

"You spoke to those humans as equals," the veteran observed. "Without contempt."

Decklan studied the flames. "They had information we needed."

"More than that," Tharak pressed. "You understood them. Their fear, their purpose." He paused. "Perhaps there is value in your divided blood after all."

Before Decklan could respond, a sentry materialized from the darkness.

"War Chief," he said tersely, "the night patrol reports movement on the western ridge. Someone's been shadowing us since sundown."

"Bloodfist scouts?" Decklan asked.

The sentry shook his head. "Movement's too deliberate. Too patient. Whoever it is, they're not trying to find us, they already know exactly where we are."

Decklan rose, hand instinctively checking his weapon. "Double the night watch. No one sleeps unarmored tonight."

As Tharak moved to relay the orders, Decklan gazed toward the western ridge, barely visible in the moonlight. The uncomfortable sensation of being observed prickled across his skin. Something was watching them—something that had been there all along, waiting for the right moment.

CHAPTER THIRTEEN

MOONLIT CONFESSION

A chill wind swept through the makeshift camp as Decklan settled against a weathered oak for his watch. The three moons hung in perfect alignment overhead, casting an eerie silver-blue light across the valley. He absently traced the edge of his father's shield with calloused fingers, feeling every nick and dent, each one a story Kargoth had shared with him through the years.

"Your father used to do that same thing when he was thinking," Krella's voice came softly as she approached. She wore her battle leather but had removed her heavier armor, her silhouette sharp against the moonlight.

Decklan nodded. "I thought you'd be resting. Your watch isn't for another few hours."

"I can't sleep." She settled beside him, close enough that their shoulders almost touched. "The moons' alignment... it unsettles the spirit."

They sat in comfortable silence for several moments before Krella spoke again. "You handled yourself well today. The warriors are beginning to see what I've seen for some time."

"And what's that?" Decklan asked, unable to keep a hint of bitterness from his voice.

It's... the way you fight like an orc, all brutal strength, but think like a human," her amber eyes catching the moonlight as she turned to face him, a depth in their gaze he might not recognize. "You see options others simply miss." A slight pause, her focus entirely on him. "Most warriors see only the direct path, the frontal assault. But you... you see around corners.

Decklan snorted softly. "That's what's always made me an outsider."

"No," Krella said firmly, placing her hand on his forearm. "That's what makes you valuable. Do you think your father became chieftain through strength alone? The strongest don't always lead, the wisest do."

The touch of her hand sent an unexpected warmth through him. They'd trained together since childhood, fought side by side countless times, but something had shifted between them since his father's death.

"I've seen you wrestle with it, your whole life," she said softly, her amber eyes filled with a deep understanding as she continued. "Putting on that mask, striving to be more orc than any orc, trying to crush anything that seemed human." She hesitated, a flicker of vulnerability crossing her face. "And all I ever felt was... admiration. For the man who dared to be different. For *you*."

Decklan's surprise was clear. "You never said anything."

"And if I had? When you were so determined to hide it?" She let the silence answer, the unspoken history stretching between them.

Decklan looked away for a moment, his jaw tight, before meeting her gaze again, tracing the moonlight on her features. "No," he finally conceded. "I just wanted... to belong. To be like him."

Krella's expression warmed with profound acceptance. "You do belong, Decklan. Because you carry the spirit of your father, yes, but also the heart of your mother."

The truth of her words struck him deeply. All his life, he'd seen his dual heritage as an obstacle to overcome, never as something that might give him strength.

"Sometimes I feel caught between worlds," he confessed, voicing thoughts he'd rarely shared. "Not orc enough for the clan, and certainly not human enough for the settlements. I don't fully belong anywhere."

"But what if being both is the truest source of your strength?" Krella challenged, stepping a fraction closer, her intense eyes, shimmering with unspoken feeling in the moonlight, fixed solely on him. "Today, when you bypassed the Blackhand war party instead of meeting them head-on... that wasn't weakness, Decklan. That was *you*. That was you seeing the bigger picture, the path only you could find."

Her words touched something deep within him, a painful hope he'd long suppressed. Before he could respond, the snap of a twig announced Grom's approach. His friend's expression was grim.

"Decklan, scouts have returned. You need to see this," Grom said urgently.

As Decklan rose to his feet, Krella caught his hand and squeezed it briefly. "Remember," she said quietly, "your vision sees more than single focus."

The moment broken, Decklan nodded to her and turned to follow Grom into the darkness, her words echoing in his mind. For the first time, he allowed himself to wonder if the very thing he'd spent his life trying to overcome might be his greatest gift after all.

CHAPTER FOURTEEN

SCOUTING MISSION

The pre-dawn air hung crisp and silent as Decklan assembled his small team. Krella stood ready, eyes alert and scanning the horizon. Grom checked his weapons one final time, the familiar ritual bringing him focus. Two other warriors—Tharak, and Lenna, known for her extraordinary night vision—completed the group.

"Five pairs of eyes should be enough," Decklan said, adjusting his father's shield on his back. "Let's see if we can find out who has been watching us. We move fast, stay silent, and learn what we can about their numbers and positions."

Krella nodded. "The eastern approach offers the most cover."

"And the most obvious route," Grom countered. "They'll expect us there."

Decklan considered this, then made his decision. "We'll take the ridge line instead. It's exposed, but they won't look for us where we shouldn't be."

They moved like shadows across the rocky terrain, using the long morning shadows for cover. When they reached the overlook above the Blackhand encampment, Decklan signaled for them to spread out and observe.

What they saw chilled him to the bone.

The valley below teemed with activity—not just Blackhand warriors but Bloodfists as well. Tents and war banners stretched across the valley floor, forge fires burning despite the early hour. Warriors drilled in formation, their numbers far beyond what the Shieldbearers could hope to match.

"There must be three hundred warriors down there," Tharak whispered, his voice tight.

"More," Lenna added. "The far side holds another camp."

Decklan's mind raced. His small war party of forty stood no chance against such numbers. Yet something else caught his attention—a circle of standing stones at the camp's center, where figures moved in what appeared to be a ritual pattern.

"Grom, look there," he pointed. "What do you make of that?"

Grom squinted. "Some kind of ritual preparation. I recognize those movement patterns—they're invoking protection wards."

Decklan focused on two figures at the center of the circle. One was unmistakably Reyn Nightshade, her distinctive silver-edged cloak catching the morning light. Beside her stood a hunched figure draped in dark robes—Vexxa Darkseer, the Blackhand shaman.

"We need to get closer," Decklan decided. "I want to hear what they're planning."

Krella touched his arm, her expression concerned. "The valley floor is too exposed."

"I wasn't thinking of the valley," Decklan replied, pointing to a narrow game trail that wound along the cliff face. "That path will take us right above their ritual circle."

Tharak frowned. "That's a small stone hopper path. Too narrow for warriors like us."

"I've used paths narrower than that," Decklan said, remembering hunting expeditions with his mother. "And I'll go alone if necessary."

"Not alone," Krella said firmly. "I'm coming with you."

They made their way carefully along the treacherous path, moving with the patience of stalking predators. Decklan led, placing his feet with a hunter's precision maintaining balance in difficult terrain.

Below them, the ritual continued. As they drew closer, fragments of conversation drifted upward.

"...alignment approaches," Vexxa was saying, her raspy voice carrying on the morning air. "The sacrifice must be prepared before the three moons reach their apex."

"The prophecy speaks of divided blood," Reyn responded. "Are you certain it refers to this Shieldbearer half-breed?"

Decklan froze, his blood turning cold. They were speaking of him.

Vexxa made a dismissive gesture. "The signs are clear. His father's death was but the first step. Now we must draw him to us."

"And the other shamans? They suspect nothing?"

"They see only what we allow them to see," Vexxa replied with a low chuckle. "The Shieldbearers believe they hunt us, while we are the true hunters."

Decklan felt Krella's hand on his shoulder, steadying him. They exchanged a glance, her eyes reflecting his own concern. They needed to hear more, but the wind shifted, carrying their scent downward. A Bloodfist sentry below lifted his head, nostrils flaring.

"We must go," Decklan whispered, pulling back from the ledge.

They retreated along the narrow path, rejoining Grom, Tharak, and Lenna at their observation point. Quickly, Decklan shared what they'd overheard.

"A prophecy? About you?" Grom's brow furrowed. "My father never spoke of such things."

"Whatever it means, we've learned enough," Decklan said. "We've confirmed they vastly outnumber us, and something larger than revenge is at play."

They began their careful withdrawal, but had covered barely half the distance back to camp when Lenna froze, raising her fist in warning. Ahead, visible through a break in the rocky terrain, a Bloodfist patrol of eight warriors moved directly across their path.

"They haven't spotted us yet," Tharak whispered. "But they'll cut off our retreat if we don't move quickly."

Decklan studied the terrain, mind racing. The patrol would reach the narrow pass before them unless intercepted. Direct confrontation meant alerting the main camp, but allowing them to pass meant being trapped.

"We need to draw them away from their course," he said, "and silence them before they can signal."

"A frontal assault is suicide," Grom argued.

"Not frontal," Decklan replied, a plan forming. "Orcs expect strength meeting strength. My mother taught me different ways to hunt."

He quickly outlined his strategy. Lenna would circle ahead through the high rocks to block their retreat. Grom and Tharak would create a distraction to one side while Decklan and Krella struck from the shadows.

Grom studied Decklan's face for a moment, doubt giving way to reluctant admiration. "Your mother's hunting techniques against Bloodfist warriors? Bold."

"Sometimes the unexpected approach succeeds where tradition fails," Decklan replied, checking his blade. "We have minutes at most. Move now."

The team dispersed silently. Decklan and Krella skirted the edge of a dried streambed, using the depression for cover. From his vantage point, Decklan watched Lenna's lithe form disappear among the rocks ahead, while Grom and Tharak positioned themselves behind an outcropping to the patrol's right.

Decklan turned to Krella. "When the distraction comes, we take the two at the rear. Swift and silent."

She nodded, her eyes gleaming with determination. In that moment, Decklan was struck by her fierce beauty—and by how completely she trusted his unconventional plan.

Minutes stretched like hours as they waited, crouched in the shadow of an overhanging rock. The patrol drew closer, their guttural voices carrying on the wind.

"...waste of time," one Bloodfist grumbled. "Nightshade sees Shieldbearers in every shadow."

"Silence," the patrol leader growled. "You question her orders?"

As the patrol passed their position, Grom's signal—a stone striking rock in the pattern of a mountain thrush's call—reached their ears. Moments later, a larger rock tumbled down the slope to their right, drawing the patrol's attention.

"Investigate," the leader barked, sending four warriors toward the sound.

This was their moment. Decklan and Krella moved in perfect synchronization, emerging from the streambed behind the remaining four warriors. With fluid precision born from his mother's hunting lessons, Decklan's blade found the gap in the first warrior's armor, between shoulder and neck. The Bloodfist fell without a sound.

Beside him, Krella dispatched her target with equal efficiency. The patrol leader spun at the sound of bodies falling, but too late—Decklan's shield crashed into him, knocking him off balance. Krella's blade ended the threat permanently.

The fourth warrior managed a strangled cry before Decklan's blade silenced him. The alarm was brief, but enough to alert the others.

"To arms!" came a shout from the rocks where the four patrol members had gone to investigate.

Grom and Tharak burst from cover, engaging two warriors immediately. Lenna's bow sang, and another Bloodfist staggered, an arrow protruding from his eye. The last warrior turned to flee, but found his path blocked as Decklan vaulted over a boulder, landing directly in his path.

For an instant, their eyes locked—the Bloodfist's widening with recognition.

"Half-breed!" he snarled, swinging his battleaxe in a vicious arc.

Decklan slipped sideways, the axe missing him by a finger's breadth. He countered with a low sweep learned from his mother's people that caught the warrior behind the knees. As the Bloodfist stumbled, Decklan's blade found its mark.

"Eight warriors, eight clean kills," Tharak said with grudging respect as they regrouped. Blood stained the rocky ground, but none of it belonged to Decklan's team.

"We need to move," Decklan urged. "More patrols will come when they don't report back."

They retreated swiftly, using every fold in the landscape for cover. Only when they reached the shadow of a deep ravine did they pause to catch their breath.

"That wasn't fighting like any orc I've seen," Grom said, studying Decklan with newfound curiosity. "The way you moved..."

"My mother taught me to hunt like her people do," Decklan replied. "Stealth before strength. Precision over power."

"It's effective," Krella observed, cleaning her blade. "They never expected such tactics from orcs."

Tharak nodded slowly. "You fight like neither orc nor human, but something new. Perhaps that is your strength, young Stormshield."

The words resonated with Decklan in a way he hadn't anticipated. All his life, he had viewed his mixed heritage as a disadvantage. But today, that same heritage had given them victory without losses.

"Whatever it is," Decklan said, sheathing his blade, "it worked. Let's get back to camp before they discover their missing patrol."

They traveled swiftly through the growing daylight, reaching their camp by midday. The other warriors gathered around eagerly as Decklan reported what they'd seen.

"Over five hundred warriors between the Blackhand and Bloodfist forces," he explained, sketching a rough map in the dirt. "They're positioned here, in the valley beyond the ridge."

The news sent a ripple of concern through the gathered Shieldbearers. They were badly outnumbered, with no hope of matching such a force directly.

"That's not all," Decklan continued, his voice lowering. "They're perform-ing rituals related to the alignment of the three moons—and they mentioned a prophecy. Something about 'divided blood.'" He hesitated, uncomfortable revealing that they had been discussing him specifically.

Krella stepped forward. "The shamans are collaborating. Whatever they're planning goes beyond simple revenge."

"We encountered a patrol on our return," Tharak added. "Eight Bloodfist warriors. All dispatched without loss." His weathered face cracked in a rare smile. "With techniques I've never seen an orc use."

The assembled warriors turned to Decklan with newfound respect. An old warrior, who had supported Decklan's claim after Kargoth's death, nodded approvingly.

"Your father would be proud," the old warrior said. "You've brought us crucial information and proven your leadership."

As the group dispersed to prepare meals and rest, Decklan returned to his tent. Inside, he found a small folded piece of bark with unfamiliar markings scratched into its surface. Cautiously, he unfolded it, recognizing the script his mother had taught him—Moongazer writing, which few orcs could read.

The message was brief but chilling: "Beware. The betrayal comes from within. Trust your blood—both sides of it. —K"

Kyra. She must have slipped into camp during their absence. Decklan crumpled the bark in his fist, his mind racing. "Betrayal from within" could only mean someone in the Shieldbearer war party was not to be trusted. But who?

He tucked the message into his belt pouch and stepped outside his tent. The camp bustled with activity as warriors prepared weapons and armor. Their earlier skepticism had been replaced by determined focus after hearing of the enemy's numbers. They were outnumbered but not defeated—not yet.

Chapter Fifteen

SUPPLY RAID

Decklan stood on a ridge overlooking the Blackhand supply trail, the morning mist curling around his ankles like pale serpents. Below him were his forty warriors, a force he silently affirmed, each one a vital part of their number.

"They're coming," Krella whispered, materializing at his side. She pointed to a faint dust cloud on the horizon where the supply caravan would soon appear. "Six wagons, maybe twenty guards. Just as the human traders informed us."

Decklan nodded, grateful for the intelligence gleaned from the settlements. "We'll use the split maneuver, half from the ridge, half from the tree line." He gestured to the rocky outcropping and then to the sparse forest opposite. "My father used this tactic against Redfist raiders three summers ago."

"And the human traders said they pause at the stream crossing," Krella added. "Perfect ambush point."

Grom approached, his eyes glittering with anticipation. "I've positioned our archers. They await your signal."

Decklan studied the terrain once more, mentally rehearsing the plan that combined frontal strength with stealth tactics. "Remember what I told everyone, wait for the wagons to reach the crossing. No one moves until my signal."

The warriors took their positions, though Decklan noted the hesitation in some of the veterans' movements, their sideways glances betraying doubt in his leadership. He pushed the concern aside, focusing instead on the approaching caravan.

When the lead wagon rumbled to a halt at the stream crossing, Decklan raised his arm. The moment the driver stepped down to check the depth, he brought his arm down sharply.

"Shieldbearers! Strike!" he roared, leading the charge down the slope.

The initial assault went perfectly, arrows rained down, pinning half the guards where they stood. Decklan's group crashed into the remaining defenders with devastating force. He blocked a sword thrust with his father's shield, feeling its comforting weight against his arm as he drove his blade through his opponent's guard.

But the coordinated assault soon unraveled. Some warriors followed Decklan's instructions to secure the wagons, while others, driven by bloodlust, pursued fleeing guards into the forest. The split forces created gaps in their formation that wouldn't have mattered in a traditional orcish charge but proved disastrous for Decklan's hybrid strategy.

"Hold positions!" Decklan shouted, trying to regain control. "Secure the perimeter first!"

Too late. The war cry of Bloodfist warriors erupted from the eastern ridge, a reinforcement patrol no one had anticipated. At least fifteen fresh warriors charged down toward the scattered Shieldbearers.

"Ambush!" Krella warned, already moving to engage the new threat. "Shield wall!"

Only half the warriors responded to the command, creating a fragmented defense. Decklan fought his way to the center, trying to organize a proper shield formation, but the damage was done. Three Shieldbearers fell before they could regroup.

Grom fought ferociously, his axe a blur of lethal motion, but even his skill couldn't compensate for their disorganization. "We're overextended!" he shouted to Decklan.

Through the chaos, Decklan made the painful choice. "Fall back to the ridge! Retreat!"

The survivors withdrew, fighting desperately. Decklan took the rear position, his shield protecting those falling back. A Bloodfist warrior charged him with a massive war hammer. Decklan deflected the first blow with his shield but staggered under its force. He recovered and countered with a swift slash across the warrior's thigh, creating space for retreat.

When they finally reached defensive positions on the ridge, Decklan tallied their losses, five dead, seven wounded. The supply wagons they'd briefly captured now burned in the distance as Blackhand reinforcements arrived.

In the makeshift camp that evening, tension hung thick as smoke. Warriors tended wounds and sharpened weapons in silence. Decklan sat apart, examining a tear in his father's shield, an apt metaphor for his fractured leadership.

Krella approached, carrying a water skin. "The wounded are stabilized," she reported, her voice low. "But Vargen won't last the night without proper treatment."

Before Decklan could respond, Tharak stood, his scarred face twisted with anger. "This is what comes of human tactics," he spat. "Kargoth would have brought overwhelming force, not this... dancing around like forest shadows."

Several warriors murmured agreement, emboldening the veteran.

"We lost good warriors today because you hesitated," Tharak continued, pointing an accusatory finger at Decklan. "Your caution makes you weak. The Bloodfists sensed it, and so they struck."

Decklan felt heat rising in his chest but kept his voice steady. "We were outnumbered three to one. A direct assault would have been suicide."

"Better to die charging than retreating!" Tharak growled. "Now we have nothing to show but our dead."

Grom stepped forward unexpectedly. "Enough, Tharak. When the ambush came, he saved many lives with that retreat order."

Tharak scoffed. "Of course you defend him. Young fools together."

"Watch your tongue," Grom warned, hand drifting to his axe.

Decklan stood, placing himself between them. "Save your strength for our enemies. We can't afford to fight amongst ourselves."

The tension remained, but Tharak backed down, returning to his bedroll with a dismissive grunt. Other warriors dispersed, leaving Decklan with Grom and Krella.

"He's wrong," Krella said firmly. "Your strategy was sound. We couldn't have anticipated that Bloodfist patrol."

Grom nodded in agreement, but Decklan noticed a flicker of doubt in his eyes.

"You have something to say, Grom. Speak it," Decklan said.

Grom hesitated, then sighed heavily. "The plan was good, but..." He looked away, choosing his words carefully. "When the Bloodfists charged, there was a moment when you could have countered immediately. Instead, you assessed, considered. It was only heartbeats, but—"

"But enough to cost lives," Decklan finished for him. He rubbed his forehead, feeling the weight of command crushing down on him. "My father would have reacted instantly."

"Your father had thirty years of battle experience," Krella countered. "This is your first command."

Decklan walked a few paces away, staring into the darkness beyond their camp. "I tried to be two things at once. Human caution and orc ferocity. Instead, I was neither."

"That's not true," Krella joined him, her voice low but intense. "You saved more than you lost. Tharak would have had us all killed for the glory of it."

Decklan turned to her, vulnerability plain on his face. "I don't know if I'm fit to lead this mission, Krella. Every decision I make feels... divided. Split between what my father would do and what my mother would counsel."

She considered this, then placed a hand on his arm. "Perhaps you shouldn't bear this burden alone. Form a war council, include Tharak, despite his attitude. Let the veterans contribute their experience while you make the final decisions."

"A war council?" Grom frowned. "We usually only form those for major defenses."

"This *is* a major defense," Decklan countered gently. "And councils *are* our way, Grom. It might work. At the very least, it would give the veterans a voice."

"And make it harder for them to complain afterward," Krella added with a grim smile.

Decklan felt a slight easing of the burden that had been crushing his chest since the failed raid. It wouldn't bring back the dead, but it might prevent more losses.

"We'll form the council at first light," he decided. "For now, help me check on the wounded."

That night, as the camp finally fell silent except for the groans of the wounded, Decklan dreamed of standing on the banks of a wide river. On the far bank stood his father, resplendent in his battle armor, shield gleaming in the sun. On the near bank stood his mother, arms outstretched, a gentle smile on her face. The current between them ran swift and deadly, and try as he might, Decklan could find no way to cross to either shore.

"Choose," whispered a voice on the wind. "You cannot be both."

Decklan woke with a start, the night still deep around him. He touched his father's shield beside his bedroll, tracing the clan emblem with his fingertips. Tomorrow would bring new challenges, but for the first time, he began to wonder if trying to be purely his father's son was the wrong path altogether.

Chapter Sixteen

AMBUSH

Dawn broke reluctantly over the Shieldbearer camp, the sky bruised purple and crimson. Decklan sat alone atop a moss-covered boulder, his father's shield resting across his lap. Its weight felt different now, heavier with responsibility, yet somehow hollow without Kargoth's arm to bear it.

The camp lay in a heavy silence, thirty warriors lost in the exhaustion of yesterday's failed raid. Five fresh graves marked the dawn. A grim reminder of the five who would never see home again. They couldn't risk the tell-tale smoke of a funeral pyre; their position had to remain hidden.

Decklan's fingers traced the shield's embossed emblem. Had his father ever doubted himself as he did now? Had Kargoth ever felt this crushing weight of lives lost under his command?

A faint sound pricked at his awareness—a whisper of movement where none should be. Decklan stiffened, his senses detecting something his full-blooded kin might have missed. The wind shifted, carrying an unfamiliar scent: oiled leather, strange herbs, bodies moving through underbrush.

He rose silently, reaching for the horn at his belt.

Before it touched his lips, shadows detached from the forest edge. Black-hand warriors, at least thirty, approaching in perfect formation.

Decklan's horn blast shattered the morning stillness. "SHIELDS! FORM RANKS!" he roared, voice carrying his father's authority.

The camp erupted. Warriors tumbled from tents, weapons in hand, some still securing armor. Tharak, the veteran who had challenged him yesterday, emerged with axe already drawn.

"Shield wall!" Decklan commanded, falling into the formation his father had drilled into him since childhood. "Second rank, prepare javelins!"

The Shieldbearers moved with practiced efficiency despite their surprise. Shields locked together as Blackhand arrows whistled through the air.

"Hold!" Decklan shouted as the first wave of attackers crashed against their shields. He felt the impact reverberate through his arm, his stance unwavering. "Push!"

The line surged forward in unison, driving back the attackers. For a heartbeat, Decklan felt his father's presence beside him, guiding his movements.

But the Blackhands regrouped quickly, circling to attack from multiple directions. A burly warrior with ceremonial face paint broke through the edge of the formation, swinging a massive war axe at Tharak.

"Gap in the shield wall!" Decklan shouted, already in motion. He slid between two warriors, intercepting the axe with his father's shield. The impact sent shockwaves up his arm, but the ancient metal held.

"I have him!" Decklan called to Tharak. "Hold the line!"

The Blackhand commander snarled, revealing sharpened teeth. "Half-breed runt," he spat. "Your father is worm food. Soon you too"

Rage flared in Decklan's chest, but he channeled it with discipline. Instead of the blind fury the commander expected, Decklan feinted left, then struck with surprising power, driving his sword into his opponent's exposed flank.

The commander howled, staggering backward.

"Reform!" Decklan shouted, sliding back into position. The shield wall closed around him.

From his elevated position, Decklan saw the Blackhand forces weren't attacking randomly. They were targeting the eastern edge of camp, trying to divide the Shieldbearers.

"Krella!" he called to where she fought nearby. "Take five warriors, circle through the creek bed. Hit their left flank when I signal!"

She nodded sharply and moved without question, selecting warriors as she went.

"Grom! Ready the fire arrows!"

His friend looked up from where he was bandaging a wounded warrior's arm. "We only have a dozen left!"

"Make them count," Decklan ordered. "Target their rear line when you hear my horn."

Decklan studied the battlefield with eyes trained by both parents, his father's tactical assessment, his mother's attention to patterns. The Blackhand commander had withdrawn to direct his forces, favoring his wounded side. Their formation was shifting, preparing for another charge.

"Second rank, prepare to advance!" Decklan called. "First rank, on my signal, drop to one knee, shields angled up!"

Tharak looked at him skeptically. "That's not how we fight," he growled, even as the enemy prepared their charge.

"It's how we win," Decklan replied firmly. "Trust me."

The veteran warrior hesitated, then nodded grimly.

The Blackhand forces rushed forward with a thunderous war cry. Decklan waited until they committed fully to their charge before raising his shield.

"NOW!"

The front rank dropped to one knee in perfect unison, angling their shields upward like a sloped wall. The charging Blackhands, expecting to meet resistance at chest height, stumbled against the unexpected formation. Some toppled forward over the shield wall, directly into the waiting weapons of the second rank.

"Second rank, ADVANCE!" Decklan commanded.

The warriors behind the shield wall surged forward, cutting down the disoriented attackers. Decklan blew three sharp blasts on his horn, signaling both Krella's flanking attack and Grom's fire arrows.

Flames arced through the dawn sky as Krella's warriors burst from the creek bed, catching the Blackhand left flank completely by surprise. Confusion rippled through the enemy ranks.

Decklan seized the moment. "SHIELDS UP! FORWARD!"

The Shieldbearers rose as one, pressing their advantage. Decklan fought at the center of the line, his movements a fluid blend of powerful strikes and swift precision. Where other warriors relied purely on strength, Decklan anticipated his opponents' movements, conserving energy and striking with deadly efficiency.

The Blackhand commander rallied his forces for one final push, charging directly at Decklan with murderous rage. This time, Decklan didn't wait for the attack. He stepped forward to meet it, using the commander's momentum against him. As the larger orc swung his axe in a powerful overhead strike, Decklan pivoted aside and struck at the commander's already wounded flank.

The commander crumpled to his knees. Decklan stood over him, sword raised for the killing blow.

"Yield," Decklan demanded, "and your warriors may retreat with their lives."

The commander spat blood. "No Blackhand yields to half-breed filth."

The commander lunged with a hidden dagger, but Decklan had anticipated the desperate move. He stepped aside and brought his sword down in a swift arc. The Blackhand commander's head hit the ground before his body.

"Retreat!" shouted the next ranking Blackhand warrior, seeing their commander fall. The surviving attackers broke formation, fleeing into the forest. Several Shieldbearers moved to pursue, but Decklan raised his hand.

"Let them go. They'll carry word of their defeat."

As the dust settled, Decklan surveyed the battlefield. Three more Shieldbearers had fallen, but they'd repelled a force nearly twice their size. The victory had been decisive.

Tharak approached, blood streaming from a gash above his eye. He studied Decklan with newfound respect.

"That formation," the veteran warrior said. "I've never seen it before."

"My mother's people use it against mounted attackers," Decklan replied. "I thought it might work against a charging line."

Tharak nodded slowly. "It did." He extended his arm in the traditional Shieldbearer gesture of respect. "You fought well... War Chief."

Decklan clasped the offered arm, feeling the weight of the moment. Around them, other warriors were gathering, watching the exchange. When Tharak released his grip, he reached down to retrieve the commander's ornate war axe and held it out to Decklan.

"The spoils belong to the victor," he said formally.

Decklan accepted the weapon, raising it for all to see. A cheer went up from the gathered warriors, not just the younger ones who had always supported him, but the veterans as well. For the first time, they were looking at him not as Kargoth's half-human son, but as their war chief.

Grom approached, grinning despite a fresh bruise darkening his jaw. "Not bad for a first battle as commander."

"We were lucky," Decklan said quietly. "If I hadn't been awake—"

"But you were," Krella interrupted, joining them. Her armor was spattered with blood, but her eyes were bright with victory. "You sensed them before anyone else could," Krella continued, wiping blood from her axe. "Your human senses and your warrior instincts. Both saved us today."

The camp bustled with activity as warriors tended wounds and secured prisoners. Decklan approached a captured Blackhand warrior, a younger orc with a broken arm and defiant eyes.

"Why attack us directly?" Decklan demanded. "Your people prefer ambush tactics."

The prisoner glared silently until Decklan knelt beside him, offering a waterskin. The unexpected gesture seemed to confuse the warrior.

"You fight for Reyn Nightshade," Decklan said, not a question but a statement. "What did she hope to gain by this attack?"

The prisoner's eyes widened slightly at Reyn's name. He took a cautious sip of water before answering.

"She wanted to test your strength," he muttered. "To see if the stories were true."

"What stories?" Decklan pressed.

The warrior's gaze flicked to Decklan's mixed features. "About the half-blood who would unite the clans."

Tharak snorted. "More likely she wanted your head to prevent any unity."

"No," the prisoner shook his head. "She seeks the one of divided blood. The prophecy speaks of one who stands between worlds."

Grom exchanged glances with Decklan. The prisoner's words echoed the message on the ritual stone they had discovered.

"Why does Reyn care about prophecies?" Krella asked.

The prisoner's expression darkened. "The shamans speak of power to be gained when the three moons align. Power in the blood of one who walks two paths."

Before Decklan could question him further, the prisoner slumped forward, foam bubbling at his lips. Decklan caught him, recognizing the signs of poison.

"Hidden tooth capsule," Grom said grimly. "Blackhand commanders use them to prevent capture."

Decklan lowered the dead warrior to the ground, disturbed by his final words. Was this why his father had been killed? Not just for clan politics, but because of some prophecy about his mixed blood?

CHAPTER SEVENTEEN

RED MIST RAVINE

Decklan stood at the edge of their camp, scanning the horizon with eyes that caught details others missed. The terrain ahead narrowed into a steep-walled ravine, perfect for an ambush, as both his hunter training and warrior instincts warned.

"Tracks lead straight through," Tharak reported, crouching beside him. The veteran tracker's respect was new, hard-won from yesterday's victory. "Blackhand forces, at least sixty warriors. Moving fast, not bothering to hide their trail."

"Too obvious," Decklan muttered. "They want us to follow."

Tharak nodded. "My thoughts exactly. But the men—" He gestured to the camp where warriors prepared for march, their faces grim with determination. "They smell blood in the air."

Decklan clutched his father's shield, tracing the worn surface with calloused fingers. "Gather the war council."

"It's a trap." Decklan stood before the assembled warriors, pointing to the crude map scratched in dirt. "The ravine narrows here. Steep walls, limited escape routes."

"So we don't enter their trap," Krella added, kneeling beside the map. "We set our own."

Murmurs of disagreement rippled through the group. "We've got them on the run!" shouted one warrior. "Strike while they're retreating!"

"Their retreat is too orderly," Decklan countered. "Too... deliberate."

"Perhaps the half-blood fears fighting like a real orc," sneered an older warrior named Kruvik. The slur hung in the air like a challenge.

Decklan met his gaze without flinching. "I fear wasting Shieldbearer lives on a fool's errand."

"Your father would have pursued them," Kruvik pressed. "Kargoth Stormshield never hesitated."

The words struck like a physical blow. Decklan felt the familiar doubt resurfacing—was he too cautious? Too human?

"We can flank them," Grom suggested, breaking the tension. "Use the ridge line instead of following directlyInto the ravine." Grom traced a path along the map's edge. "Element of surprise."

Decklan considered this, studying the terrain. "The ridge is exposed. If they're watching—"

"Always hesitating!" Kruvik interrupted. "Your father's blood runs thin in you, boy."

The warriors grew restless, many nodding in agreement with Kruvik. Decklan felt their confidence wavering. These were his father's warriors, raised on tales of Kargoth's decisive leadership and bold strikes.

"We follow the tracks," Decklan announced finally, silencing the murmurs. "But in formation, shields ready. At the first sign of ambush, we retreat to defensible ground."

Kruvik smirked in victory. Krella caught Decklan's eye, her expression concerned.

"This isn't right," she whispered as the council dispersed.

"They need to trust me," Decklan replied. "Sometimes a leader must bend to keep from breaking."

The ravine walls loomed above them, casting long shadows across the path. Decklan led from the center, his father's shield held ready. Every instinct screamed danger, but the Blackhand tracks continued clearly ahead, taunting them forward.

"Too quiet," Tharak muttered from beside him.

The ravine narrowed further, forcing the war party into a tighter formation. Loose stones clattered beneath their boots, echoing against the stone walls.

Decklan raised his fist, halting the column. Something felt wrong, a vibration in the air, a scent that didn't belong. He scanned the ridge line, squinting against the morning sun.

"See anything?" Grom asked, bow already half-drawn.

Before Decklan could answer, a low whistle cut the air. He looked up to see dark silhouettes appearing along both ridges.

"Ambush!" he shouted. "Shields up!"

The first volley of arrows rained down as warriors scrambled into defensive positions. Decklan's shield deflected three in rapid succession.

"Bloodfist markings," Krella called, examining a shaft that had landed near her feet. "They've joined with the Blackhands."

A second volley descended, followed by war cries from the ridge tops as both Blackhand and Bloodfist warriors began scaling down the ravine walls, converging on the Shieldbearers from above.

"Defensive circle!" Decklan ordered, his voice cutting through the chaos. "Backs together, shields out!"

The warriors followed his command, forming a tight ring of shields as attackers closed in. Tharak took an arrow to the shoulder but kept his position firm.

Decklan scanned for escape routes. The ravine narrowed ahead, but widened behind them. "We fall back! Maintain formation and—"

His order was cut short as an eerie crimson mist began spilling over the ravine edges, descending like blood-tinged fog. It rolled down the stone walls, unnaturally thick and flowing with purpose.

"Shaman's work," Grom warned, his eyes wide. "That's Vexxa's magic."

The red mist reached the ravine floor, swirling around their ankles before rising rapidly. Warriors coughed as it entered their lungs, its metallic taste coating their tongues.

"Don't breathe it!" Krella shouted, but too late.

Decklan felt the mist's effect immediately, a heaviness in his limbs, a clouding of his thoughts. Worse, shapes began forming in the fog, figures from memory and nightmare alike.

"Hold formation!" he commanded, even as the red haze thickened. "Don't trust what you see!"

A Bloodfist warrior lunged through the mist. Decklan met him with shield and sword, dispatching him efficiently, but two more appeared where one had fallen. The Shieldbearers fought valiantly, but confusion spread as the mist worked its dark magic.

Decklan turned to issue another order when the mist before him coalesced into his father's form. Kargoth stood tall, disappointment etched in his spectral face.

"You led them to slaughter," the apparition said, its voice a perfect echo of Kargoth's deep rumble. "As I knew you would."

"You're not real," Decklan whispered, but his sword arm faltered.

The apparition moved closer, its features sharpening in the crimson fog. "I never believed you could lead them. Too much human weakness. Too much hesitation." The phantom Kargoth's eyes burned with disgust. "You disappoint me, son."

Decklan's shield lowered slightly, the phantom words cutting deeper than any blade. Around him, other warriors battled their own visions, some crying out in terror, others striking wildly at enemies only they could see.

"Decklan!" Krella's voice seemed distant, muffled by the thickening mist. "Decklan, it's not real!"

But the specter of his father circled him, relentless. "They die because of you. Their blood is on your hands."

A Bloodfist axe swung through the mist, barely missing Decklan's exposed side. He didn't see it, his focus locked on the phantom before him.

"Your mother's blood makes you weak," the false Kargoth continued. "You were never fit to bear my shield."

Something hard struck Decklan's face, Krella's palm, delivering a stinging slap. Her face appeared before him, eyes fierce and clear despite the red fog swirling between them.

"It's Vexxa's magic!" she shouted, gripping his arm. "They're using your fears against you!"

Reality snapped back into focus. The phantom Kargoth dissolved into wisps of crimson, revealing the true battle around them. Three Shieldbearer warriors lay unmoving on the ground. Others fought desperately, some against real enemies, others against phantoms.

"We're losing," Decklan rasped, throat raw from the mist. "We need to retreat."

"There!" Grom pointed to a narrow gap in the enemy line where the ravine widened. "If we break through there—"

"On me!" Decklan roared, raising his shield. "Form wedge! We push through together!"

The remaining warriors rallied to him, forming a tight formation behind his lead. With Krella and Grom flanking him, Decklan charged toward the gap,driving his father's shield into the first Bloodfist warrior that blocked their path. The impact sent the enemy tumbling back into his comrades, creating a momentary breach in their line.

"Push through!" Decklan commanded, his voice finding new strength. The Shieldbearers surged forward, their formation holding despite the red mist swirling around them.

Two Blackhand warriors leaped into their path. Decklan parried a spear thrust with his shield while Krella's blade found the attacker's throat. Grom loosed arrows in rapid succession, forcing back warriors attempting to close the gap.

"Keep moving!" Decklan ordered as they broke into the wider section of the ravine. "Don't stop! Don't look back!"

The red mist thinned as they pushed forward, though phantoms still tugged at the edges of vision. Warriors stumbled, some wounded, others still battling the mist's effects, but the formation held.

As they neared the ravine's exit, Decklan risked a glance back. Through gaps in the crimson haze, he caught sight of a figure standing on the ridge, a woman with long dark hair and armor emblazoned with the Blackhand crest. Reyn Nightshade watched their retreat, making no move to pursue, her expression one of calculating assessment.

Their eyes met across the distance. She tilted her head slightly, as if evaluating a specimen. Then, deliberately, she turned away.

"They're not following," Tharak observed as they finally broke free of the ravine, the surviving warriors collapsing onto open ground.

Decklan took count – six warriors dead, left behind in the mist. Eight more wounded, some severely. Less than half their original force remained battle-ready.

"It wasn't a battle," Decklan realized aloud. "It was a test."

"A test?" Grom questioned, helping a wounded warrior drink from a water skin.

"Reyn Nightshade was watching," Decklan explained. "She wasn't trying to kill us all. She wanted to see how we'd fight... how I'd fight."

Krella nodded grimly. "And now she knows you're vulnerable to visions of your father."

Chapter Eighteen

TRAITOR AMONG US

ecklan sat alone outside his tent in the makeshift camp, his back against a gnarled oak, watching dying embers send weak spirals of smoke into the night air. The bitter taste of defeat clung to his mouth like old blood. His hands unconsciously traced the edge of his father's shield, feeling each dent and scrape, silent testaments to battles Kargoth had survived.

He hadn't.

The red mist from the ravine ambush had faded hours ago, but its visions lingered. His father's disappointed face, those amber eyes so like his own, judging him. *You are no son of mine. No orc. No leader.*

"Your father never spoke those words."

Decklan's hand flew to his axe before recognition dawned. "Kyra." He relaxed slightly as the slender figure emerged from the shadows. "I should hang a bell around your neck."

"Then I would be of little use to you." She settled beside him, unwrapping a bundle of herbs that released a sharp, medicinal scent. "Your wounded need these. Bloodmoss for the deep cuts. Silverleaf for fever."

"Where did you come from? How did you find us?" Decklan asked, eyeing her suspiciously.

"I've been tracking both your movements and the Blackhand clan's." Her unusual eyes, shifting between silver and violet in the moonlight, fixed on him. "What you saw in the mist was manipulation, not truth."

"It doesn't matter. Six more warriors dead. Eight wounded." Decklan's jaw tightened. "I led them into a trap because I wasn't strong enough to stand against their demands."

"And would your father have been wiser?"

Decklan fell silent, remembering Kargoth's steady leadership, his unwavering decisions.

"I bring more than herbs, Shieldbearer." Kyra reached into her cloak and produced a small cloth bundle. "I bring truth."

She unwrapped it carefully, revealing a Shieldbearer clan pendant, the distinctive shield emblem with three diagonal lines representing protection, loyalty, and honor.

"Where did you get this?" Decklan demanded, recognizing the distinctive craftsmanship. "This belongs to someone of rank within our clan."

"Indeed." Kyra's voice was measured, careful. "I found it at a meeting place between our territories and the Blackhand's. A hidden grove where someone has been meeting with Reyn Nightshade's emissaries regularly."

Decklan's breath caught. "You're suggesting a traitor among the Shieldbearers."

"I'm not suggesting. I'm stating." Kyra leaned forward, her eyes reflecting the dying fire. "Your father's assassination was orchestrated from within your clan, Decklan."

"That's impossible," Decklan growled, though doubt crept into his voice. "No Shieldbearer would—"

"The poison cup bore markings neither Blackhand nor Bloodfist. And consider this: how did the assassins at the Neutral Stones know exactly where to position themselves? How did they know precisely which delegates would attend?"

Decklan's mind raced through the possibilities. The council had been planned in relative secrecy. Few had known the details.

"This pendant was dropped at the meeting site three nights before your father's death." Kyra turned it over, revealing a small engraving on the back, a rune representing spiritual guidance. "A shaman's mark."

A twig snapped behind them. Decklan whirled to find Grom standing there, his face ashen in the moonlight.

"That's my father's pendant," he whispered. "I recognize the notch in the corner from when he caught it on his ritual knife."

Kyra nodded solemnly. "Gar'zul Wiseblood has been meeting with Blackhand emissaries for nearly a moon cycle."

"You LYING WITCH!" Grom lunged forward, but Decklan caught him, struggling to hold his friend back. "My father would DIE for the clan! He would never betray Kargoth!"

"I have more proof," Kyra said calmly, producing a small pouch. She emptied its contents: fragments of herbs, small bones, and a vial of dark residue. "These are ritual components matching those found in Gar'zul's shamanic pouch. I recovered them from the meeting site alongside this pendant. The residue contains traces of stonebite extract - the same poison that burned your hands during your trial, Decklan."

Grom's struggles intensified. "You planted this! You're trying to divide us!" His face contorted with rage as he broke free from Decklan's grip. "And you!" He jabbed a finger at Decklan's chest. "You believe this wanderer over the word of your oldest friend? My father SERVED yours for decades!"

"Grom, I haven't said I believe—" Decklan began.

"You didn't have to! It's in your eyes!" Grom snarled, drawing his hunting knife. "First you lead us into an ambush, now you accuse my father of murder? My father mourned Kargoth! He performed the death rites himself!"

"Which gave him perfect opportunity to hide evidence," Kyra interjected.

Warriors from around the camp had begun gathering, drawn by the commotion. Krella pushed through, immediately assessing the situation.

"What's happening here?" she demanded, positioning herself between the two friends.

"Ask him!" Grom spat. "Ask how quickly he believes his father's murder was arranged by mine!"

Whispers rippled through the gathered Shieldbearers. Some moved closer to Decklan, while others drifted toward Grom.

"I've known Gar'zul my entire life," Tharak said, his scarred face grim. "He's ambitious, yes, but a traitor? No."

"The shaman was against this mission from the start," countered Lenna, one of Decklan's supporters. "He wanted us to stay and fortify the camp instead of seeking vengeance."

"As any wise elder would!" Grom shouted. "We've lost eleven warriors already!"

Decklan raised his hands, trying to calm the growing division. "We don't know what's true yet. Kyra has brought evidence we must consider, but—"

"Consider?" Grom's voice broke. "My father raised me to honor the Shieldbearer ways above all else! He taught me that loyalty to clan is sacred!"

Grom's shoulders heaved with emotion as he continued, his voice hoarse with rage. "He lost my mother to the Ghosts, and he's devoted his life to protecting what remains of our people. And you would believe this... this stranger?" He gestured wildly toward Kyra.

"Grom," Decklan said, stepping closer, "think about what's happened. The trials were altered. My hands were burned with stonebite. The spirit guardian was incorrectly bound—"

"So you blame my father for your failures!" Grom lunged forward, swinging wildly.

Decklan sidestepped but refused to counterattack. "I'm not blaming anyone yet!"

Krella moved between them with practiced efficiency, shoving them apart. "Enough!" Her voice cut through the tension like a blade. "Fighting each other is exactly what our enemies want!"

The camp had fully divided now. Warriors stood in clusters, some behind Decklan, others supporting Grom, while a few remained uncertainly between the factions. Suspicious glances flew back and forth like arrows.

"We've lost too many already," Krella continued, her eyes fierce in the firelight. "If we start killing each other, our enemies won't need to finish what they started."

"She's right," Decklan said, lowering his hands. "Grom, I swear by my father's shield, I'm not accusing Gar'zul. But we can't ignore this evidence either."

"Evidence?" Grom spat on the ground. "A pendant that could have been stolen. Herbs that grow throughout our territories. The word of a wanderer who appears and disappears like mist." He sheathed his knife with trembling hands. "You want evidence of betrayal, Decklan? Look to yourself. You led us into that ravine despite every instinct warning against it."

The accusation struck Decklan like a physical blow. Several warriors murmured in agreement.

"I followed the will of the war counsel," Decklan said quietly.

"A true chief leads; he doesn't follow," Grom replied bitterly.

CHAPTER NINETEEN

DIVIDED LOYALTIES

The cold mountain air bit into Decklan's skin as he cornered Kyra near the center of camp. Dawn smeared pink across the horizon, but he felt no beauty in it, only urgency.

"No more riddles," he said, his voice low and dangerous. "No more half-truths. I want everything you know. Now."

Kyra's eyes, those strange eyes that seemed to shift color with the light, met his without flinching.

"Your father was murdered by someone he trusted," she said simply. "Gar'zul made a pact with Reyn Nightshade. Your father's peace initiatives were seen as weakness by the traditionalists. Gar'zul believed Kargoth would lead the clan to ruin."

Decklan's hands clenched. "You expect me to believe the clan's shaman, my best friend's father, betrayed us?"

"I don't expect. I know." Kyra reached into her pouch, extracting a small wooden token carved with Gar'zul's personal sigil. "This was found where Blackhand messengers met with a Shieldbearer representative. Three times before your father's death."

The evidence was like a knife between his ribs. "But why poison? Gar'zul could have challenged him openly."

"The agreement was never to kill Kargoth," Kyra said, her voice softening. "Only to force him to step down. The poison was meant to weaken, not kill. Reyn betrayed that agreement. She wanted war, not merely a change in leadership."

The realization hit Decklan like a physical blow. "We're being played. All of us."

"Yes. The Shieldbearers are caught between the Blackhand-Bloodfist alliance. Gar'zul never anticipated this outcome."

A rustling sound made them both turn. Grom stood there, face ashen, having heard enough.

"You filthy liar," he spat at Kyra. "My father would never—"

"Use your truth-seeking spell," Kyra challenged calmly. "The one he taught you in secret. Test my words."

Grom's face contorted with rage and pain. For a moment, he seemed ready to lunge at Kyra, but instead, his hands began weaving the intricate gestures of a shaman's spell. Blue-white light gathered around his fingertips.

"How do you know of this ritual?" he demanded as the light intensified. "Only shamans of our clan—"

"That doesn't matter now," Kyra said. "Test my words, Grom Wiseblood. See the truth for yourself."

Grom completed the spell, sending the spectral light toward Kyra. It surrounded her, pulsing as she repeated her accusation. The light remained steady, showing no flicker of falsehood.

"No," Grom whispered, the color draining from his face. "It cannot be."

Decklan moved toward his friend. "Grom—"

"Stay away from me!" Grom's eyes blazed with betrayal, but Decklan couldn't tell if it was directed at him, Kyra, or the father who had apparently sold out their clan.

"I need to speak with him," Grom said, suddenly resolute. "Now."

"That's not possible," Krella said, emerging from the shadows. She had been listening too. "We're days from camp."

"There is a way," Grom said grimly. "A ritual my father taught me for emergencies. It requires blood."

Without waiting for permission, Grom withdrew to his tent. Decklan followed, watching as his friend prepared a small ritual circle using ashes from their campfire.

"You shouldn't be here," Grom said without looking up.

"If what Kyra says is true—"

"If?" Grom's laugh was bitter. "The truth-seeking spell doesn't lie, Decklan. You saw it yourself."

"Then I should be here," Decklan insisted. "This concerns all of us."

Grom worked in silence for several moments before pricking his finger with a ritual knife. A drop of blood fell onto the ash circle, which began to glow with eerie green light.

"Father," Grom whispered. "I call to you across the distance. Blood to blood, spirit to spirit."

The ash circle flared, smoke twisting upward to form a semblance of Gar'zul's weathered face. Even in this spectral form, the shaman looked haggard, his eyes hollow with exhaustion or guilt.

"Grom? Why do you call? Is Decklan—" The smoky visage faltered when it noticed Decklan standing behind Grom. "I see."

"Is it true?" Grom's voice cracked. "Did you conspire with the Black-hands against Kargoth?"

A heavy silence hung between them. The smoke-face seemed to age before their eyes.

"Not as you think," Gar'zul finally answered, his voice distant like wind through stone. "Kargoth's peaceful ways would have destroyed us. I sought only to force him to step aside."

Decklan stepped forward, rage burning in his chest. "You got him killed!"

"No!" For the first time, real emotion broke through Gar'zul's stoic facade. "Reyn betrayed our agreement. The poison was to weaken, not kill. She added something... something dark from her shaman's craft."

"You poisoned my father." Each word felt like a stone in Decklan's mouth.

"To save our clan," Gar'zul insisted. "The Blackhands promised alliance against the humans pushing into our territories. Instead, they formed a pact with the Bloodfists. Now they hunt us all."

Grom's hands trembled as he maintained the ritual. "You betrayed everything we stand for. Everything I believed about you."

"I did what was necessary for our survival." Gar'zul's gaze shifted to Decklan. "Your father was too trusting, too willing to compromise. We are warriors, not diplomats."

"And now we're caught between two enemies because of your actions," Decklan said, his voice dangerously quiet.

The smoke began to dissipate as Grom's concentration wavered with his growing anger.

"Return to camp," Gar'zul urged. "We need every warrior. The Blackhands and Bloodfists gather for, " His voice faded as the connection broke. The smoke figure of Gar'zul dissolved into wisps of gray that curled like dying fingers before fading entirely. The ash circle, once luminous with green energy, now lay cold and inert on the ground between them.

Grom remained kneeling, his shoulders hunched, head bowed as if bearing an impossible weight. When he finally looked up at Decklan, his eyes burned with accusation and betrayal.

"My father..." he whispered, voice raw with contempt. "All my life I wanted to be like him. And you've destroyed that with these... lies."

Decklan knelt beside his friend, reaching for his shoulder. "Grom, I—"

"Don't touch me!" Grom snarled, jerking away violently. "You were like a brother to me, and now you stand there believing the words of this... stranger over a man who's guided our clan for decades."

"I saw the truth spell. We both did."

"Magic can be twisted," Grom spat. "Just like loyalty, apparently."

Outside the tent, morning had fully broken. Raised voices carried on the cold mountain air, the war party arguing, dividing. Word had spread quickly. By the time Decklan emerged, warriors had formed into two distinct groups.

Kruvik, the old warrior, approached Decklan with six warriors at his back. "We're returning to camp," he said, voice flat with finality. "The clan needs defenders, not vengeance-seekers."

"And what of Kargoth's killer?" asked Krella, who stood firmly at Decklan's side. "Do we let Reyn escape justice?"

"Justice?" Kruvik scoffed. "Look around, girl. We started with forty. We're down to twenty-three, with eight wounded. This isn't justice, it's suicide."

Decklan surveyed what remained of his war party. Faces he'd known since childhood stared back, some accusatory, others uncertain. The unity forged through years of clan life lay shattered like his father's poisoned cup.

"Each warrior must decide," Decklan announced, his voice carrying across the camp. "Those who wish to return, go with Kruvik. Those who would continue, stay. There is no dishonor in either choice."

Grom emerged from the tent, his face hardened into stone. "I will stay," he said, deliberately standing apart from Decklan. "Not for you, but to learn the truth about my father. And because Reyn Nightshade must pay for her deceptions."

In the end, eleven warriors chose to follow Kruvik back to the clan. Twelve remained with Decklan, including Grom and Krella. The division cut like a physical wound through what had once been a unified force.

As Kruvik's group gathered their supplies, the veteran warrior approached Decklan one last time.

"I don't envy your position," he said quietly. "Leading with a divided heart is like fighting with a broken blade." He clasped Decklan's forearm in the traditional warrior's farewell. "May Gallant guard your path."

When the departing warriors had disappeared over the ridge, Krella came to stand beside Decklan. The morning light caught the determination in her eyes as she gazed at the diminished camp.

"They call this betrayal," she said softly. "But I see it differently. The true betrayal came when Gar'zul poisoned your father."

"And now we stand divided when we most need unity." Decklan's gaze drifted to where Grom sat alone, sharpening his blade with furious strokes.

"What will you do now?" Krella asked.

Decklan felt the weight of his father's pendant against his chest. The symbol of leadership that now seemed to mock him with all it represented: protection, unity, strength. Things he had failed to provide.

"We continue," he said finally. "Not for vengeance, but for truth. Reyn Nightshade must be exposed for what she's done, to all our clans."

Krella studied his face, her eyes searching. "That path leads through blood and fire, Decklan Stormshield. Choose wisely. Your path affects us all."

As she walked away, Decklan felt the truth of her words settle into his bones. Bridge or breaker, the prophecy had said. With the war party now split, with his best friend turned cold toward him, with enemies closing in from all sides, the choice before him had never seemed more significant, or more difficult.

CHAPTER TWENTY

BLOOD OF TWO WORLDS

The three moons hung in perfect alignment above, bathing the night in silver light that seemed to pulse with ancient magic. Decklan sat alone on a ridge overlooking the valley, his father's shield propped against a rock beside him. The firelight from their diminished camp flickered below, each flame representing a warrior who had chosen to remain despite mounting losses and uncertainty.

He closed his eyes, attempting the meditation his mother had taught him. *Find your center*, she would say. But his center felt like a battlefield where his orc and human heritages waged endless war.

"What would you have done, father?" he whispered to the night. The question hung unanswered in the cool air.

A vision formed behind his closed eyelids, his father standing tall, axe raised, every inch the orc chieftain commanding respect through strength. Beside this image appeared another: his mother in her healing pose, palms open, offering life rather than dealing death.

Two paths. Two bloodlines. Two destinies.

"Always chasing shadows instead of seeing what's before you," came a familiar voice.

Decklan's eyes snapped open. Kyra stood nearby, her form almost translucent in the moonlight.

"You appear and disappear like a spirit," Decklan said, not entirely surprised by her presence anymore.

"Perhaps I am one," she replied with that mysterious smile. "What troubles you, Decklan Stormshield?"

He gestured toward the camp. "Half my warriors have abandoned me. The other half question every decision. My best friend believes I've betrayed him. My clan faces destruction while I chase vengeance." He picked up a handful of dirt, letting it sift through his fingers. "And I'm still no closer to understanding why my father had to die."

"Is vengeance truly what you seek?" Kyra asked, settling beside him.

Decklan stared at the distant horizon. "What else is there?"

"Justice. Truth. Understanding. Peace." She touched the shield gently. "Your father carried this not to strike down enemies, but to protect those he loved."

The moonlight seemed to intensify as Decklan considered her words. For the first time since his father's death, he realized that vengeance alone would not honor Kargoth's memory.

"My father was never consumed by hatred," Decklan said softly, tracing the shield's emblem with his fingertips. "Even when facing enemies, he sought justice, not blood."

"And your mother?" Kyra prompted.

"She sees beyond clan boundaries, finds healing where others see only conflict." Decklan looked up at the three aligned moons. "I've been trying to be wholly one or the other, the perfect orc warrior or the thoughtful human mediator."

"And failing at both," Kyra observed without cruelty.

Decklan nodded slowly. "Two halves never make a whole when you keep them divided."

He stood, lifting the shield and studying its surface in the moonlight. For the first time, he noticed how the emblem incorporated elements of both cultures, the angular strength of orcish design surrounding the flowing, protective curve of human craftsmanship.

"I am both Shieldbearer and Moongazer," he said, his voice growing stronger. "My divided blood gives me sight others lack."

As dawn approached, Decklan returned to camp where the remaining warriors were preparing for departure. Some packed to return home, others readied for what they assumed would be a final vengeful assault.

Decklan called them to gather around the dying embers of the night's fire. Krella stood at his side, her eyes alert, watching his transformation with quiet amazement.

"My father was murdered," Decklan began, meeting each warrior's gaze in turn. "But rushing blindly into battle has cost us dearly. Reyn Nightshade doesn't just want me dead—she needs chaos between our peoples. The prophecy speaks of divided blood as bridge or breaker." He placed a hand over his heart. "I choose to be a bridge."

Murmurs rippled through the group. Grom stood apart, arms crossed, expression guarded.

"Our mission changes now," Decklan continued. "Not vengeance, but justice. Not destruction, but truth. We will expose Reyn's manipulation of all clans and end this cycle of bloodshed."

Tharak stepped forward. "Fine words, but what does that mean in blood and steel, War Chief? Our kin need protection, not philosophy."

Decklan met the weathered warrior's skeptical gaze unflinchingly. "It means we stop fighting the battle Reyn wants us to fight. She's manipulating the Bloodfist and Blackhand clans against each other and against us. We need evidence of her treachery that all clans will recognize."

He pointed toward the distant peaks. "We continue north, but not as raiders seeking blood. We move as shadows, gathering proof of Reyn's deceptions. We capture, not kill. We learn, not destroy."

"And if we're discovered?" another warrior asked.

"Then we fight with the discipline of Shieldbearers," Decklan replied, his voice steady. "We use terrain to our advantage. We strike only when necessary. We preserve our strength."

Several warriors nodded their approval, but others exchanged doubtful glances. Three more announced they would return to defend the clan directly. Decklan accepted their decision without anger, giving each departing warrior a respectful clasp of forearms.

As the gathering dispersed, Grom finally approached, his face a mask of conflicted emotions.

"So you've abandoned vengeance," he said, his voice low enough that only Decklan could hear.

"I've found a better purpose," Decklan replied. "One that honors both my father's strength and my mother's wisdom."

Grom's jaw tightened. "My father may have betrayed yours, but I won't abandon this mission. Not because I follow you, Decklan, but because I need to learn the truth. And because Reyn Nightshade used my father like a tool and discarded him. She will pay for that."

Decklan nodded, recognizing that while their paths ran parallel for now, their motivations remained different. "I welcome your strength, Grom Wiseblood, whatever your reasons."

After Grom walked away, Krella stepped closer, her eyes reflecting the morning light.

"Your words have changed," she observed, a slow smile playing on her lips. "And something else too... I like it."

Decklan met her gaze, a touch of curiosity in his eyes. "How so?"

"You stand differently," she said, letting her eyes linger on him for a moment. "More balanced. Before, you always seemed to be leaning forward, rushing toward something or away from something else."

A smile touched the corner of his mouth. "Perhaps I've finally stopped running from half of myself."

Krella reached out, her calloused fingers lightly touching the shield emblem that hung at his chest. "I think you're becoming what your father always hoped you would be."

"And what's that?"

"Something new," she said simply. "Neither purely orc nor human, but something stronger than either alone." She stepped back with a warrior's formality, but her eyes held something deeper. "I stand with you, Decklan Stormshield. Not because you are Kargoth's son, but because you are becoming your own man."

From her position near the edge of camp, Kyra observed their exchange with an approving smile. The morning light seemed to shimmer around her as she watched Decklan begin to transform from a warrior seeking vengeance into something far more powerful, a leader who might truly unite what generations of conflict had divided.

Decklan lifted his father's shield, feeling its weight differently now. Not as a burden of legacy he had to carry, but as a symbol of protection he chose to uphold. The rising sun caught its surface, reflecting light that seemed to bridge the distance between earth and sky.

Blood of two worlds flowed through his veins. And for the first time, Decklan embraced them both as one.

Chapter Twenty-One

THE WEB TIGHTENS

Decklan stood, his eyes scanning the rolling plains below. Three days had passed since the revelation about Gar'zul's betrayal had fractured their war party. Three days of uncertainty and growing dread.

Tharak approached, his weathered face grim. "Bad news, War Chief," he said, dispensing with formalities. "Blackhand and Bloodfist forces are surrounding our home. My scouts report at least three hundred warriors moving in from the east and north."

Decklan nodded, unsurprised. "And the south?"

"Nothing yet, but the river would slow their advance. They'll come eventually."

"They're boxing us in," Decklan said, tracing imaginary lines on the landscape before them. "Not just our camp, the entire clan."

A shout from the perimeter drew their attention. One of their scouting parties returned, two warriors supporting a third between them. Blood darkened the wounded scout's leggings.

"Specialized trackers," the lead scout reported as Decklan knelt beside the wounded warrior. "Like nothing I've seen before. They found our false trail, ignored it completely. They're hunting us systematically."

The wounded scout grimaced. "They knew exactly where to find us. Ambushed us near the split oak. Bloodfists, but not regular warriors. Moved like shadows."

Krella joined them, her expression hardening at the sight of the wounded warrior. "That's three ambushes in two days. They're getting closer."

Decklan helped the wounded man to the healing tent before returning to Krella and Tharak. "We can't stay in open country. We need shelter, somewhere defensible."

"There's an abandoned human outpost half a day's journey west," Tharak suggested. "Riverstone traders used it before the troubles started."

"No," countered Grom, approaching with his spear resting casually on his shoulder. Despite his relaxed posture, tension radiated from him like heat from a flame. "If we go west, we move further from the clan. They need us, Decklan. We can't abandon them when enemy forces are closing in."

Decklan felt the familiar tug of conflict between his responsibilities to his warriors and to the larger clan. He closed his eyes briefly, centering himself before responding.

"We're no use to anyone dead," he said finally. "The outpost gives us walls, shelter, and time to assess our situation. The clan's defenses are stronger than ours, they can hold longer."

Grom scowled but didn't argue further.

As they prepared to move, Kyra approached Decklan, motioning him away from the others. Her mysterious comings and goings had become commonplace, though no less unsettling.

"Reyn has eyes watching you," she said quietly. "Vexxa is using blood magic to track your movements."

"Is that even possible?" Decklan asked.

"For one with her skills? Yes. The ritual requires something personal, blood, hair—"

"My blood was spilled at the ravine ambush," Decklan realized.

Kyra nodded. "I can teach you how to block her scrying. It won't be pleasant."

The ritual was indeed unpleasant, a mixture of bitter herbs that made Decklan's stomach heave, followed by meditative chants that seemed to vibrate in his very marrow. But when they finished, Kyra seemed satisfied.

"It will hold for now," she said. "But be vigilant."

They reached the abandoned outpost by dusk, a simple palisade surrounding a few stone buildings. The gate had rotted away, but the walls were mostly intact. As the warriors secured the perimeter, Decklan explored the main building, finding scattered evidence of hasty departure, upturned furniture, forgotten cooking utensils, a child's wooden toy.

In what had once been some sort of meeting room, he discovered a chest partially hidden beneath collapsed roof beams. Inside lay correspondence between the outpost commander and various settlements, including Riverstone.

One letter caught his eye:

Third incident this month. Blackhand raiders attacking our northern farms while Bloodfist raiders hit the southern mines. Impossible timing unless coordinated. Request investigation into claims that a human mercenary group led by woman named Giath is orchestrating these attacks. Our scouts report seeing her meeting with both clan leaders separately. Believe she may be deliberately inciting conflict to profit from weapons trade.

Decklan spread the letters across a dusty table as Krella entered.

"Look at these dates," he said, pointing to several messages. "Five years ago, raids on Moongazer settlements blamed on Shieldbearers. Three years ago, attacks on Blackhand hunting grounds attributed to humans. Every single conflict... manipulated."

"She's been playing the long game," Krella said, tracing the timeline with her finger. "Positioning herself as ally to each group while turning them against each other."

Decklan clenched his fist. "My father was getting too close to the truth. That's why she needed him gone."

A commotion outside interrupted them. A messenger had arrived, a young Shieldbearer warrior, exhausted and dust-covered.

"War Chief," he gasped, dropping to one knee before Decklan. "I bring grave news. The clan is under siege. Combined Blackhand and Bloodfist forces surround our camp. Elder Varkus sent me to find you three days ago."

"How many?" Decklan demanded.

"At least five hundred. They've cut off access to the river. Elder Varkus says they're preparing for defensive stand, but without reinforcements..." The messenger left the sentence unfinished.

A heavy silence fell over the gathered warriors. Grom gave Decklan an accusatory glance that needed no interpretation: *We should have returned sooner.*

"What of Gar'zul?" Decklan asked.

The messenger shook his head. "Missing since before the siege began."

Decklan paced the room, acutely aware of his warriors watching, waiting for his command. Their numbers had dwindled to less than twenty effective fighters, against five hundred besieging the clan.

"We need to move quickly," Tharak advised. "Return to the clan before the noose tightens completely."

"And do what?" Krella challenged. "Twenty warriors against five hundred won't turn the tide."

"We die with our clan then," Tharak growled. "As honor demands."

Decklan raised his hand for silence, his mind racing. The blunt pragmatism of his orcish upbringing told him to return and fight alongside the clan, even if it meant certain death. But the analytical thinking his mother had instilled urged caution, a strategic approach.

"There's another way," Decklan said finally. "This evidence proves Reyn has been manipulating all the clans, including the Blackhands and Blood-fists. If we can expose her deception, we might fracture their alliance."

"While our people die waiting?" Grom's voice was harsh. "The clan needs warriors, not accusations and parchment!"

"And what good are twenty more corpses?" Decklan countered, facing Grom directly. "My father did not sacrifice himself for us to throw our lives away in a glorious but futile last stand."

He spread the letters across the table, motion for the others to gather around. "These prove a pattern. For years, Reyn has played all sides, creating conflict where none existed. If we can gather more concrete evidence, proof the clan leaders can't ignore, we might save not just our clan, but end this cycle of manufactured hatred."

Tharak studied the letters, his weathered face thoughtful. "You speak like your father now," he said grudgingly. "He too believed in finding solutions beyond the blade."

"But what of our people in the meantime?" Grom demanded.

"The Shieldbearer defensive position is strong," Krella interjected. "Elder Varkus is a skilled strategist. If they've already held for days, they can hold longer."

Decklan nodded, his decision crystallizing as he studied the map. "We need to expose Reyn's deception. That's the only way to save our clan, not by adding twenty more shields to a defensive line of hundreds."

"And where will you find such evidence?" Tharak asked, skepticism heavy in his voice.

"There," Decklan pointed to a location marked on one of the maps they'd found. "The trading post at Three Rivers Ford. According to these letters, it's where Reyn meets with her various contacts. If she's coordinating all this, that's where we'll find proof."

A murmur passed through the gathered warriors. Some nodded in agreement, while others exchanged troubled glances.

"Our clan fights for survival while we chase parchment and rumors," Grom said, his voice tight with barely controlled anger. "What good is evidence when our people lie dead?"

"What good is rushing to our deaths?" Decklan countered. "Think, Grom. Five hundred warriors against our twenty? We wouldn't even slow them down. But if we can prove Reyn has manipulated both the Blackhand and Bloodfist clans, we might fracture their alliance."

Tharak stroked his graying beard, his expression conflicted. "It's a gamble, War Chief. One that places your father's clan at risk while we hunt for truth. Not all warriors understand the value of patience in battle."

Decklan met each warrior's gaze in turn, seeing their doubt, their fear, and in some, their resentment. The weight of command pressed down on him like never before. He thought of his father, what would Kargoth do in this impossible situation?

"My father died because someone feared the alliances he was building," Decklan said finally. "I will not dishonor his memory by abandoning his vision. We cannot win this war with blades alone. We need truth as our ally."

After a long silence, Krella stepped forward to stand beside him. "I follow Decklan. His path is difficult but right."

One by one, most of the warriors nodded their agreement, though several remained visibly unconvinced.

"We leave for Three Rivers Ford at first light," Decklan announced, hoping his decision would prove wise and not doom them all. As the warriors dispersed to prepare, Decklan couldn't shake the feeling that the web around them was tightening with every passing hour.

Later that night, as most of the camp slept, Decklan studied his father's shield by torchlight. The metal was dented and scratched from years of battle, but the clan emblem remained proud at its center, a stylized shield with mountains in the background.

"You can't sleep either." Krella's voice came from the shadows before she stepped into the torchlight, her expression somber.

"I keep wondering if I'm making the right choice," Decklan admitted. "Tharak and Grom aren't wrong. Every warrior is taught to stand with their clan, to fight and die together if necessary."

Krella sat beside him, her shoulder brushing his. "And that thinking has perpetuated endless cycles of violence. Your father recognized this. That's why he sought alliances, tried to build peace."

"And ended up poisoned for his efforts." Decklan traced the emblem on the shield. "What if we're too late? What if the clan falls while we search for proof?"

"Then we avenge them by exposing the truth," she said firmly. "Your plan has merit, Decklan. You're thinking beyond just the immediate battle. That's what a true leader does. That is why I continue to follow you."

CHAPTER TWENTY-TWO

BETRAYAL AT DAWN

awn broke with an unnatural silence over the makeshift camp. Decklan stirred, his body instinctively sensing something was wrong before his mind fully awakened. The camp felt emptier, the usual sounds of warriors preparing morning meals absent from certain quarters.

He rose quickly, the fine hairs on his neck rising as he surveyed the camp. His worst fears were confirmed when he reached the eastern perimeter, where Borkan and seven others had made their sleeping area. Nothing remained but cold fire pits and indentations in the grass.

Krella approached, her expression grim. "They left before first light. Slipped away like shadows."

"Bite the Storm," Decklan growled, punching the ground where Borkan's bedroll had been just hours before. The earth absorbed his anger as he examined the carefully erased traces of their departure. "Cowards couldn't even face me before leaving." His voice trembled with frustration as he traced the deliberate way they'd obscured their tracks. They hadn't fled in panic, they'd methodically removed themselves from his command, a calculated betrayal that stung worse than any battle wound.

Tharak emerged from the tree line, holding a scrap of bark with crude markings scratched into it. "Found this secured to the old oak."

Decklan took the message, reading the abbreviated Orcish script:

Gone to defend clan. Honor demands it. Follow or continue your path. Either way, the oath remains.

Though not signed, Decklan recognized Borkan's distinctive method of marking the glyphs. He crushed the bark in his palm, letting the fragments fall.

"Eight warriors," he said finally. "That leaves us twelve."

"Eleven," Krella corrected quietly. "Mezzik's fever worsened in the night."

Decklan closed his eyes briefly, absorbing this additional blow. The wounded warrior had seemed to be improving yesterday.

"We continue to Three Rivers Ford as planned," he announced, turning to face the remaining warriors. Their expressions ranged from resigned acceptance to barely concealed doubt. "Our path hasn't changed. Exposing Reyn's manipulations might save more lives than rushing into a siege with our small numbers."

Grom approached, eyes hard with barely contained anger. "These warriors chose honor over your scheming. Perhaps they're the wiser ones."

"Perhaps," Decklan acknowledged, refusing to rise to the bait. "Gather your things. We move in twenty minutes."

They traveled in tense silence through the forest growth, maintaining a tight formation. Decklan took point, his senses heightened to their surroundings. The departure of eight warriors had left them dangerously vulnerable, and the remaining group knew it.

By midday, they reached the edge of Blackhand territory, a boundary more sensed than seen, where the forest subtly changed character. Older, darker trees dominated here, their massive roots creating natural barriers. Decklan halted the group with a raised fist, his nostrils flaring.

"Blood," he whispered, drawing his sword. "Fresh."

Krella moved to his side, her bow already nocked. "Ambush?"

"Maybe." Decklan scanned the heavy undergrowth ahead. His mixed heritage gave him advantages here, orc sense of smell combined with human discernment for patterns. "Something's not right. The birds stopped singing."

Grom stepped forward, staff gripped tightly. "We should pull back. Find another route."

But before they could retreat, the forest erupted in violence. A massive figure burst from concealment, followed by five others, elite Bloodfist Slaughterlords, their bodies decorated with ritual scars and red paint.

"Zoggorn," Krella hissed, recognizing the hulking orc leader.

Snarlgar Zoggorn, chieftain of the Bloodfist clan, towered above his warriors, wielding twin axes with practiced ease. His scarred face split in a terrible grin.

"The half-breed pretender," Zoggorn rumbled, his voice like stones grinding together. "Cowering in the shadows while your clan burns."

Decklan raised his father's shield, heart hammering against his ribs. "Form circle!" he shouted to his warriors. They reacted instantly, backs to each other as more Bloodfist warriors emerged from the trees.

The battle exploded around them. Decklan deflected Zoggorn's first axe strike with his shield, the impact numbing his arm. He countered with a swift slash that the massive orc barely avoided. Around him, his warriors engaged the Bloodfist forces with desperate intensity.

"Reyn sends her regards," Zoggorn taunted, pressing his attack. "She wants your blood, half-breed."

Decklan ducked another vicious swing, feeling the air displacement above his head. "Strange company you're keeping these days, Zoggorn," he grunted, driving forward with his shield to create space. "Blackhands were gutting Bloodfists in the borderlands just last season."

The massive orc chieftain laughed, a sound like breaking bones. "Rivalries die for richer prey."

A scream cut through the chaos, one of Decklan's warriors fell, a Bloodfist axe buried in his chest. The circle tightened, but another warrior stumbled back with a Bloodfist spear protruding from his shoulder.

"Declan, your flank!" Grom shouted, his voice cutting through the chaos of battle.

Decklan turned a heartbeat too late. A Bloodfist warrior had circled behind him while he was engaged with Zoggorn, blade already arcing toward his exposed back. In that frozen moment, Decklan saw death approaching with terrible clarity.

Then Grom was there, pushing past his own opponent, throwing himself between Decklan and the descending blade. The weapon bit deep into Grom's side instead of Decklan's spine, drawing a spray of crimson that painted the forest floor. Grom's pained roar mingled with Decklan's shout of dismay.

"No!" Decklan abandoned his position, smashing his shield into Zoggorn's face with desperate strength before pivoting to Grom's aid. His sword found the attacker's throat in a single fluid motion, driven by a rage that burned hotter than any he'd felt before. The Bloodfist warrior collapsed gurgling as Grom sank to one knee, clutching his wound.

"Hold the line!" Krella called from somewhere to his left, her arrows singing their deadly song through the air, but the truth was undeniable, they were hopelessly outnumbered.

Decklan crouched beside Grom, shield raised to protect them both as he surveyed the bleeding gash. "Why did you—" he began, but Grom cut him off with a pained grimace.

"Bite the storm," Grom hissed through clenched teeth, blood seeping between his fingers. "We can discuss my stupidity later."

Decklan gripped Grom's arm, helping him to his feet. "Stay with me," he urged, deflecting another attack that came too close. "We need to move now."

Blood soaked through Grom's tunic, but the shaman's son gritted his teeth and forced himself to stand. "I can fight."

"There!" Krella shouted, pointing to a narrow ravine cutting through the forest. "We can funnel them through there!"

Decklan nodded. "Fall back to the ravine! Retreat!"

The Shieldbearers moved as one, maintaining formation as they withdrew. Decklan and Tharak formed the rear guard, holding off the Bloodfist warriors long enough for the others to reach the ravine entrance.

"Go," Tharak urged, shoving Decklan toward safety. "I'll hold them."

Before Decklan could protest, Tharak roared and charged at Zoggorn, buying precious moments for the others to escape. It was the last Decklan saw of the veteran warrior, a silhouette against the forest, axe and sword dancing in a final, desperate display of courage.

"Keep moving!" Decklan commanded, supporting Grom's increasingly heavy weight as they scrambled up the ravine. The narrow passages twisted through rocky outcroppings, forcing their pursuers into single file. Krella and two remaining archers positioned themselves at choke points, loosing arrows at the Bloodfists who followed.

"I know... where to go," Krella gasped, taking Grom's other arm as the shaman's son stumbled. "Cave system... not far... we can lose them."

Grom's face had grown alarmingly pale, his breathing shallow. "Leave me," he muttered, eyes glazed with pain. "I'll slow you down..."

"Shut up," Decklan snapped, tightening his grip. "I'm not losing anyone else today."

They climbed higher, the sounds of pursuit growing fainter behind the rocky twists of the ravine. Two more warriors fell covering their retreat, their sacrifice buying the survivors precious time. By the time they reached the hidden entrance Krella had mentioned, a narrow crack in the mountainside concealed by dense foliage. Only seven remained of their original force.

Inside, the cave opened into a small chamber with a ceiling just high enough for them to stand. Krella immediately located a small spring trickling from the rear wall and began filling waterskins while Decklan eased Grom onto a relatively flat stone. The clean, cold water was a blessing they desperately needed—both for drinking and for cleaning Grom's wound.

"How bad?" Decklan asked, carefully pulling away the blood-soaked cloth from Grom's side.

"Bad enough," Grom replied through gritted teeth. The wound was deep, still bleeding freely. Without proper healing, infection would set in within hours.

While Krella organized the survivors to create makeshift bedding and fortify the entrance, Decklan tore strips from his undershirt to bind Grom's wound. His fingers worked swiftly, applying pressure to stem the bleeding, but he knew basic field dressings wouldn't be enough.

"Why did you do it?" Decklan asked quietly. "Why did you save me after everything?" Decklan finished, his voice barely above a whisper.

Grom's eyes, clouded with pain, fixed on Decklan's face. "Because," he rasped, "I might hate your decisions... but you're still my blood-brother. And I've seen... enough betrayal." A wet cough interrupted him, flecks of blood appearing on his lips.

Decklan pressed down harder on the wound, fear twisting in his gut. The bleeding wasn't stopping. "Save your strength," he murmured, but Grom gripped his wrist with surprising force.

"Listen," Grom insisted. "The prophecy... my father feared it because... change always frightens those in power." His breathing grew more labored. "But I think... the divided blood was never meant to be feared."

Before Decklan could respond, a voice from the cave entrance made them all turn.

"He's right. The prophecy was twisted by those who feared what it truly meant."

Kyra stood there, having found them despite the hidden entrance. She carried a worn leather satchel that clinked softly with the movement of glass vials inside.

"How did you—" Decklan began, but she brushed past him, kneeling beside Grom.

"Questions later. Your friend is dying." She opened her satchel, withdrawing several small containers. "Hold him still."

Kyra worked with practiced efficiency, cleaning the wound with a stinging solution that made Grom hiss through clenched teeth. She applied a poultice of herbs Decklan didn't recognize, chanting softly as she worked. The language wasn't Orcish or Common, but something older that made the fine hairs on Decklan's arms stand on end.

"This will slow the bleeding and fight the poison," she explained.

"Poison?" Decklan's head snapped up. "The blade was poisoned?"

Kyra nodded grimly. "Nightshade extract. Subtle but deadly. The Bloodfist Slaughterlords coat their blades with it." She bound Grom's wound with fresh bandages from her satchel. "This will slow the bleeding and fight the poison," she explained.

Decklan sat back on his heels, the full weight of the day's events crashing down on him. Eight warriors had abandoned him before dawn. Now, after the ambush, only five remained besides himself, Krella, and the gravely wounded Grom.

"How did you find us?" Krella asked Kyra, her voice edged with suspicion.

Kyra continued working, not looking up. "I've been tracking you since you left camp. When I heard the fighting, I followed."

"Impossible," one of the remaining warriors growled. "No one could have followed us without us knowing."

Kyra simply shrugged, unbothered by the accusation. "Yet here I am."

Decklan stood, moving to the cave entrance where the others had arranged defensive positions. Outside, twilight was settling over the forest. They'd need to post watches through the night.

"I have more news," Kyra said, her voice suddenly solemn. "The Shieldbearer camp is under full siege. Combined Blackhand and Bloodfist forces have surrounded it completely."

The words fell heavy in the cave, each warrior absorbing the implications.

"How many?" Decklan asked.

"At least five hundred warriors. They've blocked all routes in or out."

Silence filled the cave, broken only by Grom's labored breathing and the soft drip of water from the cave wall. Decklan felt Krella's intent gaze upon him, her normally fierce expression now tempered with exhaustion and concern.

"Maybe they were right to leave," Krella said quietly, wringing blood-soaked cloth into a small puddle beside her. "The others who returned to the clan. Perhaps we should have gone with them."

Decklan turned to face her, moonlight from a small fissure in the cave ceiling casting half his face in silver, the other half in shadow. His expression hardened, but there was no anger in it, only grim resolve.

"Even with our full strength, we couldn't have broken that siege," he said, running his thumb along the worn edge of his father's shield emblem. "Seven warriors against five hundred? That's not a battle—that's extinction."

He looked around at their diminished group, Krella, wounded Grom, and the four exhausted warriors who'd survived the ambush. Each face bore the hollow-eyed look of those who'd witnessed too much death in too short a time. The weight of their lives now rested on his decisions, a burden heavier than any shield.

He moved closer to where Grom lay, the shaman's son's breathing now more even under Kyra's ministrations, though his face remained pallid in the dim light. Decklan placed his hand gently on his friend's shoulder.

"Our mission remains what it always was. Not vengeance, but truth. Not a glorious death, but a difficult path forward."

Chapter Twenty-Three

BREAKING POINT

Decklan sat alone on a boulder overlooking the narrow entrance to the cave system where his remaining warriors had taken refuge, his father's shield propped against his knee. The three moons hung in the night sky, their alignment creating an eerie triangular pattern that cast triple shadows across the landscape. Their light seemed to mock him, illuminating the path of failures that had led him here.

Six days since his father's death. Six days of decisions that had whittled his war party from forty proud Shieldbearer warriors to a mere nine, most wounded, all exhausted, none with much hope remaining.

He traced the emblems on his father's shield with calloused fingers. The metal felt cold, unresponsive. What would Kargoth have done differently? Everything, probably.

"Tormenting yourself won't heal Grom's wounds," came Krella's voice from behind him.

Decklan didn't turn. "You should be resting."

"You should be leading," she countered, settling beside him on the boulder. Her arm brushed his, warm in the night chill. The touch anchored him momentarily before guilt pulled him back into the depths.

"I've led enough," Decklan said bitterly. "Look where it's gotten us."

Krella's face hardened. "Self-pity doesn't become you, Stormshield."

"It's not self-pity. It's accounting." Decklan gestured toward the cave where Grom lay fevered from Snarlgar's poisoned blade. "We started with forty warriors. Eleven are definitely dead. Eight abandoned us to return to a clan that's now surrounded by hundreds of enemies. Most of the rest are wounded. And for what? What have we accomplished?"

"We're still alive," Krella said firmly. "We know more about our enemy today than we did yesterday."

Decklan laughed hollowly. "My human heart makes me hesitate; my orc blood makes me reckless. I'm trapped between two natures, and neither serves me well."

From the shadows near the cave entrance, Kyra emerged like a spirit, her unusual eyes reflecting the triple moonlight. "You still insist on seeing yourself as divided, even after everything that's happened?" She approached them, her movements fluid and silent. "When will you recognize that you are uniquely whole?"

"Whole?" Decklan's voice cracked with sudden anger. "Look at me! I'm too slow to be human, too weak to be orc. I've spent my entire life caught between worlds that never fully accepted me."

"And yet you're the one mentioned in prophecy," Kyra replied calmly. "Not despite your heritage, but because of it."

"Then the prophecy chose poorly." Decklan stood abruptly. "A true orc leader would have led a direct assault on Reyn's forces and died honorably alongside his warriors. A true human commander would have negotiated alliances before ever leaving camp. I've done neither effectively."

"Perhaps because you're trying to be one or the other," Kyra suggested, "instead of being Decklan Stormshield."

"Enough!" Decklan snatched up his father's shield. "I don't need riddles. I need answers. I need to decide what to do next."

Krella reached for his arm, but he pulled away.

"I need to be alone," he said, softer this time. "Check on Grom. His fever should have broken by now."

Without waiting for a response, Decklan strode into the darkness, away from the cave mouth. Behind him, he heard Kyra whisper something to Krella, but he didn't turn back.

The night embraced him as he climbed higher along a narrow game trail. His orc blood gave him excellent night vision, one advantage of his heritage he'd never denied. The image of Grom taking that strike meant for him replayed endlessly in his mind. His dearest friend, now delirious with poison, alternating between cursing Decklan's name and pleading for forgiveness for past slights.

He found a flat outcropping overlooking the valley below and sat cross-legged, his father's shield before him. In the distance, beyond the hills that sheltered them, campfires flickered, the combined forces of the Blackhand and Bloodfist clans surrounding the Shieldbearer territories.

"What would you do, father?" he whispered to the night air. "I've tried to be the leader you wanted. I've tried to be the warrior the clan needed. I've failed at both."

The alignment of the three moons—Calanthir, Harmony, and Morvak—cast an unnatural glow across the shield's surface. Their light revealed subtle engravings he'd never noticed before: fine lines connecting the central emblem to the rim in patterns that reminded him of the web-like drawings in his mother's healing books.

Decklan pulled parchment and charcoal from his pouch and began sketching plans. If they couldn't match their enemy in strength, perhaps they could outsmart them. He outlined approaches to the Blackhand camp, possible diversions, routes of escape. With each revision, the plans grew more desperate, more unlikely to succeed.

Hours passed. The moons shifted position, their perfect alignment beginning to wane. Decklan's head drooped as exhaustion claimed him.

In dreams, he stood between his parents. Kargoth, tall and imposing in battle gear, frowned down at him. "You hesitate when you should strike," his father's shade said. "A chieftain must be decisive."

"You strike when you should heal," his mother countered, her hands glowing with Moongazer healing energy. "A leader must protect more than destroy."

"I'm trying to do both," Decklan told them. "I don't know how."

Both parents turned away, disappointment etched on their faces. "Then you will fail at both," they said in unison, their voices fading as they walked in opposite directions.

Decklan woke with a gasp, cold sweat making his skin glisten in the predawn light. His sketched plans lay scattered around him, some crushed beneath him as he'd tossed in fitful sleep.

As the eastern sky lightened, Decklan gathered his father's shield and the rumpled parchments. He had made his decision during the night, somewhere between planning and dreaming. Whether it was wisdom or desperation, he couldn't say.

But he knew one thing with certainty, they could not afford to wait any longer. The time for caution had passed. The time for decisive action had come.

Reyn Nightshade would pay.

CHAPTER TWENTY-FOUR

DESPERATE GAMBIT

D ecklan studied his father's shield once more, tracing the worn emblem with calloused fingers. The decision had crystallized in his mind during those dark hours, No more hiding, no more caution. The time had come for action.

He found the others gathered around a small fire in the cave, their faces haggard from days of retreat and nights of restless sleep. Grom sat propped against the wall, his skin pale but his eyes clearer than they had been since taking the poisoned wound. Krella tended the fire, her movements efficient but weary.

"We're going after Reyn Nightshade," Decklan announced without preamble. "Directly."

The silence that followed was broken only by the soft crackle of flames.

"You've seen their numbers," Krella finally said, her voice carefully neutral. "Three hundred warriors at least."

"We're not going to fight them all," Decklan replied, kneeling to sketch a rough map in the dirt floor. "We're going to infiltrate their camp during the ritual I witnessed. Capture Reyn herself. Force her to confess her manipulations."

"Suicide," Tuhak,one of the remaining warriors muttered.

Kyra stepped from the shadows where she'd been mixing herbs. "There are other ways, Decklan. The human settlements could provide allies. With time—"

"Time is something we don't have," Decklan cut her off, his voice harder than intended. "My father died because he was too careful. The clan falls while we hide in caves."

"And they'll fall permanently if we throw our lives away," Kyra countered.

Decklan stood again, drawing himself to full height. "I'm not asking anyone to follow me who doesn't wish to. But I'm going."

Krella moved to stand beside him, her loyalty evident though concern lined her face. "How do you propose we do this? Even if we reach Reyn, she'll be surrounded by elite guards."

Grom cleared his throat, wincing as he shifted position. "The eastern perimeter," Grom said. "It's their weakest point. The Blackhands believe the ravine there is impassable."

Everyone turned toward him, surprised at his contribution after days of resentful silence.

"You know this how?" Decklan asked.

Grom's eyes darkened. "My father... he shared their defensive positions with me once. Information gained during his... negotiations." The word tasted bitter in his mouth. "The ravine has a hidden path. Difficult, but navigable."

Decklan nodded slowly. "Go on."

"Their camp rituals follow a pattern. The third night after the moon alignment, Reyn will conduct a ceremony to honor their victories. All eyes will be on the central fire." Grom's gaze met Decklan's directly for the first time in days. "That's your window."

Decklan knelt beside his blood-brother. "You don't have to come. Your wound—"

"I'm coming," Grom interrupted, struggling to sit straighter. "Not for you. For the truth about my father. And to make Reyn pay for using him."

Kyra approached, medicinal herbs in hand. "This plan is born of desperation, not wisdom."

"Sometimes desperation is all we have," Decklan replied, turning to the remaining warriors. "I need to know who stands with me."

One by one, they nodded, some immediately, others after hesitation. Even Tuhak, who had called it suicide gave a reluctant nod.

Krella pulled Decklan aside as the others prepared. "You've changed," she said quietly. "There's something different in your eyes."

"Clarity," he answered. "For too long I've tried to prove myself as either orc or human. But tonight, I fight as Decklan Stormshield."

As dusk approached, Decklan led them through the Shieldbearer pre-battle ritual, his voice faltering occasionally over the traditional words. The warriors gathered in a circle, each holding a small stone to symbolize their collective strength.

"May Gallant watch over us," Decklan concluded, placing his stone in the center of their circle. "And if we fall, may we fall with honor."

The others added their stones, forming a small cairn that would remain long after they departed. Perhaps the only monument they would ever have.

As the warriors dispersed to prepare, Decklan caught Grom staring at him, his expression unreadable in the dying firelight.

"What?" Decklan asked.

"You've never led that ritual before," Grom observed. "Always said it was your father's place."

Decklan tightened the straps on his armor. "Things change."

"Yes," Grom agreed, his voice low. "They do." He hesitated, then pulled something from his pouch, a small leather cord with a carved wooden charm. "My mother made this for me before she died. Said it would protect me from evil spirits." He held it out awkwardly. "You might need it more than I do."

Decklan took the offering, recognizing it as the peace offering it was meant to be. He tied it around his wrist without comment, but the slight nod between them carried weight.

Krella approached, her weapons checked and ready. "If this works, we'll need to move quickly afterward. The entire camp will be after us."

"If we capture Reyn," Decklan said, buckling his father's shield to his arm, "we gain leverage. The Blackhand respect strength but follow the strongest. We show them their leader's weakness, and the alliance might fracture."

"And if it doesn't?" Kyra asked from the cave entrance.

Decklan met her gaze steadily. "Then at least I die trying to save my people, not hiding while they fall."

The night deepened around them as they moved through the forest, each carrying the weight of what might be their final mission. Decklan led them forward, his father's shield gleaming dully in the moonlight, no longer a burden but a promise.

Chapter Twenty-Five

INFILTRATION

Decklan crouched in the shadow of a massive oak, his eyes fixed on the distant Blackhand encampment. Fires dotted the valley below like fallen stars, their glow revealing the massive scale of the combined Bloodfist and Blackhand forces. The scent of woodsmoke mingled with the metallic tang of weapons being sharpened. War songs drifted upward, carried by the night breeze.

"At least five hundred warriors," Krella whispered beside him. "Maybe more."

Decklan nodded grimly. "And we're nine." He studied the camp's layout, noting the patrol patterns, the main gathering areas, and what appeared to be a central stone circle where several larger fires burned.

Their small group had gathered in a tight circle behind the treeline. Besides Decklan, Krella, and a still-recovering Grom, there remained only six warriors: Lenna with her exceptional night vision, a young tracker named Tuhak, the twins Varo and Loktar, the seasoned fighter Dornach, and Zirka, a quiet woman skilled with throwing blades.

"This is madness," Tuhak muttered, voicing what they all thought.

Decklan unrolled a crude map on the ground between them. "Then we'll need to be methodical in our madness. Each of you was chosen because your skills complement our mission." He looked at each face in turn, finding a mixture of doubt, determination, and fear.

"Lenna, Tuhak, you'll take the high eastern approach through the ravine Grom identified. Your task is observation only, map guard rotations, locate prisoners, and signal us when the ritual begins." He marked their path with a stick. "Varo, Loktar, you're our diversion. When you receive Lenna's signal, create chaos at the northern edge, but keep mobile. Draw attention, not confrontation."

The twins nodded, their identical faces solemn in the moonlight.

"Dornach, Zirka, you'll be our extraction. Station yourselves here," he pointed to a narrow pass, "and prepare for a rapid retreat, clearing any pursuit."

"And us?" Krella asked. Decklan turned to Krella and Grom, his expression resolute. "We're the infiltration team. The three of us will enter through the supply routes on the western edge that Grom identified. While the twins create their diversion, we'll move to the central area where Reyn is likely conducting her ritual."

Grom winced as he shifted his weight, his hand instinctively moving to the bandaged wound in his side. "And once we're inside?"

"I'll confront Reyn," Decklan said simply. "Force her to reveal her manipulations."

"And if she refuses?" Zirka asked, her fingers unconsciously touching the throwing blades at her belt.

Decklan's jaw tightened. "Then we take her. Bring her back to face the clan's justice."

Krella studied his face. "You don't sound convinced of our success."

"I'm not," Decklan admitted. "But I am convinced of our necessity." He looked around at each of them. "If any wish to leave now, do so with honor. This mission offers little glory and much risk."

No one moved. After a moment, Dornach spoke, his weathered face serious in the dim light. "My father served your father. My axe serves you."

The others murmured agreement, though Tuhak's eyes still showed doubt.

Decklan nodded, grateful for their loyalty. "Then let's prepare. Grom, help me with disguises."

While the others readied weapons and equipment, Grom and Decklan worked on transforming their appearances. Using mud, charcoal, and pieces of scavenged Blackhand clothing, they made themselves resemble messengers from outlying scouts.

"The dialect, can you still mimic it?" Grom asked as he smeared dark mud across Decklan's distinctively lighter skin.

"Well enough," Decklan replied, adopting the harsher consonants of Blackhand speech. "Only need it long enough to pass the outer guards."

As Grom worked, he paused, meeting Decklan's eyes. "This isn't just about your father anymore, is it?"

Decklan considered the question. "No," he admitted. "It's about all of us, Shieldbearer, Bloodfist, Blackhand. We've all been manipulated, played against each other while someone else pulls the strings."

"And what if we're too late?" Grom's voice was low. "What if the Shieldbearers have already fallen?"

"Then we ensure they didn't fall in vain," Decklan replied, securing his father's shield to his back, concealed beneath a ragged Blackhand cloak. "The oath remains"

Grom nodded, though his expression remained troubled. The poison wound had sapped his strength, but his determination remained undiminished.

Krella joined them, her distinctive red hair hidden beneath a hood. "The oath remains."

They synchronized their timing using the position of the three moons overhead. The alignment was nearly perfect now, Calanthir, Harmony, and Morvak forming an equilateral triangle in the night sky. Whatever ritual Reyn planned would likely coincide with the apex of this alignment.

"May the moons guide your paths," Decklan told the group as they separated. "We meet at the extraction point before dawn—with or without me."

Krella shot him a sharp look at these words, but said nothing.

The descent toward the Blackhand camp proceeded more smoothly than Decklan dared hope. Lenna and Tuhak disappeared like shadows into the eastern ravine, while the twins circled north. Decklan led Krella and Grom down a barely visible game trail that wound toward the supply lines Grom had identified.

As they approached the perimeter, Decklan raised a hand, halting their progress. Ahead, two Blackhand sentries stood beside a supply cart, sharing a wineskin.

"Follow my lead," Decklan whispered. He hunched his shoulders, adopted a hurried gait, and stepped boldly onto the path, gesturing for Krella and Grom to follow.

"Ho, brothers!" he called in the harsh Blackhand dialect. "Word from the eastern scouts!"

The sentries straightened, hands moving to weapons. "What word?" the larger one demanded. "And why so late?"

Decklan manufactured an expression of urgency, stalking closer with the confident gait of someone with important news.

"Movement in the eastern passes. The Shieldbearer remnants may be gathering for a desperate strike," Decklan growled, his voice roughened to match Blackhand speech patterns. He gestured toward Grom and Krella. "We need to report directly to Captain Gorash."

The sentries exchanged glances. The smaller one squinted at them. "Don't recognize you."

"Perimeter scouts," Grom interjected, moving forward to draw attention from Decklan's lighter skin. "Been watching the eastern ridges three days now."

The larger sentry relaxed slightly, but his companion remained suspicious. "Why three messengers for one report?"

Decklan nodded toward Krella. "She spotted the movement. I confirmed it. He knows the terrain best to guide Gorash's response." He leaned in, lowering his voice conspiratorially. "Reyn's paying extra for confirmed Shieldbearer kills tonight. Thought we'd share the opportunity."

At the mention of payment, the sentries' attitudes shifted. The larger one chuckled. "Gorash is at the western quadrant. Follow the main path, turn at the red banners."

They stepped aside, and Decklan led his companions past with a curt nod. Once beyond earshot, Krella whispered, "That was too easy."

"Their arrogance is our advantage," Decklan replied, maintaining his hunched posture as they wove between supply tents and cooking fires. "They don't expect anyone would dare infiltrate their camp."

The encampment sprawled across the valley floor, larger than any gathering Decklan had ever seen. Blackhand and Bloodfist warriors mingled around fires, sharpening weapons or engaged in boisterous competitions of strength. Banners bearing the symbols of both clans hung side by side, unthinkable months ago.

"This alliance isn't natural," Grom muttered. "These clans have been enemies for generations."

Decklan nodded grimly. "Reyn's influence is greater than we imagined."

They worked their way deeper into the camp, passing groups of warriors without challenge.

CHAPTER TWENTY-SIX

DARK RITUAL

A s they penetrated deeper into the Blackhand encampment, the atmosphere shifted. The raucous laughter and warrior songs faded behind them, replaced by an eerie stillness punctuated by low, rhythmic chanting. Ahead, the firelight took on an unnatural crimson hue.

"Something's wrong with that light," Krella whispered, her hand instinctively moving to her blade.

Decklan nodded, feeling a chill that had nothing to do with the night air. They crouched behind a stack of supply crates, observing the central clearing. What he saw made his blood run cold.

A perfect circle of standing stones dominated the area, each carved with symbols that seemed to writhe in the firelight. Between them, black iron braziers burned with that unnatural red flame. In the center stood an altar stone, its surface gleaming with fresh blood.

Reyn Nightshade stood before the altar, her tall figure commanding and terrible in elaborate ceremonial armor that combined Blackhand and Bloodfist symbology. Beside her, Vexxa Darkseer moved in slow circles, her hands weaving complex patterns in the air as she chanted in a language Decklan didn't recognize.

"Blood of the divided lineage," Vexxa's voice carried to them, "bridge between worlds, vessel of prophecy. When the three moons align, your sacrifice will seal our power."

"Nyxthera demands completion," Reyn responded, raising a curved ceremonial dagger. "The half-blood's life force will feed her hunger."

Decklan felt Grom stiffen beside him. "Nyxthera," Grom whispered, his face pale. "The Devourer of Light. My father spoke of her, an ancient entity even the shamans fear to invoke."

"They're performing blood magic," Krella added, her voice tight with disgust. "Forbidden even among the Bloodfist."

As Reyn stepped aside, Decklan could finally see what lay upon the altar, and his heart nearly stopped. Tharak, the Shieldbearer warrior, bound and barely conscious, struggled weakly against his restraints. Behind the altar, at least a dozen more of his clan members were bound to wooden posts, their faces drawn with exhaustion and fear.

"They've been taking our people," Decklan breathed, horror congealing in his chest. "Using them for their rituals."

"Look at the markings on their chests," Grom pointed out, his voice trembling. "They're testing them."

Each captive bore different symbols painted in what appeared to be blood, swirling patterns that centered on their hearts. Tharak's markings were noticeably different, more elaborate than the others.

"They're looking for someone specific," Krella whispered. "Someone with..."

"Divided lineage," Decklan finished, a cold realization washing over him. "They're looking for me."

The perfect alignment of the three moons now formed a perfect triangle in the night sky above the ritual site. Their combined light cast an otherworldly glow over the proceedings, the moon-shadows seeming to move of their own accord.

Vexxa approached Tharak, examining the markings on his chest with a disapproving frown. "The blood responds, but incompletely. He carries only a trace of human ancestry, too diluted for our purpose."

Reyn's face twisted with impatience. "We've tested dozens. Where is the half-blood warrior? The prophecy was specific, the Shieldbearer of divided blood."

"I need to stop this," Decklan whispered, reaching for his weapon.

Grom caught his arm. "We're outnumbered thirty to one. We need the diversion first."

"There's no time," Decklan hissed, watching as Reyn raised her ritual dagger over Tharak's chest.

Before they could move, a commotion erupted at the perimeter of the ritual ground. Tuhak, who had been positioned to signal the others, was dragged into the firelight by two massive Blackhand warriors, his slight form struggling against their iron grip.

"Intruders!" a guard shouted, and immediately the encampment erupted into chaos.

"They've found one of us," Decklan whispered urgently. "We need to act now before they discover the rest."

"Signal the twins for the diversion. Bite the storm" Grom said, already reaching for the small fire crystal in his pouch.

Krella's hand closed over his. "Wait. Look at Reyn."

The Blackhand leader had gone completely still, her ritual dagger suspended in mid-air. A slow, predatory smile spread across her face as she turned away from Tharak toward the captured Tuhak.

"Search the perimeter," she commanded, her voice cutting through the chaos. "The half-blood is here. I can feel it." She approached Tuhak, gripping his chin with cruel fingers. "Where is Decklan Stormshield?"

Tuhak spat at her feet. "Death comes for you, witch."

Reyn's laugh was cold as winter. "No, boy. It comes for your half-breed leader."

Decklan's mind raced. Their element of surprise was evaporating with every heartbeat. He glanced at the captives, then to his companions, then up at the three moons perfectly aligned in their celestial triangle.

"New plan," he whispered. "Grom, signal the twins, but tell them to target the northwest supply tents. Krella, can you reach Tharak and the others if I create a distraction?"

"Yes," she replied without hesitation, "but what are you—"

"I'm going to give Reyn exactly what she wants." Decklan's voice hardened with resolve as he removed his disguise. "Me."

Grom's eyes widened. "That's suicide."

"We have no choice. They'll find us any moment. Free our people while I keep them occupied. The oath remains."

Before either could protest further, Decklan stood and stepped into the clearing. The murmurs of the gathered warriors fell silent as he walked forward, his father's shield gleaming in the eerie light of the three moons.

"I am Decklan Stormshield," he announced, his voice ringing with authority he didn't entirely feel. "Son of Kargoth Stormshield and Skye of the Moongazers." He fixed his gaze on Reyn. "I understand you've been looking for me."

Reyn's face transformed with triumphant hunger. "The divided blood comes willingly to the altar. Seize him."

A dozen elite warriors moved to surround Decklan, but he stood his ground, keeping their attention fixed on himself rather than his companions still hidden in the shadows.

"Before you take me," Decklan called out, his voice carrying across the ritual ground, "tell me why. What is this prophecy that makes my blood so valuable?"

Reyn approached, her movements predatory and fluid. In the crimson light, her features were sharp as a blade, beautiful and terrible. "The divided blood will either unite the clans or destroy them all," she said, circling him slowly. "I simply ensure it will be destruction, but for our enemies, not for us."

From the corner of his eye, Decklan caught a glimpse of movement, Krella slipping from shadow to shadow toward the captives. He needed to keep Reyn talking.

"That's why you killed my father? For a prophecy?"

"Kargoth was an obstacle. He understood too much, too late." Reyn smiled coldly. "He died protecting the future you represent, a future where orcs and humans might stand as equals. Such weakness cannot be allowed."

A sudden explosion rocked the northern edge of camp, the twins' diversion. Flames leapt skyward, warriors shouting in confusion as they rushed toward the disturbance. Reyn barely glanced in that direction.

"A desperate attempt," she said dismissively. "Your friends cannot save you."

Decklan shifted his stance, positioning his shield. "I don't need saving."

He lunged forward, shield first, driving directly at Reyn. Her guards moved to intercept, but Decklan was faster than they anticipated, his movements blending power with agility. His sword flashed in the moonlight, drawing first blood from a surprised Blackhand warrior.

"Take him alive!" Reyn commanded sharply. "The ritual requires his living blood!"

The warriors adjusted their approach, trying to subdue rather than kill. Decklan used this to his advantage, fighting with calculated ferocity. He caught glimpses of the rescue effort. Krella cutting Tharak's bonds, Grom creating a wall of smoke to cover their escape.

Then Vexxa stepped forward, her eyes glowing with unnatural light. She raised gnarled hands toward Decklan, chanting words that seemed to twist the air around them. From her fingertips erupted tendrils of crimson energy that cut through Decklan's defenses as if his shield were made of parchment.

Pain unlike anything he'd ever experienced tore through him. Every muscle seized, every nerve igniting with agony. He fell to one knee, shield arm trembling against the magical onslaught.

"The blood calls to blood," Vexxa intoned, her voice echoing unnaturally. "Your resistance only strengthens the binding."

Through the haze of pain, Decklan saw Krella had freed Tharak and was working on the other captives. On the far side of the camp, a second explosion erupted. Grom had successfully signaled the others.

The momentary distraction weakened Vexxa's concentration. Decklan forced himself to his feet, muscles screaming in protest. With a defiant roar, he raised his father's shield against the magical assault. To his astonishment, the shield's central emblem began to glow with a silvery light, partially deflecting Vexxa's magic.

"The old power still lives in the bloodline," Vexxa hissed, her eyes narrowing.

Reyn stepped forward, drawing a slender black blade that seemed to drink in the moonlight. "Enough games. The alignment reaches its peak."

She moved with unnatural speed, closing the distance before Decklan could reposition. Her first strike he caught on his shield, the impact sending shockwaves through his already weakened body. The second sliced across his upper arm, drawing blood that sizzled when it touched her blade.

"Perfect," she whispered, examining the dark crimson stain. "The divided blood responds to the calling."

A horn sounded from the eastern perimeter of the camp, the signal that Grom's diversion had succeeded. Warriors were rushing in all directions, flames now spreading through the storage tents.

"Reyn!" A Blackhand captain rushed forward. "The prisoners are escaping!"

Rage flashed across Reyn's face. "Secure them! The ritual must not fail!"

The distraction gave Decklan the opening he needed. He slammed his shield into Reyn with all his remaining strength, sending her staggering backward. In that moment of imbalance, Decklan seized his chance, swinging his sword in a desperate arc that forced her guards to retreat.

"Decklan!" Grom's voice cut through the chaos. He had appeared at the edge of the ritual circle, bow drawn, covering the escape of the freed prisoners. "We have to go, now!"

Vexxa had recovered, her hands weaving a new spell that made the very air shimmer with malevolent energy. "You cannot escape the prophecy, half-breed," she snarled, dark power coalescing around her fingers.

The magic erupted toward Decklan like a wave of liquid darkness. He raised his shield instinctively, the emblem flaring with that same silver light, but it wasn't enough. The magic crashed against him, shattering his defense and sending him sprawling to the ground. Pain exploded through every nerve, his vision blurring as blood trickled from his nose and ears.

"The blood price will be paid," Vexxa intoned, advancing on his fallen form. "Willingly or not."

"Not today, witch."

The voice came from the shadows beyond the ritual circle. A figure stepped into the firelight, Kyra, her simple traveling clothes replaced by a silver-embroidered cloak that seemed to capture and refract the moonlight. She moved with fluid grace, hands tracing patterns in the air that mirrored Vexxa's but with a difference that made the hair on Decklan's neck stand up.

Where Vexxa's magic was dark and consuming, Kyra's shimmered with pale light that reminded Decklan of his mother's healing herbs.

"Who dares?" Vexxa snarled, redirecting her attack toward the newcomer.

The two magical forces collided in a thunderclap of energy that sent both shamans staggering. In that moment of confusion, Krella appeared at Decklan's side, helping him to his feet.

"Can you run?" she asked urgently, her eyes wide with concern.

Decklan nodded, though every movement sent fresh waves of pain through his body. "The others?"

"The others are clear," Krella reported, supporting Decklan's weight as his legs threatened to buckle. "Tharak is leading them to the eastern ravine where Dornach waits."

Across the ritual ground, Kyra and Vexxa circled each other, their magics clashing in bursts of silver and crimson. The very air between them seemed to bend and ripple with power. Kyra called out without taking her eyes from her opponent, "Go! I cannot hold her much longer!"

Reyn had recovered, her face contorted with rage. "Stop them!" she commanded, and a dozen warriors moved to block their escape.

Grom loosed three arrows in rapid succession, each finding its mark with deadly precision. "This way!" he shouted, gesturing toward a narrow path between two supply tents.

Decklan pushed through the pain, forcing his body to move. His sword arm felt leaden, but he managed to parry a thrust from a Blackhand warrior as Krella pulled him toward the escape route. Behind them, the magical duel reached a crescendo, culminating in an explosion of light that temporarily blinded everyone in the vicinity.

They tumbled through the gap between tents, Grom behind them unleashing a final volley of arrows before following. Alarm horns sounded throughout the camp, warriors scrambling to intercept them.

"The northwestern passage is blocked," Krella reported, her breath coming in sharp gasps.

"There," Decklan pointed with his sword toward a shadowy gap between two guard posts. The guards were distracted, looking toward the flames now leaping skywards from the supply area.

They sprinted across open ground, every step an agony for Decklan. Whatever Vexxa had done to him, it went beyond physical injury—he could feel it coursing through his veins like ice, sapping his strength with each heartbeat.

"He's wounded," Grom told Krella, notching another arrow. "Magical attack. I've seen my father treat similar injuries."

Behind them, a terrifying sound, Reyn's enraged voice cutting through the chaos: "The blood price must be paid! Find him!"

They reached the perimeter, slipping between unmanned guard posts. Beyond lay darkness and the promise of escape, if they could reach the rendezvous point where Dornach would be waiting with the freed prisoners.

The forest closed around them like a protective embrace. Decklan stumbled, the world tilting sickeningly as Vexxa's magic continued to work through his system.

"Keep moving," Krella urged, her arm firm around his waist. "There will be trackers right behind us."

They pushed deeper into the woods, following a barely visible game trail. Decklan's breath came in ragged gasps, each inhale like drawing fire into his lungs. His father's shield, once a comforting weight, now felt impossibly heavy on his arm.

CHAPTER TWENTY-SEVEN

BROKEN SHIELD

Darkness blanketed the mountains in suffocating waves, casting long shadows that seemed to reach for Decklan like grasping fingers. Each breath came labored, as if the night itself pressed down upon their chests, squeezing the hope from their lungs with each desperate step forward. He staggered along the narrow path, one hand clutching his blood-soaked side where Vexxa's blood magic had torn through his defenses. Pain radiated through his body with every heartbeat, the corrupted magic spreading like poison through his veins.

"Move faster," he hissed to the others, though his own legs trembled with exhaustion. "They could be right behind us."

Their small band scrambled through the darkness, hearts pounding in their throats. Twice they'd heard the distant howls of Bloodfist trackers, and each sound sent fresh terror coursing through their veins. Lenna had stumbled and nearly fallen into a ravine, saved only by Dornach's quick reflexes. Varo supported his twin brother Loktar, whose face was gray with pain from a deep gash in his thigh.

Kyra moved like a ghost ahead of them, navigating treacherous ravines and hidden paths that appeared and vanished in the moonlight. "This way," she whispered, changing direction so abruptly that Decklan nearly lost her in the shadows. "The path narrows here. Watch your footing."

A branch snapped somewhere behind them, and they froze, breath held, eyes wide in the darkness. Grom clutched his side where his partially healed wound had reopened, his breath coming in short, painful gasps.

"We can't outrun them much longer," he murmured, voice tight with fear and pain.

Decklan stumbled, nearly falling as a wave of dizziness washed over him. Krella was at his side instantly, her strong arm wrapping around his waist for support.

"I've got you," she whispered, her voice steady despite the fear in her eyes. "Just a little further."

The night seemed endless, each moment stretched into hours as they pushed forward, jumping at every sound, flinching at every shadow. The mountains loomed around them, impassive witnesses to their desperate flight.

"There," Kyra announced, her voice barely audible over their labored breathing. "The sanctuary."

Dawn's first tentative light revealed a narrow cleft in the mountainside, almost invisible unless one knew exactly where to look. Kyra guided them through the opening, which widened into a spacious cavern. Ancient stone pillars, carved with symbols that predated even the oldest clan markings, supported the high ceiling.

"We'll be safe here," she said, though her eyes betrayed uncertainty. "For a time."

Decklan collapsed against a smooth stone wall, his father's shield clattering beside him. The pain in his side had spread to his chest, and dark tendrils crawled beneath his skin like spiderwebs. Sweat beaded on his forehead despite the cave's chill.

"Let me see," Kyra knelt beside him, gently pulling aside the blood-soaked fabric. Her sharp intake of breath told him everything.

"That bad?" he managed, forcing a weak smile.

"Vexxa's blood magic is... powerful." Kyra's fingers hovered over the wound, not quite touching. "It continues to spread."

Grom slumped down nearby, his expression a mixture of pain and accusation. "This is what comes of challenging Reyn Nightshade directly." His voice was bitter. "Our clan scattered, our warriors dead or captured, and for what?"

No one answered him. The silence hung heavy in the air, broken only by the ragged breathing of wounded warriors.

Krella organized the survivors, setting watches and tending to injuries as best she could with their limited supplies. Dornach and Lenna secured the entrance while the twins huddled together, Varo attempting to stem the bleeding from his brother's leg.

Fever took Decklan before midday. He drifted in and out of consciousness, plagued by nightmares in which his father stood before him, face twisted in disappointment. In his delirium, he reached for Kargoth, but his fingers found only the cracked surface of his father's shield.

"No..." he mumbled, forcing his eyes open to see what his fingers had discovered. The shield, carried through so many battles, had cracked nearly in half during their escape, a jagged line running from the outer edge to the central emblem. The metal was warped and scorched from Vexxa's blood magic. The mighty Stormshield, symbol of his father's strength and leadership, lay broken beside him like an omen.

Decklan tried to sit up, but pain lanced through him, driving him back down with a grunt. Krella appeared at his side immediately, pressing a cool cloth to his forehead.

"Don't move," she said, her voice gentle but firm. "The magic is still spreading."

"My father's shield..." he whispered, fingers tracing the crack. "Like everything else I've touched."

"It's just metal," Krella replied, though her eyes betrayed her understanding of its significance.

Dornach approached, his weather-worn face grim. "Scouts returned. The news isn't good." He glanced at Decklan, hesitating.

"Tell me," Decklan commanded, struggling to focus through the fever.

"The Shieldbearer camp has fallen." Dornach's voice was hollow. "Those not killed in the siege were captured or scattered to the winds. Elder Varkus led the final defense but..." He trailed off, the silence completing his sentence.

The news struck like a physical blow. Decklan closed his eyes, the knowledge settling like a stone in his gut. Their home, their people, gone. And he had not been there to fight alongside them.

"This is your doing," Grom's voice cut through the silence, sharp as a blade. He stood, swaying slightly from his own injuries, eyes burning with rage. "While you chased your grand schemes and prophecies, our clan fought and died without their war chief."

"Grom—" Krella warned.

"No," Grom interrupted, his voice rising. "I followed you into this disaster, Decklan, because I believed you could avenge your father. Instead, you've led us from one defeat to another. For what? A broken shield and a dying clan?"

Decklan had no answer. The accusation stung all the more because it echoed his own thoughts.

"I'm done," Grom continued, gathering his meager possessions. "When I'm strong enough to travel, I'll find the survivors. Someone needs to rebuild what's left of our clan, and it clearly won't be you."

His words hung in the air like poison darts. No one spoke as Grom limped to the far side of the cavern, isolating himself from the others.

Krella knelt beside Decklan, her eyes reflecting the torchlight. "He's speaking from pain," she said softly. "We've all lost much."

Decklan turned away, unable to meet her gaze. "He's right," he whispered. "I abandoned the clan to chase vengeance. My father would never have—"

"Your father made choices too," Krella interrupted, her voice firm but gentle. "Not all of them were perfect."

Decklan closed his eyes as another wave of pain washed through him. The dark tendrils had spread across his chest now, visible even through his skin. Kyra had tried various remedies, but the blood magic resisted her efforts, feeding on his life force like a parasite.

As night fell, his fever worsened. In his delirium, he saw his father standing before him, disappointment etched in every line of his face.

"You were meant to protect them," Kargoth's specter accused. "Instead, you led them to ruin."

"I tried," Decklan pleaded. "I wanted to make you proud."

The apparition shook its head. "A leader sacrifices his pride for his people. You sacrificed your people for your pride."

Decklan reached toward the vision, but Kargoth dissolved into mist. "Father, wait!" he called out. "Tell me how to fix this!"

Kargoth's voice echoed as he faded: "The shield was never the strength..."

Decklan jerked awake with a gasp, sweat-soaked and shivering. The cavern was dim, lit only by a small fire. Kyra sat beside him, grinding herbs in a stone mortar.

CHAPTER TWENTY-EIGHT

PROPHECY'S TRUTH

The rhythmic drip of water echoed through the cavern, each drop like a heartbeat marking time. Decklan's consciousness returned slowly, his body leaden, limbs unresponsive. His blood felt like molten metal in his veins, burning where Vexxa's magic had seeped into him. Through half-open eyes, he glimpsed a blurred figure kneeling beside him, hands moving in careful patterns over his chest.

Kyra's face swam into focus, her features set with concentration. Around her fingertips, a pale bluish light pulsed in time with his heartbeat. Not herbal medicine, but something else, something ancient and powerful.

"What are you—" Decklan's voice cracked like parched earth.

Kyra's eyes snapped to his, the strange light disappearing as she quickly withdrew her hands. "Healing herbs," she said, too quickly. "Rest. The blood magic still spreads."

Before he could question further, a distant sound reached them, the unmistakable clash of metal on stone. Kyra's head turned sharply toward the cavern entrance.

"They've found us," she whispered, rising to her feet in one fluid motion.

The sanctuary erupted into frantic movement. Their small band, reduced to a pitiful handful of warriors, grabbed weapons and took defensive positions. Decklan struggled to stand, his body protesting with waves of pain. Krella appeared at his side, supporting him with a strong arm.

"You shouldn't be standing," she said, concern evident beneath her stern expression.

"Neither should they," Decklan managed, nodding toward the cavern entrance.

From outside came battle cries, distinctly Bloodfist in their guttural intensity. Moments later, Snarlgar Zoggorn himself appeared in the entrance, massive frame silhouetted against the dying daylight, his war axe gleaming with fresh blood.

"Found you, half-breed," he growled, satisfaction evident in his voice. Behind him, elite Bloodfist Slaughterlords poured into the sanctuary like a tide of death.

The battle that followed was chaos. Despite his weakness, Decklan fought alongside what remained of his warriors, his every movement sending fresh waves of agony through his poisoned veins. Dornach fell first, overwhelmed by three Bloodfists. The twins Varo and Loktar battled back-to-back near the western alcove, their blades a blur of desperate defense.

"Fall back to the inner chamber!" Decklan shouted, parrying a vicious overhand strike. His arms trembled with the effort, the blood magic draining his strength with every heartbeat.

Through the melee, Decklan caught glimpses of Kyra moving with impossible grace, her form seeming to shift between shadows as she avoided blades that should have found her. Not fighting, but not falling either.

As their small force retreated deeper into the cavern system, a new figure entered, Vexxa Darkseer, her robes billowing around her skeletal frame as if alive with malevolent purpose. The Bloodfist warriors parted before her, creating a path.

"The half-blood still stands," she rasped, her voice like stone grinding on stone. "How... resilient."

She raised gnarled fingers toward Decklan, dark energy crackling between them. "But you cannot resist what is already inside you."

Pain erupted anew in Decklan's chest, the blood magic responding to her call. He fell to one knee, gasping as darkness clawed at the edges of his vision. Through sheer force of will, he raised his father's cracked shield, though he knew it offered no protection against such power.

"Your blood betrays you," Vexxa hissed, approaching slowly. "It always has. It always will."

With a sudden gesture, she sent a pulse of crimson energy into Decklan's chest. The world around him dissolved, replaced by visions that tore through his mind like serrated blades.

He stood before a massive stone altar, ancient and worn by countless seasons. Above him, three moons hung in perfect alignment, Calanthir, Harmony, and Morvak. Their light casting triple shadows at his feet.

"Behold the truth," Vexxa's voice echoed around him. "The prophecy you've glimpsed only in fragments."

*Words appeared in fiery script upon the altar, burning themselves into his mind:

"When the three moons align and cast their threefold light, the one of divided blood shall stand at the crossroads of fate. Through their sacrifice, the old ways shall either be preserved eternal or broken forever. The bridge or the breaker, the healer or the destroyer, the choice is written in blood, but the ending is not yet carved in stone."

The vision shifted, showing countless orcs kneeling before a figure whose face was obscured in shadow. Human settlements burned in the distance.

"This is what the prophecy truly foretells," Vexxa's voice rasped. "A half-blood leader who will bring either salvation or destruction to all orcs. Reyn understands what your father refused to see, that your existence threatens everything."

Another shift. Decklan saw himself bound to the stone altar, his blood flowing into channels carved in the rock. Reyn Nightshade stood over him, a ritual dagger gleaming in the moonlight.

"Your blood will serve a greater purpose," Vexxa continued. "Through your sacrifice to Nyxthera, we ensure the prophecy bends toward our salvation, not our destruction. The purity of orc dominance will be preserved."

The vision shattered as something interfered, a pulse of blue-white light cutting through the crimson magic. Decklan gasped as his senses returned to the cavern. Kyra stood before him, one hand raised toward Vexxa, blue energy crackling between them.

"Enough of your lies, shadow-weaver," Kyra said, her voice suddenly resonant with power that hadn't been there before.

Vexxa hissed in recognition. "You! How dare you interfere, light-spawn!"

Their confrontation was cut short as the sanctuary's defenses began to collapse. Stone groaned as an ancient support pillar fractured under the weight of a Bloodfist warrior thrown against it. Dust and debris rained down from the cavern ceiling.

"We cannot hold!" Zirka shouted, blood streaming from a gash across her forehead.

Decklan struggled to his feet, his vision swimming with the effort. Through the chaos, he saw Snarlgar engage Krella. Her blade moved with deadly precision, but the Bloodfist chieftain was a force of pure brutality. With a savage backhand swing, he knocked her blade aside and drove his shoulder into her chest, sending her crashing against the stone wall.

"No!" Decklan roared, lurching forward. His legs betrayed him, and he fell to his knees as Vexxa's magic pulsed through him once more.

Grom appeared from the chaos, charging Snarlgar with reckless fury. "The Oath Remains!" he bellowed, delivering a devastating strike that forced the Bloodfist chieftain away from Krella's crumpled form.

Their duel was brief and vicious. Though Grom fought with all the skill and strength he possessed, he was injured and Snarlgar was the more seasoned warrior. A feint, a pivot, and Snarlgar's war axe swept through Grom's defense, catching him across the ribs. Grom staggered but remained standing, blood spreading across his tunic.

191

"Take the son of Gar'zul alive," Vexxa commanded as two Bloodfist warriors seized Grom from behind, forcing him to his knees.

Decklan, fighting both Vexxa's magic and his own failing strength, crawled toward Krella. Blood matted her hair where her head had struck the stone. She stirred weakly at his touch, eyes unfocused.

"Run," she whispered.

"Not without you," Decklan replied, pulling her arm across his shoulders.

Kyra appeared beside them, her face resolute. "The passage behind the third pillar," she said quietly. "I will hold them."

"They'll kill you," Decklan protested.

"Trust me," Kyra replied with a strange smile. "Some things cannot die so easily. Now go, Krella needs immediate attention."

Decklan hesitated, torn between saving Krella and helping the others. His gaze met Grom's across the chamber. Despite everything that had happened between them, he couldn't abandon his blood-brother.

"I can't leave Grom," he said.

"You must," Kyra insisted, her voice taking on that strange resonance again. "The prophecy is not yet fulfilled. If you fall here, all is lost."

A sudden explosion of blue light flared from Kyra's hands, momentarily blinding everyone in the chamber. When Decklan's vision cleared, she stood between them and their pursuers, her form shimmering with energy that seemed to hold the Bloodfist warriors at bay.

"GO!" she commanded.

With a final agonized look at Grom, Decklan half-carried, half-dragged Krella toward the hidden passage. He heard Grom's voice rise above the battle sounds.

"RUUUUNNNN!"

The last thing Decklan saw before entering the narrow tunnel was Vexxa advancing on Kyra, shadows writhing around her outstretched hands. Then darkness swallowed them as they fled deeper into the mountain.

CHAPTER TWENTY-NINE

DARK NIGHT

T he deeper tunnels of the mountain cave system echoed with Krella's ragged breathing. Decklan sat beside her makeshift bed of cloaks and furs, watching helplessly as she fought for each breath. Her normally copper skin had faded to an ashen gray, the wound in her side seeping a dark fluid that smelled wrong, tainted with whatever foul magic Snarlgar's blade had carried.

"Hold on, Krella," Decklan whispered, though he wasn't sure she could hear him anymore. "Just hold on."

The torchlight cast long shadows across the rough stone walls. Beyond their small circle of light, the cave mouth opened to the night, where stars glimmered coldly in a sky that seemed utterly indifferent to their suffering.

Kyra knelt on Krella's other side, grinding the last of her healing herbs into a paste with a small stone mortar. Her hands moved with practiced efficiency, but Decklan could see the worry in her eyes.

"This will help stabilize her," she said, spreading the poultice over Krella's wound, "but I can't promise more. The blade carried old magic, blood magic. It resists conventional healing."

Krella moaned, her head turning fitfully from side to side as fever gripped her. Decklan took her hand, feeling its unnatural heat. He'd seen warriors die before, had delivered death himself many times, but watching Krella fade was different. Each labored breath felt like a personal failure.

"My father's dead," he said quietly, his voice hollow. "My clan scattered, my friends wounded or captured. Because of me."

Kyra didn't look up from her work. "Because of Reyn Nightshade."

"No." Decklan's hand tightened around Krella's. "I led them into this. I failed them."

When Kyra finished applying the poultice, she bound Krella's wound with clean strips of cloth torn from her own cloak. "I've done what I can," she said, washing her hands in a small bowl of water. "Now we wait."

Decklan nodded, unable to speak the question that burned in his mind: *Wait for what? Her recovery or her death?*

Krella's breathing hitched, then steadied slightly. The poultice was working, at least temporarily, but Decklan knew that blood magic couldn't be countered with herbs alone. He'd seen such wounds before, warriors who seemed to improve only to fade suddenly hours later, the corruption reaching their hearts.

"I don't know who I am anymore," Decklan confessed, his voice barely above a whisper. "I tried to be my father's son, a true Shieldbearer warrior, but I hesitated when I should have acted. I tried to be clever like my mother's people, planning instead of fighting, and I led everyone into disaster."

He glanced at his father's broken shield, propped against the cave wall. The crack running through its center seemed to mock him, a physical manifestation of his fractured identity.

"Grom was right," he continued. "I'm not enough orc to lead through strength, not enough human to succeed through wisdom. I'm nothing but a half-measure."

Rising to his feet, Decklan paced the small cave. He moved to Krella, placing a hand on her forehead in a traditional orcish gesture meant to comfort the wounded. When that felt insufficient, he whispered a Moongazer prayer for healing his mother had taught him. Neither seemed to help.

"I can't even do this right," he growled, frustration bubbling into anger. "Can't fight like a proper orc, can't heal like a proper human."

Kyra watched him silently, her eyes reflecting the torchlight as he spiraled deeper into despair.

Without warning, Decklan grabbed the broken shield and stormed toward the cave entrance, pushing past the carefully placed scrub branches that concealed their hiding place. Outside, the night air struck his face, cold and indifferent. Moonlight, the three moons now perfectly aligned, cast an eerie glow across the mountain slope, illuminating the steep drop beyond the narrow ledge. The valleys below were shrouded in mist, punctuated by the distant pinpricks of enemy campfires that seemed to mock his failures.

With a roar of anguish that echoed across the mountainside, Decklan hurled the broken shield into the darkness. It tumbled end over end, the silver emblem catching moonlight in brief flashes before disappearing into the mist-shrouded depths below. The sound of it striking stone and bouncing away grew fainter until silence reclaimed the night, leaving only the hollow emptiness in his chest.

He sank to his knees at the ravine's edge, the echo of the shield's impact fading into silence. In that void, only the distant water's whisper remained, indifferent to his pain.

"What have I accomplished?" Decklan asked the darkness. "Nothing but death."

He sat in the cave's cold embrace for what felt like hours, staring into the abyss. The moons would be aligned perfectly now, their light falling on whatever ritual Reyn Nightshade had planned. With Grom captured and Krella dying, there was no one left but him, a half-blood who'd failed at everything he'd attempted, and even he was injured.

Perhaps there was one final way he could serve his people.

The thought formed slowly in his mind, terrible and tempting. If Reyn wanted his blood so badly, if the prophecy truly centered on him, perhaps surrender was the answer. He could offer himself in exchange for the release of his captured warriors. His blood for theirs.

"If my blood brings only destruction," he whispered to the darkness, "maybe it should be spilled."

The cavern offered no answer beyond the hollow drip of distant water. Decklan closed his eyes, imagining himself walking into the enemy camp, laying down his weapons, offering his throat to Reyn's blade. Would it be enough to save what remained of his clan? Or would his sacrifice simply complete whatever dark ritual Reyn had planned?

He didn't know. And in this moment, crushed beneath the weight of his failures, he wasn't sure he cared anymore.

Chapter Thirty

HEALER'S TRUTH

The pale light of dawn crept through the cave mouth, painting the rough stone walls in shades of ash and blood. Decklan sat motionless at the edge, his back against cold rock, eyes fixed on the fading stars. The three moons had passed their perfect alignment during the night, yet their unnatural proximity still dominated the sky, Calanthir's silver light, Harmony's soft blue glow, and Morvak's crimson stain forming a triangle that seemed to focus directly on him.

Behind him, Krella's labored breathing punctuated the silence. Each ragged inhale twisted something in his chest. Her wound festered with Vexxa's blood magic, darkening the veins around it like poison roots seeking her heart.

"You've been sitting here all night," Kyra's voice came softly as she approached, her footsteps making no sound on the stone.

Decklan didn't turn. "What does it matter? I've failed them all."

"Have you?" Kyra settled beside him, her strange eyes reflecting the dawn light. "Or have you simply failed to be something you were never meant to be?"

A bitter laugh escaped him. "And what was I meant to be? Not orc enough for my father's people. Not human enough for my mother's. A half-measure in both worlds."

"Half?" Kyra's voice sharpened. "Is that truly how you see yourself? As incomplete?"

"What else would you call it?" Decklan gestured at the ravine below where fragments of his father's shield lay scattered. "I couldn't save my father. Couldn't protect my clan. Couldn't even keep my shield whole."

Kyra was silent for a long moment, studying him with those unsettling eyes that seemed to shift color with the growing light.

"Your blood is not your fate, Decklan Stormshield. Your choices are." She leaned forward. "The prophecy speaks of divided blood not as weakness, but as potential. The bridge or the breaker, two paths, not two halves."

"Pretty words. They won't heal Krella. Won't bring back Grom."

"No," Kyra acknowledged. "But neither will yourself-pity."

Decklan's head snapped up, anger flaring in his amber eyes. "Self-pity? My clan is scattered, my father murdered, my friend—" His voice caught. "Grom is captured because of me."

"Yes," Kyra said, her voice firm but not unkind. "And what will you do about it?"

She reached toward him, and for the first time, he noticed a small leather pouch in her hand.

"Look," she said, opening it to reveal shimmering dust that seemed to capture the dawn light. "Do you know what this is?"

Decklan frowned. "Moon dust. My mother used it for healing rituals."

"Yes, but not just any moon dust. This comes from the crystal caverns, where all three moons' light converges during alignment. It's sacred to both your bloodlines, though few orcs remember this."

"What are you saying?"

"I'm saying that your dual heritage is not a burden but a gift." Kyra's eyes softened. "You see what pure-blooded orcs cannot. You understand what humans miss. You stand at the crossroads between worlds."

Decklan turned away. "It hasn't helped much."

"Because you've been trying to be one or the other," Kyra said, her voice gaining a strange resonance that made Decklan look at her sharply. "Orc warrior or human diplomat. Your father's son or your mother's child. You've never embraced what you truly are, both at once."

She gestured toward Krella's sleeping form. "Your friend fights for her life because she believes in you. Not in spite of your heritage, but because of it. She sees what you refuse to acknowledge."

"And what's that?" Decklan asked, bitterness still edging his voice.

"That you carry the wisdom of two worlds in your blood. That you can see solutions others cannot." Kyra rose to her feet, suddenly seeming taller in the growing light. "Did you ever wonder why your father carried a shield rather than a greatsword like most orc chieftains?"

Decklan blinked at the unexpected question. "He valued protection over aggression."

"Yes," Kyra said, her voice carrying a weight that demanded attention. "Protection. Not just of himself, but of others." She offered a hand to help Decklan rise. "Your father understood something many orcs forget, true strength lies not in how many you can defeat, but in how many you can defend."

Decklan took her hand and stood, joints stiff from his night-long vigil. "My father was a warrior of renown."

"And a protector without equal," Kyra added. "The Stormshield name was earned generations ago not through conquest but through salvation. Your ancestors stood between warring factions and created peace."

She moved to the cave entrance, gesturing at the valley below where enemy campfires still smoldered. "Did you know that 'Shieldbearer' originally meant something different? In the ancient tongue, it meant 'those who bridge the divide.' Your clan began not as warriors, but as mediators between human settlements and orc tribes."

Decklan's brow furrowed. "That can't be right. The clan has always valued martial prowess."

"Because they forgot their purpose," Kyra said softly. "As generations passed, they remembered only that they were strong, not why that strength mattered." Her gaze pierced him. "Your father was beginning to remember, before Reyn silenced him."

"How could you possibly know this?" Decklan demanded, suspicion edging into his voice.

Kyra smiled, the expression transforming her face. "I know many things, Decklan Stormshield. Just as I know that Gar'zul's betrayal came not from malice but from fear. Fear of change. Fear of what you represent."

She turned toward Krella's prone form. "Even now, he regrets his actions. He never intended your father to die, only to be weakened enough that tradition could prevail."

"You speak as if you've seen into his heart," Decklan said, following her gaze to Krella. The warrior woman's face was pale, her breathing shallow.

"Perhaps I have." Kyra knelt beside Krella, placing a cool hand on her forehead. "Just as I see into yours. You blame yourself for everything that has happened, but your failure wasn't in your divided blood. It was in refusing to accept it."

Decklan watched as Kyra examined Krella's wound, her fingers tracing the dark veins with surprising tenderness. "Even if what you say is true, what good does it do now?"

"That depends," Kyra said, looking up at him with eyes that seemed to shift from amber to an unearthly blue-green. "On whether you continue to see yourself as broken or begin to understand you are uniquely whole."

She stood again, her movements fluid and graceful. "The divided blood prophecy doesn't dictate your path, Decklan. It merely describes your potential. Bridge or breaker, the choice remains yours."

Decklan looked down at his hands, stronger than a human's but more dexterous than an orc's. Hands that had both dealt death and attempted healing. "My father—"

"Would be proud of your struggle," Kyra interrupted gently. "He understood far more than he could express to you. Why do you think he insisted you train in both orcish combat and your mother's healing arts?"

A memory surfaced, his father watching silently as his mother taught him to identify healing herbs, a rare look of approval crossing Kargoth's stern features when Decklan correctly named them all. He had assumed his father merely tolerated these lessons.

"Your mother's prayers reached deeper than you know," Kyra continued, her voice taking on an almost musical quality. "She never asked the gods for your victory, only for your wholeness."

The rising sun cleared the mountain ridge, sending a shaft of golden light through the cave entrance. It caught Kyra's form, making her seem momentarily translucent, her outline blurring into the light itself.

"Who are you?" Decklan asked, the question emerging as barely more than a whisper.

Kyra smiled, neither confirming nor denying his suspicions. "Someone who has watched your journey longer than you know. Someone who believes in what you might become." She gestured to Krella. "As does she."

CHAPTER THIRTY-ONE

TWILIGHT VIGIL

D ecklan settled beside Krella's still form, her breathing shallow and un-
even. Dark veins spread from her wound like spiderwebs beneath her
skin, the magic of Vexxa's curse slowly consuming her.

"You should rest," Kyra said softly from the shadows. "Your wounds are still
not completely healed."

"I can't," Decklan replied, his voice hollow. He reached for Krella's hand,
careful not to disturb the poultice Kyra had applied. "Not while she fights for
her life because of me."

Kyra said nothing, only nodded and retreated deeper into the cave, leaving
him alone with his thoughts and the ragged sound of Krella's breathing.

Outside, the three moons hung unnaturally close in the night sky, their
alignment still potent even as it began to wane. Decklan closed his eyes, exhaustion threatening to overtake him. But sleep meant dreams, and dreams meant
his father's disappointed face, Grom's accusations, and the faces of all those
who had fallen following him.

Instead, he settled into the cross-legged position his mother had taught him
long ago, when she would speak of Viviana, the Life Weaver. "Find your center,"
she would say, guiding his small hands to rest on his knees. "Breathe in life,
breathe out fear."

The familiar ritual calmed his racing thoughts. As his breathing slowed,
he found himself recalling more of his mother's teachings. Gentle wisdom he

had often dismissed as too weak, too soft for a warrior's path. But now, with strength having failed him so utterly, perhaps there was value in softness.

"The Life Weaver teaches that healing begins within," his mother's voice echoed in his memory. "We cannot mend others until we accept our own wounds."

His wounds ran deep, not just the lingering effects of Vexxa's blood magic, but the gashes in his spirit. A lifetime of rejection for being neither fully orc nor fully human. The weight of his father's legacy. The desperate need to prove himself worthy.

As the night deepened, Decklan's meditation shifted. He began incorporating the endurance rituals of his father's people, the rhythmic chanting that Shieldbearers used to withstand pain in battle. Without conscious thought, he found himself weaving together his mother's peaceful breathing techniques with the guttural strength of orcish battle meditation.

The two traditions, so often at odds in his mind, now flowed together like tributary streams joining a river. His breathing deepened, his posture straightened, and something settled within him, not peace exactly, but a momentary stillness in the storm of his thoughts.

In this strange clarity, Decklan opened his eyes and looked at Krella. The dark veins beneath her skin seemed to pulse with the rhythm of his breathing. He placed one hand gently over her wound and the other on her forehead, feeling the unnatural heat of her fever.

"I don't know if you can hear me," he whispered, his voice rough with exhaustion. "But I'm not leaving you. Not this time. You are so important to me."

The words stirred something deep within him. A memory of his mother treating a child with fever in their clan. She had sung a Moongazer healing song while applying her remedies, her hands gentle but sure. The melody came to Decklan now, hesitant at first, then stronger. The language was not his father's harsh Orcish but the flowing syllables of his mother's people.

As he sang, he began to incorporate the low, resonant throat singing tones that Shieldbearer shamans used to drive out malevolent spirits. The combination was strange, discordant at first, then finding an unexpected harmony as he continued.

Hours passed as Decklan maintained his vigil, alternating between song and silence, meditation and prayer. Sometime in the deepest part of the night, when even the cave's shadows seemed to have weight, he felt Krella's breathing change. The rasp that had accompanied each breath eased slightly. Her skin, though still fever-hot, no longer burned like forge-fire beneath his palm.

"Decklan." Kyra's voice broke his trance. She stood at the edge of the small fire she'd built, her features half-hidden in shadow. "You need to see this."

He reluctantly left Krella's side and approached the fire. In Kyra's outstretched palm lay something small and glinting. The central emblem from his father's shield, broken free from the shattered remains he had cast away in despair.

"Where did you find this?" he asked, taking it carefully. The metal was cool against his skin, the familiar weight of it somehow comforting.

"At the bottom of the ravine," Kyra replied. "The shield broke, but this piece endured." She watched him closely as he traced the worn design with his fingers. "Perhaps it was meant to."

Decklan stared at the emblem, the stylized shield within a shield that had been his father's symbol for so long. He had never noticed before, but the design contained elements of both orcish angular patterns and the flowing circular motifs of his mother's people. Not fully one or the other, but something unique born from both.

"She's stabilized," Kyra said, nodding toward Krella. "Whatever you did... it helped."

Decklan looked back at Krella's sleeping form, surprise momentarily displacing his weariness. "I didn't do anything. I just... sang to her."

"Sometimes that's enough." Kyra moved to a small leather pouch and withdrew something that caught the firelight, a cord braided from leather and silver thread. "Your mother made this. She thought you might need it someday."

Decklan accepted the cord, feeling the intricate pattern of the weave between his fingers. Without speaking, he began threading it through the small ring at the top of the shield emblem, fashioning it into a pendant. When he had finished, he slipped it over his head, the weight of it against his chest oddly reassuring.

"I've been a fool, Kyra," he said quietly. "Trying to be my father. Trying to be what everyone else wanted. I forgot who I am."

"And who are you?" she asked, her voice gentle but probing.

He touched the pendant at his chest. "I'm still figuring that out. But I know I'm not just half of something. I'm... whole. Different, but whole."

Kyra smiled, her eyes reflecting the firelight in a way that seemed almost too bright to be natural. She moved to her travel pack and withdrew a worn leather scroll case.

"Then perhaps it's time you saw this," she said, extracting an ancient-looking parchment. As she unrolled it on the stone floor, Decklan saw it was a map unlike any he'd seen before. The ink seemed to shimmer with a faint silvery glow in the firelight.

"What is this?" he asked, leaning closer.

"A path," Kyra replied. "One that few know exists, a hidden passage into the heart of the Blackhand ritual grounds."

Decklan studied the map, recognizing landmarks he'd seen during their previous infiltration, but also noting routes that hadn't been visible, narrow crevices between rock formations, underground passages beneath seemingly impassable terrain.

"Where did you get this?"

"From those who walked between worlds long before you were born," Kyra said cryptically. "The question is not where it came from, but what you'll do with it."

Decklan traced a finger along one of the secret paths. "Reyn still has Grom. And the other prisoners."

"Yes." Kyra watched him carefully. "What does that mean to you now?"

Decklan was quiet for a long moment, touching the shield emblem at his chest. When he spoke, his voice carried a new certainty.

"It means I need to help them. Not for vengeance, not to prove anything, but because they need me." He looked up at Kyra. "My father carried a shield, not a sword. I never understood until now. His strength wasn't in what he could destroy, but in what he could protect."

He turned to look at Krella, whose breathing had steadied further. "I won't defeat them with strength alone, but with wisdom from both my bloodlines."

For the first time in days, Decklan felt something like purpose returning. The weight of failure still pressed on him, but it no longer threatened to crush him entirely. There was a path forward. Different from the one he had imagined, but perhaps the one he was always meant to walk.

"They'll be expecting us to run," he said, studying the map again. "They won't expect us to return. Not with so few warriors, not when we've been so thoroughly defeated." He traced the hidden path with his finger again, a new determination hardening in his eyes.

"We won't fight them directly," Decklan continued. "We'll move like shadows, freeing the captives before they realize we've returned."

Kyra nodded approvingly. "And what of Reyn Nightshade? What of vengeance?"

Decklan looked down at the shield emblem resting against his chest, then back to Krella's sleeping form. The anger that had driven him these past weeks still burned, but differently now, less consuming, more focused.

"Justice, not vengeance," he said, his voice low but firm. "Reyn must answer for what she's done, but killing her won't bring back my father or heal our clan." He looked up at Kyra, a new clarity in his gaze. "My mother always said that the right path isn't always the easiest or most direct."

"And what is that path?" Kyra asked, though her eyes suggested she already knew his answer.

"To break this cycle of bloodshed. To find a way forward that doesn't end with more graves." He stood straighter, shoulders squared. "My father died because someone feared what unity might bring. I won't make the same mistake."

CHAPTER THIRTY-TWO

UNEXPECTED ALLIES

T he shield emblem hung heavy against Decklan's chest as he watched Krella's chest rise and fall with each labored breath. The dark lines of Vexxa's blood magic still traced ominous patterns beneath her skin, but something had changed through the night. Her fever had broken, and her face seemed less contorted with pain.

For the first time in days, Decklan felt a flicker of hope stirring within him. The healing song had worked—not perfectly, but enough to buy them time. Perhaps there was truth to what Kyra had told him about his divided blood being a strength rather than a weakness. If he could blend his mother's healing traditions with the resilience of his father's people, maybe he could forge a new path forward. One that neither pure-blooded orc nor human could walk alone.

He touched the shield emblem lightly, tracing its intricate design with his fingertips. It wasn't broken after all, just as he wasn't half of anything. He was whole and in that wholeness lay possibilities he was only beginning to understand.

"We need to move her," Kyra said, appearing silently beside him. "This location is too exposed."

Decklan nodded, his jaw set with determination. "The eastern caves might offer better shelter. If we follow the ridgeline—"

A sound from below stopped him mid-sentence, the soft crunch of footfalls on stone. Decklan dropped to a crouch, drawing his blade in a single fluid motion.

"Wait," Kyra whispered, placing a restraining hand on his arm. Her eyes narrowed as she peered into the silvery morning mist. "Look carefully before you strike."

The figures emerged from the fog like ghosts, a dozen or so travelers moving with the practiced stealth of those accustomed to hostile territory. Their clothing bore the pale blues and silvers of the Moongazer clan, and at their head walked a woman whose posture Decklan would recognize anywhere.

"Mother?" The word escaped him in a breath of disbelief.

Skye Stormshield's head snapped up, her keen eyes finding her son instantly despite the distance. For a moment, she stood frozen, then broke into a run, scrambling up the rocky slope with surprising agility.

Decklan met her halfway, nearly stumbling as she threw her arms around him. Her embrace was fierce, almost desperate, as if trying to confirm he was real.

"I feared the worst," she whispered against his shoulder. "When we heard the Shieldbearer camp had fallen..."

"How did you find us?" Decklan asked, his voice rough with emotion.

Skye pulled back, studying his face with the intensity only a mother could manage. "The three moons guided me. And..." she hesitated, glancing toward where Kyra stood watching them. "I had help."

Before Decklan could question this cryptic statement, his mother's attention shifted to Krella's prone form.

"She's been touched by blood magic," Skye said, her healer's eyes assessing the dark lines beneath Krella's skin. She knelt beside the fallen warrior, fingers hovering over the wound. "Strong magic. Vexxa's work?"

Decklan nodded grimly. "We've managed to slow its spread, but..."

"You've done well," his mother said, unpacking herbs from a leather pouch at her belt. "Better than I would have expected from someone with no formal training."

There was a question in her words, but Decklan chose not to answer it directly. Instead, he looked toward the Moongazer band that had followed his mother up the slope. Among them were familiar faces, his mother's cousin Lyara, the scout Tannin, but also several humans he didn't recognize, dressed in the earthen tones of Riverstone traders. Then there was one orc he did recognize.

"Bite the storm. Tharak, you made it"

"When Krella cut me loose I was able to sneak out in the commotion." Tharak beamed.

"Can't keep a strong orc down. You've brought humans with you?" Decklan asked, surprise evident in his voice.

Skye nodded while examining Krella's wound. "The threat Reyn poses isn't limited to orcs, my son. The human settlements have suffered raids as well, coordinated attacks designed to drive them westward."

One of the humans stepped forward, a broad-shouldered man with graying temples and a trader's shrewd eyes. "Your mother convinced us this fight concerns us all. I'm Harran, of Riverstone. These are my sons, Teren and Joss." He gestured to two younger men who stood warily at his side, hands never straying far from their weapons.

Decklan noticed how they studied his features, the blended characteristics of orc and human ancestry that had made him an outsider among both peoples.

"You look like your father," Harran said unexpectedly. "He and I traded salt for furs for fifteen seasons. He was a hard bargainer, but he kept his word."

Harran's words stirred a mix of emotions within Decklan, pride, sorrow, and a renewed sense of purpose. He remembered his father's unyielding stance, his commitment to his clan, and his unwavering honor. Kargoth Stormshield had been a formidable chieftain, respected even by those who had been his adversaries.

"Thank you," Decklan said, his voice steady despite the turmoil inside him. "My father valued his word above all else."

Harran nodded, his expression softening slightly. "We've lost much to these raids. Homes, friends, family. Your mother convinced us that standing together is our best hope."

Skye looked up from tending to Krella, her eyes holding a quiet strength. "The prophecy speaks of a divided blood bringing unity or destruction. Decklan, you are that bridge. We must unite, orcs and humans, to face this threat."

Decklan felt a surge of resolve. His mother's words echoed the vision he had been forming in his own mind. "We need to move Krella to a safer location. The eastern caves should provide better shelter."

Skye nodded in agreement. "Lyara, Tannin, gather the others. We move out immediately. Harran, can your men carry Krella on a stretcher?"

Harran signaled to his sons, who quickly began fashioning a makeshift stretcher from branches and their cloaks. Decklan watched as they worked efficiently, their movements practiced and coordinated. It was a stark reminder of the potential that could be harnessed when diverse peoples worked together.

Kyra, who had been silent until now, stepped forward. "Your mother speaks wisely, Decklan. The path ahead will not be easy, but it is the right one."

Decklan looked at Kyra, a sense of understanding passing between them. She had been a mysterious figure throughout their journey, but her presence had been a guiding force, helping him to see beyond the limits of his own perceptions.

As the group prepared to move out, Decklan took a moment to address them all. "We face a common enemy, one who seeks to divide and conquer. Reyn Nightshade has manipulated our clans and settlements for her own gain, sowing discord and chaos. But we are not pawns to be moved at her whim. We are orcs and we are humans, and we stand together."

The group moved quickly through the mountain paths, with Harran's sons bearing Krella's stretcher and Moongazer scouts ranging ahead and behind. As they traveled, Skye shared what she had learned about the captured Shieldbearers.

"Gar'zul is among the prisoners," she said quietly to Decklan. "Reyn turned on him after your father's death, claiming he had outlived his usefulness. The Blackhand clan now controls what remains of the Shieldbearer territory."

Decklan absorbed this news with a mix of emotions. Gar'zul had betrayed them all, yet he was still Grom's father and had been manipulated by Reyn's schemes. "What of the other captured warriors?"

"They're being held for some ritual," Skye explained. "The alignment of the three moons approaches its peak. Whatever Reyn plans, it will happen soon."

As they reached the eastern caves, tension arose between the different groups. The Moongazers kept to themselves, while Harran's men eyed the unfamiliar surroundings warily. Some muttered about trusting orcs, even half-blooded ones.

Decklan stepped forward, addressing the growing divide. "I know what you see when you look at me," he said, his voice carrying through the cave. "Neither fully orc nor fully human. But that's precisely why we must work together. Our differences can be our strength, not our weakness."

The cave fell silent as Decklan continued, his voice gaining strength. "Each of us brings something unique to this fight. The Moongazers' knowledge of healing and stealth, the humans' tactical thinking and resourcefulness, the Shieldbearers' strength and courage. Together, we're stronger than any single group alone."

He moved among them, addressing each faction directly. "Tannin, your tracking skills rival any Shieldbearer scout. Harran, your trading routes give you knowledge of paths even the Blackhand warriors don't know. Lyara, your healing abilities complement my mother's perfectly. We need all of these skills."

As if to emphasize his point, Krella stirred on her stretcher, mumbling in pain. Skye and Lyra immediately moved to tend her, working in seamless coordination. The others watched as Moongazer healing techniques visibly eased Krella's suffering.

"See?" Decklan gestured to the healers. "Already we're stronger together."

Kyra stepped forward, her presence somehow making the cave feel larger. "Decklan speaks truth. The enemy counts on our divisions. Every moment we spend distrusting each other is a victory for Reyn Nightshade."

Harran's elder son, Teren, spoke up. "Fine words, but how do we rescue prisoners from an entire clan's stronghold? We're barely two dozen fighters."

"By using what makes us different," Decklan replied. He moved to a clear patch of ground, kneeling to sketch a rough map in the dirt. "The Blackhand clan expects either a frontal assault from warriors or perhaps some attempt at stealth. They don't expect us to combine both."

The group gathered around as Decklan outlined his plan, drawing on each group's strengths. The Moongazers would create diversions using their nature magic, while Harran's knowledge of trading paths would get them close to the prisoner camp.

As the night deepened, Kyra drew Decklan aside. "You need to learn something before tomorrow," she said softly. "Your mother's healing gifts flow in your blood as surely as your father's warrior strength," Kyra continued, leading Decklan to a quieter corner of the cave. "It's time you learned to access both."

Decklan settled cross-legged beside her, watching as she arranged several small stones in a circle. "I've never had the patience for healing arts," he admitted. "The meditation, the careful study of herbs, it always felt too passive compared to warrior training."

"That's because you were trying to learn as a human would," Kyra replied, her voice carrying an ancient wisdom that made Decklan wonder again about her true nature. "Or perhaps as an orc would. But you are neither, and both. Your path to healing will be uniquely your own."

She placed her hands over the stone circle, and a soft light began to emanate from between her fingers. "Watch carefully. Feel the energy flow, like blood through veins, like the tide of battle through warriors' ranks."

Decklan closed his eyes, trying to sense what she described. To his surprise, he could feel something, a subtle pulse that reminded him of the rhythm he found during combat.

"Now," Kyra instructed, "reach for that energy as you would reach for your weapon, but instead of taking, give. Instead of striking, support."

The sensation was strange, almost uncomfortable. Decklan felt the power gathering in his hands, but rather than the familiar surge of combat strength, this energy flowed like water seeking its own path.

"I don't understand," he admitted. "It feels... wrong. Uncontrolled."

"Because you're trying to dominate it like a warrior." Kyra's voice held a hint of amusement. "Healing isn't about control. It's about guidance. Like steering a river rather than damming it."

Decklan thought of his mother's gentle hands tending wounds, how she seemed to work with the body's natural healing rather than forcing it. He relaxed his grip on the energy, letting it flow more naturally.

"Yes," Kyra whispered. "Now you begin to understand."

The energy responded, gathering more strongly in his palms. When he opened his eyes, a soft silvery light emanated from between his fingers, reminiscent of moonlight on water.

"The strength was always there," Kyra said. "You just needed to stop fighting yourself to find it."

The light faded, leaving Decklan drained but somehow more complete than before. He looked at his hands with new appreciation, understanding that they could do more than just destroy.

Hours passed as Kyra guided him through exercises that blended combat focus with healing intention. By dawn, Decklan had managed to ease most of the remaining injuries he suffered from Vexxa's magic. A small achievement, but one that filled him with a new kind of pride.

"Remember," Kyra said as they concluded, "healing is not weakness, and fighting is not strength. They are two halves of the same whole, just as you are."

Decklan nodded, finally understanding. He wasn't caught between two worlds; he was building a bridge between them.

The others were stirring now, preparing for the rescue mission ahead. As Decklan rose to join them, he caught sight of his reflection in a pool of water. The face that looked back at him was neither orc nor human, but something new, something whole.

CHAPTER THIRTY-THREE

FOREST APPROACH

D ecklan moved silently through the ancient forest, his footsteps finding the gaps between fallen leaves with practiced precision. Behind him followed their unlikely alliance, Moongazers with their fluid grace, the other humans from Riverstone with their practical weapons, and Tharak with his imposing form. The combined force moved like a single organism through the shadows of towering pines.

The forest grew denser as they approached Blackhand territory, the canopy overhead filtering the early morning light into a verdant haze. Decklan paused, raising his fist in the Shieldbearer signal for halt. The movement rippled backward through their ranks.

"Blackhand scouts ahead," he whispered as Skye and Harran from Riverstone crept forward to join him. "Two, maybe three."

Skye nodded, her eyes narrowing as she studied the barely visible movement through the underbrush. "They're using a standard Blackhand patrol pattern. Predictable."

Harran grunted softly. "We could circle around. Add half a day to our approach, but safer."

Decklan considered both perspectives, feeling the familiar internal tug-of-war that had plagued him his entire life. The Shieldbearer in him wanted to eliminate the threat directly; the Moongazer blood counseled avoidance. For the first time, he didn't perceive these impulses as contradictions, but as complementary tools.

"No," Decklan decided. "We don't have half a day. Grom and the others are being prepared for the ritual sacrifice." He turned to his mother. "Can your Moongazers create a distraction?"

Skye's eyes lit with understanding. "Lyara's connection with forest creatures is strong. She could scatter the birds, make the scouts look east."

"While we move in from the west," Decklan finished her thought. "Harran, your sons know how to move without disturbing the underbrush. They'll lead the flanking party."

The Riverstone hunter nodded with grudging respect. This half-orc understood the strengths of each group without favoring one approach over another.

When everyone understood their roles, Decklan made a signal to advance.

Lyara moved forward at Skye's gesture. Crouching beneath a twisted oak, she closed her eyes and began a soft, melodic humming that barely disturbed the air. After several heartbeats, the forest canopy above erupted with movement—dozens of birds suddenly taking flight eastward with alarmed calls.

The Blackhand scouts reacted instantly, their attention drawn toward the commotion. In that moment, Decklan signaled and Harran's sons slipped through the underbrush with near-supernatural stealth. Within moments, two scouts were subdued, not killed, but rendered unconscious with precise pressure to their necks.

The third scout, however, spotted the movement. He opened his mouth to sound an alarm, but Decklan was already moving. With a burst of strength and speed, he crossed the distance in three silent strides, one hand clamping over the scout's mouth while the other delivered a precise blow to the temple.

"Bind them," Decklan whispered. "No blood spilled unless absolutely necessary."

Tharak, frowned. "The Blackhand wouldn't show us such mercy."

"That's precisely why we must," Decklan replied, meeting the veteran's eyes. "We're not fighting just for survival, but for a different way forward."

As the scouts were secured, Decklan consulted the ancient map Kyra had provided. "The ravine entrance should be just beyond that ridge. According to this, it leads directly to the eastern edge of the ritual grounds."

"It won't be unguarded," Skye cautioned.

"No," Decklan agreed, "but they'll expect an assault from the main paths, not a small team through a supposedly impassable ravine."

He turned to address the gathered force. "We divide here. Harran, take half our numbers and create a distraction at the northern approach. Mother, your Moongazers position near the western ridge—if we need to retreat quickly, we'll need your pathfinding."

Decklan selected five warriors, a mix of Moongazers, Tharak, and one of Harran's sons named Teren, for his infiltration team. "We'll find the prisoners and open a path from inside," he said, securing the shield emblem pendant around his neck. "No heroics. This is a rescue, not a war."

Skye approached her son, her expression a mixture of pride and concern. "You've grown into something neither your father nor I could have imagined," she said softly.

"Thank you," Decklan said. He hesitated, then added, "I understand now what father meant about trusting my whole self. It's not about choosing between orc and human ways. It's about knowing when each serves best."

Skye's eyes glistened. "He would be proud to see you now."

The groups separated, each moving toward their designated positions. Decklan led his small team toward the hidden ravine entrance, navigating through increasingly difficult terrain. The forest floor gave way to rocky outcroppings, forcing them to climb rather than walk. When they reached the ridge overlooking the ravine, Decklan motioned everyone down.

Below, a narrow cleft in the earth cut between two sheer rock faces. At its mouth stood two Blackhand guards, looking bored but alert.

"Two at the entrance," Decklan whispered. "Likely more farther in."

Tharak growled softly. "Frontal attack?"

"No," Decklan replied. "We need stealth, not strength." He considered the terrain, the position of the guards, the patterns of their movement. An idea formed, one that combined Shieldbearer tactics with Moongazer observation techniques.

"They're rotating watch positions every fifty heartbeats," he observed. "And the one on the left keeps checking something in his pocket, probably counting time until relief comes."

Teren nodded. "I see it too. Getting antsy."

Decklan reached into his pouch and removed a small vial Layra had prepared. "Sleeping essence. Strong enough to drop a war wolf, but we need to get close."

He outlined his plan quickly, pointing to a small outcropping of rock twenty paces from the guards. "Teren, your aim is best. When the guards switch positions again, I need you to hit that rock with an arrow. Make them think it's an animal."

Tharak looked skeptical. "And when they investigate?"

"Only one will check. The other will stay on guard. That's when I'll move in with the sleep essence."

Decklan gave precise instructions, and they waited until the guards made their routine position change. At Decklan's signal, Teren released an arrow that struck the rocks with a sharp clack before falling into the underbrush. As predicted, one guard jerked his head toward the sound, said something to his companion, and moved cautiously to investigate.

The moment the guard's back was turned, Decklan slipped down the embankment with almost supernatural silence, a skill learned from his mother. He approached the remaining guard from behind. In one fluid motion, he pressed a cloth dampened with the sleeping essence over the guard's mouth and nose.

The guard struggled briefly before slumping in Decklan's arms. By the time the second guard returned from investigating the noise, Tharak and a Moongazer had joined Decklan. They quickly tackled the guard to the ground. The confused guard had no chance to raise an alarm before he too succumbed to the sleeping essence.

"Impressive," Tharak admitted grudgingly. "I would have simply charged in."

"And we'd be fighting the entire Blackhand clan by now," Decklan replied. "Bind them and hide them among the rocks. They'll sleep until morning."

The small team moved into the ravine, which narrowed until they were walking single file between walls of striated stone. The air grew cooler, carrying the scent of damp earth and something else, the bitter tang of ritual incense and smoke.

After navigating the winding passage for nearly an hour, they reached a point where the ravine widened slightly before ending at a rock face. Decklan studied the ancient map, then ran his fingers along the seam in the stone.

"There should be a passage here," he whispered, pressing against various projections in the rock. When his hand brushed against a symbol etched almost invisibly into the stone, a trio of interlocking circles, part of the rock face shifted inward with the grinding protest of long-unused stone.

"Moongazer path marking," said Selene, one of Skye's companions, her voice barely audible. "Our ancestors must have used this route."

"Single file," Decklan instructed. "Watch for triggers or wards."

They followed the tunnel for what felt like an eternity, the air growing warmer and the distant sounds of drums becoming audible. Eventually, the passage opened onto a small ledge overlooking a vast clearing. Decklan signaled for everyone to stay low as they crept to the edge.

Below them spread the Blackhand and Bloodfist encampment, illuminated by dozens of ritual fires. At its center stood a massive stone altar, around which Vexxa Darkseer and several acolytes moved in synchronized patterns. Reyn Nightshade stood at the altar's head, arms raised toward the darkening sky where the three moons, Calanthir, Harmony, and Morvak—hung in ominous proximity.

"There," Tharak whispered, pointing to the eastern edge of the clearing. "The prisoners."

Decklan's breath caught when he saw them. At least twenty Shieldbearers confined in a makeshift pen, guarded by Blackhand warriors. Among them, he could make out Grom's slumped form, apparently unconscious.

"And there," Teren added, indicating another group of captives separated from the Shieldbearers. "Humans from the eastern settlements."

Decklan's gaze swept the encampment, noting patrol routes, guard positions, and the rhythm of movement. Unlike his earlier, emotion-driven observations, he now processed everything with a clarity born of his dual perspective.

"The patrols change every hundred heartbeats," he whispered. "And look there. They've positioned most guards facing the main approaches, not internal pathways."

Tharak nodded. "Expecting an attack from outside, not infiltration."

"Their mistake," Decklan replied. "We'll wait until nightfall. When the ritual intensifies, their attention will focus on the altar."

The team retreated slightly from the edge, establishing a hidden observation point among a cluster of weathered boulders. As darkness fell, they watched the encampment transform. Additional fires were lit, casting long shadows across the clearing. The drumming increased in tempo and volume, becoming a primal heartbeat that echoed through the ravine.

Decklan observed Vexxa leading a procession of acolytes around the altar, each carrying a bone staff topped with a different symbol. Behind them walked Reyn Nightshade, resplendent in ceremonial armor inlaid with obsidian and bloodstones. Her voice carried across the clearing as she addressed the gathered warriors.

"The prophecy foretold this night! When the three moons align, the divided blood shall decide our future!" The Blackhand and Bloodfist warriors roared their approval, weapons clanging against shields. "Tonight, we ensure that future belongs to the true children of the earth, not the weak soft-skins who would dilute our strength!"

Decklan's hand instinctively went to the shield emblem hanging at his chest. The contempt in Reyn's voice echoed the doubts he'd carried his entire life, but now those words rang hollow. He no longer felt divided, but whole. Unique in a way neither pure-blooded orcs nor humans could understand.

Chapter Thirty-Four

BREAKING CHAINS

The three moons hung like ethereal sentinels in the night sky, their light casting long shadows across the combined Blackhand and Bloodfist encampment. Decklan crouched behind a cluster of weathered stones, studying the movements of the guards. Beside him, Tannin of the Moongazers and Harran from Riverstone waited in silence, their breath misting in the cold night air.

"The guard change comes soon," Decklan whispered, his eyes never leaving the makeshift prison pen. Through the gaps in the wooden stakes, he could make out the forms of orc prisoners. His heart leaped when he spotted Grom's distinctive broad shoulders, though his blood-brother's head hung low.

Skye approached silently, pressing a small vial into Decklan's palm. "More sleeping essence," she whispered.

Decklan nodded, feeling the weight in this moment. "We move when the horns sound for the ritual."

As if summoned by his words, deep-throated horns bellowed from the center of the camp. Vexxa Darkseer's voice rose above the assembled warriors, proclaiming the coming of a new age. The guards at the prison pen straightened, attention drawn toward the ceremony.

"Now," Decklan breathed.

They moved like shadows. Decklan approached the first guard from behind, smothering her with the sleeping essence before the orc could turn. The guard's eyes rolled back as Decklan eased her to the ground without a sound.

Tannin and Harran dispatched the remaining guards with similar efficiency. No deaths, no alarm raised. Just as Decklan had planned.

"This isn't the orc way," Tannin observed quietly as they reached the pen.

"Nor is it entirely the human way," Decklan replied, working at the lock on the prisoner's pens. "It's my way."

The lock gave way beneath his hands, and Decklan pulled the gate open. The prisoners stared at him with disbelief in their hollow eyes. Grom was the first to rise, his face gaunt and marked with fresh bruises, but his amber eyes sparked with recognition.

"You came," he said, voice hoarse.

"Did you doubt I would?" Decklan extended his hand.

Grom hesitated, the weight of their past conflict hanging between them. "I didn't think you'd be foolish enough," he finally replied, clasping Decklan's forearm in the traditional grip.

As the other prisoners stirred, Decklan signaled for silence. "We have three paths out," he whispered, "but little time. Harran will lead the first group through the eastern ravine. Tannin, take the second along the moonpath. I'll escort the third through the western approach where my mother and the others wait."

The prisoners divided quickly, their movements betraying both fear and desperate hope. Decklan was about to send them on their way when Grom gripped his shoulder.

"Not all of us," Grom said gravely. "My father is held separately."

Decklan's expression hardened. Despite everything, Gar'zul was still Grom's father. "Where?"

"The shaman's tent. Near the ritual site."

Harran stepped forward. "That's suicide. The ritual is gathering all their forces."

"Then they won't expect us there," Decklan said with quiet determination. He turned to the others. "Proceed with the escape. Grom and I will find Gar'zul."

Skye touched her son's cheek, her eyes reflecting the three moons above. "Be careful. The alignment peaks in less than an hour."

Decklan nodded, feeling the pendant of his father's shield emblem warm against his chest. "We'll meet at the western ridge."

As the rescued prisoners dispersed with their guides, Decklan and Grom slipped into the shadows of the camp. The ritual drums intensified, their rhythm pulsing through the ground beneath their feet. Warriors streamed toward the central clearing, leaving the outlying areas less guarded.

"They've taken all the shamans prisoners," Grom whispered as they ducked behind a supply cart. "Reyn doesn't trust anyone with power that isn't completely loyal."

Decklan studied the layout ahead. "Smart. Dangerous, but smart."

The shaman's tent stood apart from others, marked by totems and surrounded by four guards, two Blackhand, two Bloodfist, further evidence of the unusual alliance. Decklan reached for the sleeping potion, but Grom stopped him.

"Too many for that trick," he warned. "And they're alert. They expect someone to try for the shamans."

Decklan considered their options. Pure orcish strength would suggest charging in, but his human side recognized the foolishness of that approach. Neither extreme would work here.

"We need a distraction," he murmured, eyes shifting to a row of ritual braziers nearby. "And a different kind of stealth."

He explained his plan quickly. Grom nodded, a hint of his old respect returning. "Now that's pure Decklan Stormshield."

They separated. Decklan circled around the tent while Grom approached a brazier filled with glowing coals. With powerful movements that belied his wounded state, Grom tipped the brazier, sending embers cascading into a pile of ceremonial hides. The dry pelts caught immediately.

The guards shouted in alarm as flames leapt skyward. Three rushed to battle the fire, leaving just one at the tent entrance. Decklan approached openly, stumbling like a drunken warrior returning from celebration.

"Brother," he called in slurred Blackhand dialect. "The ritual... they call for more guards."

The remaining sentry hesitated, torn between duty and the spectacle of Reyn's ceremony. Decklan swayed closer, then lunged with unexpected speed. Before the guard could utter a sound, a cloth dowsed with sleeping potion was firmly applied to his face. The warrior slumped to the ground, breathing but unconscious.

Decklan sliced through the tent's back wall with his blade, slipping inside rather than using the guarded entrance. The interior was dim, lit only by a single brazier. The air stank of blood and herbs.

In the center, bound to a ritual post, knelt Gar'zul. The old shaman's face was a mask of bruises, one eye swollen shut. His ceremonial vestments had been stripped away, leaving him in tattered undergarments stained with his own blood.

"Decklan?" Gar'zul's voice was barely a whisper. "Have you come to kill me then?"

"No," Decklan said, kneeling to cut the bindings. "Though I might have, not long ago."

Grom slipped into the tent behind him, freezing at the sight of his father. "Father," he breathed, his voice cracking.

Gar'zul's good eye widened. "My son. You should not have come. Reyn... she knows more than we realized. The prophecy—"

"Later," Decklan interrupted, helping the old shaman to his feet. "We need to move now."

Outside, the fire had drawn more attention. Warriors rushed past the tent, shouting orders. The drums at the ritual circle beat faster, more insistently.

"I cannot walk," Gar'zul confessed as his legs buckled beneath him.

Without hesitation, Grom lifted his father onto his back. "I have you."

Decklan led them toward the western edge of the camp, away from the growing commotion. They had almost reached the shadows of the outer perimeter when a shout went up behind them.

"Prisoners! The half-breed is here!"

Decklan spun to face six Blackhand warriors charging toward them, weapons drawn. "Grom, get your father to the ridge. I'll hold them."

"You can't face them alone," Grom protested.

"I'm not alone," Decklan replied, touching the shield emblem at his chest. "I never was."

Decklan stood his ground as the Blackhand warriors charged. His father's shield emblem seemed to pulse with warmth against his chest as he drew his blade.

The first warrior reached him with a bellowing war cry. Instead of matching force with force as an orc would, Decklan sidestepped, redirecting the warrior's momentum. The Blackhand stumbled past, exposing his flank. Decklan struck not to kill but to disable, his blade slicing across the back of the warrior's knee.

"Go!" he shouted to Grom, who hesitated at the edge of darkness, his father still slumped across his shoulders.

Two more warriors converged on Decklan, their axes gleaming in the moonlight. He parried the first blow, the impact jarring up his arm, then ducked beneath the second. His counter was precise—a thrust that pierced an attacker's shoulder rather than his heart. The wounded orc dropped his weapon, howling.

Decklan fought defensively, creating space rather than pressing the attack. This wasn't about killing; it was about protecting. Each move was calculated to delay, to give the others time to escape. The remaining warriors circled warily, confused by his unfamiliar fighting style.

"The half-breed fights like a soft-skin," one sneered, spitting on the ground.

Behind him, alarm horns blared from the prisoner pens. The escape had been discovered. Time was running out.

The warriors attacked simultaneously, hoping to overwhelm him. Decklan gave ground deliberately, drawing them away from Grom's escape route. One warrior overextended, and Decklan's blade found the gap beneath his arm guard. Another received a stunning blow from Decklan's pommel to the temple.

But the odds were shifting against him. One blade sliced across his forearm, drawing blood. Another narrowly missed his neck. Four warriors remained standing, and more shouts suggested reinforcements approached.

Suddenly, fire arrows arced overhead, raining down on the Blackhand warriors. Decklan glanced back to see Krella, bow in hand, standing at the edge of the darkness with two other Shieldbearer archers.

"Move!" she shouted.

Decklan didn't hesitate. He broke away as the warriors scattered from the flaming projectiles, racing toward his companions.

"I thought you were supposed to stay with the wounded?" Decklan said as he reached Krella.

Her eyes flashed with familiar defiance. "And leave you to die gloriously? Not while I can still draw a bow." Her face was still pale from her wounds, but determination burned in her eyes.

Together they retreated into the forest, where Grom waited with Gar'zul. The old shaman lay propped against a tree, breathing heavily.

"You shouldn't have risked yourselves," Gar'zul wheezed. "Not for me."

"It wasn't just for you," Decklan replied, checking that their escape route remained clear. "I need answers."

Gar'zul's remaining good eye fixed on Decklan. "The prophecy. You've begun to understand it, haven't you?"

"Parts of it." Decklan crouched beside him. "But I need to know why Reyn wants me so badly."

A commotion from the camp interrupted them, horns blowing in different patterns, warriors shouting. The prisoners' escape had been fully discovered.

"We need to move," Krella urged. "The others are waiting at the western ridge."

Decklan nodded, but Gar'zul gripped his arm with surprising strength.

"Listen to me," the old shaman whispered urgently. "Reyn didn't just want Kargoth removed. She wanted you to take his place, to be manipulated. She believes your blood is key to some ancient power."

"What power?" Decklan asked.

"I don't know fully. But the ritual—" Gar'zul's words were cut short as a wall of flame erupted between them and their escape route.

Vexxa Darkseer stepped through the flames, her eyes gleaming with malevolent power. Behind her, a dozen Blackhand and Bloodfist warriors formed a semicircle, weapons ready.

"The divided blood returns to us," Vexxa intoned, her voice carrying an unnatural resonance. "How convenient."

Decklan positioned himself between the shaman and his companions, mind racing through their limited options. The forest behind them offered some cover, but Krella was still weakened from her wounds, and Gar'zul could barely stand.

"You've lost, Vexxa," he said, playing for time. "Your prisoners are gone."

The dark shaman's lips curled into a smile. "Pawns, nothing more. It was always you we sought, Decklan Stormshield. The vessel of divided blood." She gestured toward the three moons overhead. "The alignment reaches its peak. Reyn will be most pleased when I deliver you."

"I'm not going anywhere with you," Decklan replied, his hand tightening on his weapon.

"You misunderstand," Vexxa said, raising her staff. "I wasn't offering a choice."

The staff's tip glowed crimson as she began to chant in an ancient tongue. The air around them thickened, making breathing difficult. Decklan felt a strange pulling sensation in his veins, as though his blood were responding to her call.

"Krella," he gasped, fighting the magical compulsion, "get them out through the eastern path."

"I won't leave you," she protested.

"You must." He reached for his father's shield emblem, which burned against his chest. "This is my fight."

Vexxa's spell intensified. The warriors with her began to advance slowly, confident in their prey's entrapment. Decklan felt his knees weaken as the blood magic pulled at him.

Then Gar'zul, barely conscious, began to whisper a counter-chant. The old shaman's voice was weak but determined, his good eye fixed on Vexxa. The pulling sensation in Decklan's veins eased slightly.

"Traitor," Vexxa snarled at Gar'zul, redirecting part of her spell toward him. The old shaman cried out in pain.

"Father!" Grom moved to protect him, but Decklan held him back.

"Get them out," Decklan said, his mind racing for a solution. The shield emblem against his chest continued to burn, almost as if responding to his desperation.

A memory flashed through his mind, Kyra's lessons on healing, on channeling energy not for destruction but for protection. Without fully understanding what he was doing, Decklan pressed his palm against the emblem and drew upon that warmth, that connection to both sides of his heritage.

"Shield us," he whispered, closing his eyes.

For a heartbeat, nothing happened. Then the emblem blazed with light, bright enough to cast shadows across the clearing. A translucent barrier of silvery energy expanded outward from Decklan, pushing back Vexxa's crimson spell. More importantly, it created a protective dome around himself and his companions.

Vexxa's eyes widened in shock. "Impossible! No half-blood could—"

"I am not half of anything," Decklan declared, his voice steady despite the strain of maintaining the shield.

The magical barrier held, but Decklan could feel it draining his strength rapidly. He wouldn't be able to sustain it for long.

"Decklan," Krella whispered, touching his shoulder, "you're bleeding."

Crimson droplets traced paths down his face from his eyes, nose, and ears—the price of channeling power he barely understood.

"The fire wall is weakening on the eastern side," Grom observed, supporting his father. "If we move now..."

Decklan nodded, holding the shield steady with pure determination. "Run for the eastern ridge. I'll be right behind you."

Grom hesitated only briefly before lifting Gar'zul and guiding him through the gap in the flames. Krella lingered, her eyes locked with Decklan's.

"I'll follow," he promised, managing a tight smile despite the pain building behind his eyes.

With a reluctant nod, she finally followed Grom and Gar'zul, disappearing through the wavering flames.

The warriors advanced, weapons gleaming in the moonlight. Decklan retreated backward step by step, his strength waning. Every heartbeat drummed with painful urgency in his temples. The blood from his eyes blurred his vision, but he kept moving, drawing them away from his companions' escape route.

He had led them away from his companions deliberately, but now found himself being herded toward the center of the Blackhand encampment rather than away from it. The three moons hung in perfect alignment overhead, bathing everything in their eerie combined light.

After putting enough distance between himself and his friends, he made a desperate decision. Instead of continuing to flee, he would confront the source of this conflict directly. Drawing on his last reserves of strength, Decklan changed direction, moving purposefully toward the ritual grounds at the camp's heart.

"If Reyn wants me so badly," he muttered, wiping blood from his eyes, "then let her face me."

As he contemplated his next move, a sharp pain pierced the back of his skull. He tried to turn, but his limbs wouldn't respond. The world tilted sideways as he collapsed.

CHAPTER THIRTY-FIVE

HEART OF DARKNESS

Decklan struggled to remain conscious as rough hands dragged him into the clearing. Through blurring vision, he saw Reyn's face split into a triumphant smile.

"The guest of honor arrives," she announced, approaching him with slow, deliberate steps. "Decklan Stormshield. So eager to join us that you walked right into our arms." Reyn circled him, her amber eyes gleaming in the moonlight. "The mighty half-blood. Kargoth's disappointment."

Decklan fought against the paralyzing effect of whatever had struck him. His muscles burned with the effort, but he managed to raise his head. "My father was never disappointed in me," he spat. "He saw what you fear, strength you don't understand."

Reyn laughed, the sound echoing unnaturally across the ritual grounds. "Kargoth was weak. He spoke of peace while our enemies grew stronger. The soft-skins encroach on our lands, yet he sought to trade with them rather than drive them back." She gestured toward the prisoners. "Look where his vision has led your clan."

Two Blackhand warriors dragged Decklan to his feet. As the paralysis slowly receded, he took stock of his situation. His weapons had been taken, though they'd missed the small knife hidden in his boot. His father's shield emblem still hung around his neck, a cold weight against his chest.

"Bring him to the altar," Vexxa commanded, her voice resonating with unnatural power.

As they hauled him forward, a commotion erupted at the edge of the clearing. Snarlgar Zoggorn entered, dragging a struggling figure, Grom. Blood trickled from a wound on his temple, but his eyes burned with defiance.

"Found this one trailing your patrol," Snarlgar announced, throwing Grom to the ground. "Says he's the shaman's son."

Reyn's lips curved into a smile. "How fitting. The traitor's son returns to witness his friend's sacrifice."

Decklan felt an unexpected surge of emotion. Despite everything that had passed between them, Grom had returned. "You should have stayed with the others," he said softly.

"And miss seeing you finally put these dogs in their place?" Grom managed a pained grin despite his injuries. "Not a chance, blood-brother."

Vexxa waved her hand dismissively. "Bring the shaman's son closer. His blood carries power too, corrupted, but useful."

Warriors dragged Grom forward until he knelt beside Decklan at the base of the altar. The stone loomed above them, its surface etched with symbols that seemed to drink in the moonlight.

"You see, Stormshield," Reyn said, approaching with measured steps, "your bloodlines were never meant to mix. The prophecy speaks of the divided blood standing at a crossroads, but prophecies can be interpreted in many ways." She gestured to the stone circle around them. "These markings are older than any clan. They speak of power that flows when blood is spilled under the three-fold light."

Decklan strained against his captors, but their grip remained firm. "If you know so much about the prophecy, then you know it names me as either bridge or breaker. Not your sacrifice."

"That's where you're wrong." Vexxa stepped forward, her fingers trailing wisps of green energy. "The prophecy states the divided blood will determine the fate of our peoples. We've simply chosen which fate that will be." She smiled, revealing teeth filed to points. "When your blood flows upon this altar during perfect alignment, it will empower me to ensure orc dominance for generations."

Decklan's mind raced. He needed time. The rescue must have succeeded. The absence of alarms suggested his mother and the others had escaped with the first group of prisoners.

"Tell me, Reyn," he called, forcing strength into his voice. "Did my father know what you planned? Or did you deceive Gar'zul just as you've deceived these warriors?"

A flicker of uncertainty passed through the assembled ranks. Reyn's expression hardened.

"Your father was becoming dangerous," she hissed, lowering her voice. "He spoke of alliances with humans, of shared territories. He would have weakened us all."

"He saw a future beyond endless bloodshed," Decklan replied, his voice carrying across the clearing. "That's what you truly fear."

Reyn struck him across the face, the blow snapping his head sideways. "I fear nothing, half-blood. Especially not your attempt to turn my warriors against me." She turned to address the gathered forces. "The half-blood tries to confuse us with words, as his kind always do."

Vexxa approached, her hands glowing with sickly green energy. "The moons reach their apex. The time comes. Prepare him."

The warriors forced Decklan onto the stone altar, binding his wrists and ankles with leather straps reinforced with metal. The stone felt unnaturally cold against his back, as though it had never known the warmth of the sun. Above him, the three moons formed a perfect triangle in the night sky converging directly overhead.

"You see," Reyn whispered, leaning close enough that her breath warmed his ear, "your father never understood true power. He thought strength came from compromise, from building bridges between peoples who should remain separate."

Vexxa raised her hands, silencing the whispers with a pulse of dark magic. "The alignment peaks. Begin the ritual."

She approached Decklan with the bowl, dipping her fingers into the dark substance. With practiced movements, she drew symbols across his forehead and chest, the liquid burning wherever it touched his skin. He recognized blood mixed with crushed herbs and something else, something that smelled of decay.

"Blood of the unworthy," Vexxa chanted, "blood of the divided, blood that stands between worlds." Her voice gained a resonant, unnatural quality that echoed across the clearing. "Blood that must choose, bridge or breaker."

Reyn stepped forward with the ceremonial dagger, its edge glinting with an oily sheen that suggested poison. "Tonight, we choose for him."

Decklan struggled against his bonds, but they only tightened. Above him, the three moons seemed to pulse in unison, their light intensifying as they reached perfect alignment. He could feel something shifting in the air around them. A thinning of reality itself, as though unseen eyes now watched from beyond a veil.

"Nyxthera, Devourer of Light," Vexxa intoned, raising her hands toward the moons, "accept this offering of divided blood. Let it fuel your hunger and strengthen your chosen."

The air above the altar began to shimmer and darken, forming a swirling vortex of shadow that seemed to drink in the moonlight. Decklan felt his strength ebbing, drawn upward into that hungry darkness.

"My blood... won't... serve you," he gasped, each word an effort as the ritual drained his vitality.

Reyn smiled cruelly, raising the dagger. "Your blood serves whatever purpose I choose, half-breed. Your father couldn't protect you. Your mother couldn't save you. No one can stand against what we've unleashed."

The dagger descended toward Decklan's chest. In that moment, a blinding flash of silver light erupted at the edge of the ritual grounds. Warriors cried out, shielding their eyes as a figure strode forward through their ranks. Those who moved to intercept were flung aside by an invisible force.

"I beg to differ," came a familiar voice, and Decklan turned his head to see Kyra approaching. But she no longer looked like the mysterious woman who had guided him. Her form seemed to shimmer between solid and ethereal, her simple clothing replaced by flowing robes that caught the moonlight like liquid silver.

"You!" Vexxa snarled, recognition and fear mingling in her voice. "Light-spawn!"

Reyn's eyes widened. "Kill her!" she commanded, and this time her warriors moved with practiced precision, surrounding Kyra with blades drawn.

"You cannot stop what has begun," Kyra called out, her voice carrying unnaturally across the clearing even as four Blackhand warriors seized her. Despite her struggle, they forced her to her knees, binding her arms behind her back with ritual cords that seemed to dim the strange aura that had briefly surrounded her.

Vexxa approached Kyra, dark energy coiling around her fingertips. "You thought yourself clever, infiltrating our camps, whispering to the half-blood." She traced a symbol in the air that made Kyra wince in pain. "But your interference ends tonight."

Decklan's mind raced through foggy confusion. Kyra was something more than she appeared, that much was clear, but her powers seemed diminished now, contained by whatever binding Vexxa had placed upon her.

"The alignment peaks!" Vexxa announced, turning back toward the altar with renewed urgency. "The veil thins! She cannot stop us now."

Above the altar, the vortex of darkness pulsed, growing larger. Decklan felt his life force draining more rapidly, feeding the hungry void. Reyn had recovered from her momentary distraction and now positioned the dagger over his heart.

"Your meddlesome friend will watch you die," Reyn spat. "The ritual completes now!"

Chapter Thirty-Six

BLOOD SACRIFICE

The moonlight bathed the ritual site in an eerie silver glow as Decklan struggled against the iron bindings that secured him to the stone altar. Blood trickled from intricate patterns Vexxa had carved into his flesh, symbols that burned like fire yet froze like ice. Around him, the massive stones of the ancient circle hummed with power, resonating with the perfect alignment of the three moons overhead.

"The time has come," Reyn Nightshade declared, her voice carrying across the assembled warriors of the orc clans. She stood tall and imperious, dressed in ceremonial armor adorned with the symbols of Nyxthera. "Tonight, we harness the power of divided blood to ensure our dominance for generations to come!"

Vexxa Darkseer moved around the altar with practiced precision, her fingers trailing dark energy that seeped into the carvings on Decklan's skin. Each touch sent waves of agony through his body, drawing involuntary cries that he fought to suppress.

"You feel it, don't you?" Vexxa whispered, her voice carrying despite the chaos around them. "The power in your veins, neither fully orc nor fully soft-skin. A perfect vessel for Nyxthera's blessing."

From his position on the altar, Decklan could see Grom bound to one of the standing stones, blood streaming from a wound reopened during his capture. Their eyes met briefly. Grom's filled with a mixture of rage and regret.

"I told you to run," Grom mouthed silently.

"And leave my brother?" Decklan managed through gritted teeth.

A commotion erupted at the edge of the circle. Krella, her body still weakened from Vexxa's earlier attack, fought against three Blackhand warriors. For a moment, she broke free, charging toward the altar with desperate determination.

"Decklan!" she cried, before a Bloodfist warrior tackled her from behind. She crumpled to the ground, still fighting as they bound her hands.

Snarlgar Zoggorn dragged her before Reyn, grinning with malicious pleasure. "Another sacrifice for Nyxthera's glory?" he asked, his yellow eyes gleaming with cruel anticipation.

Reyn considered Krella thoughtfully. "No. Not yet. Let her witness what becomes of those who defy me. Let her see what true power looks like." She turned to the gathered warriors. "Let all witness the fate of the divided blood!"

Vexxa completed a circle of dark symbols around the altar, stepping back as they began to glow with malevolent purpose. She raised her hands, channeling energy from the three moons into the ritual space. The air itself seemed to thicken, making it difficult to breathe.

"The prophecy speaks of the one of divided blood," Vexxa intoned, her voice resonating with unnatural power. "Who shall stand at the crossroads of fate. Tonight, we ensure that crossroad leads only to our ascendance!"

Decklan writhed against his bonds as the carved symbols on his skin burned with increasing intensity. The pain was unlike anything he had ever experienced. Not just physical, but reaching into the very essence of who he was. It felt as though two halves of his being were being forcibly torn apart.

Reyn approached the altar, a ceremonial obsidian dagger gleaming in her hand. The blade appeared to drink in the moonlight rather than reflect it, creating a void in the shape of a weapon.

"Your father died because he was weak," Reyn taunted, leaning over Decklan. "Just like you. Too concerned with peace, too willing to compromise." She traced the dagger along Decklan's chest without breaking the skin. "The Shieldbearers were once great warriors, before chieftains like your father made them soft. But your blood, your special, divided blood, will restore us to glory."

Through the haze of pain, Decklan saw Kyra bound to another stone, her form flickering between solid and ethereal as strange runes etched into her bindings prevented her from using her powers. She caught his gaze, her eyes filled with sorrow and something else, a silent message he couldn't quite decipher.

Vexxa began a low, rhythmic chant that the assembled warriors took up, their voices merging into a thunderous drone that vibrated through the stones beneath the altar. The three moons seemed to pulse in rhythm with their voices, casting overlapping shadows across Decklan's bound form.

Dark energies swirled above him, coalescing into a vortex that drew blood from his carved flesh. Each droplet rose into the air, suspended momentarily before being consumed by the growing darkness overhead. With each drop, Decklan felt something essential being pulled from his core.

"Your struggle is pointless," Reyn said, her voice cutting through the chanting. "The prophecy will be fulfilled tonight, but on our terms. Your divided blood will not unite the clans. It will ensure our dominance over all who oppose us."

Decklan's vision blurred as the pain intensified. In this moment of extreme agony, memories flashed through his mind: his father's stoic pride after his first hunt, his mother's gentle hands healing wounds after training, Krella's unwavering support, Grom's brotherhood despite their differences. All paths that had led him here, to this altar.

"I wanted your respect," Decklan gasped, his words barely audible above the chanting. "All my life... trying to be... enough."

Reyn leaned closer, the dagger hovering above his heart. "What did you say, half-breed?"

"I spent my life trying to choose," Decklan continued, his voice strengthening despite the pain. "Orc or human. Warrior or healer. My father's son or my mother's. Always choosing, always divided."

Something shifted in the ritual's energy. The vortex above faltered momentarily.

239

"It doesn't matter now," Reyn snapped, raising the dagger. "Your struggle ends tonight."

Through the excruciating pain, a moment of perfect clarity struck Decklan. The prophecy, his father's final words, Kyra's counsel—suddenly, all aligned in his mind like the three moons overhead.

"My divided blood was never my weakness," he whispered, the realization blooming within him like dawn breaking through storm clouds. "My refusal to accept it was."

The dark vortex above pulsed, responding to his words. For the briefest moment, the agony receded, replaced by a sense of wholeness Decklan had never known.

"Enough talk," Reyn snarled, raising the obsidian dagger higher. "Vexxa, complete the binding!"

The shaman's hands moved in complex patterns as she drew more power from the aligned moons. The symbols carved into Decklan's skin flared with renewed intensity, and his momentary clarity dissolved back into overwhelming pain. His back arched against the stone altar, a scream tearing from his throat.

"The vessel is ready," Vexxa announced, her eyes glowing with an unnatural light. "His resistance only strengthens the ritual. The divided blood fights against itself, creating the perfect tension to channel Nyxthera's blessing."

Reyn positioned the dagger precisely above Decklan's heart, the tip hovering just above his skin. The obsidian blade seemed to pulse with hunger, eager to complete its purpose.

"With this sacrifice," she proclaimed to the assembled warriors, "the prophecy is fulfilled on our terms. The divided blood shall not unite the clans, but ensure our dominance forever!"

Decklan's eyes found Krella's across the ritual space. Despite her bonds, she struggled toward him, tears streaming down her face. Her lips formed words he couldn't hear but somehow understood: "Fight, Decklan."

As Reyn began the downward stroke that would end his life, time seemed to slow. In this suspended moment, Decklan finally understood what his father had meant by his dying words: "Trust your whole self." Not just the orc, not just the human, but the unique being formed at their intersection.

The shield emblem around his neck, the one he'd fashioned from his father's broken shield, began to warm against his skin, glowing with a silvery light that matched the three moons above.

Reyn's dagger descended toward his heart—

And the night exploded into blinding light.

CHAPTER THIRTY-SEVEN

GODDESS REVEALED

The obsidian blade descended toward Decklan's heart, Reyn's face twisted in savage triumph. Time seemed to slow, each heartbeat stretching into eternity as the ritual reached its climax. The dark energy vortex above the altar pulsed hungrily, drawing more blood from the symbols carved into Decklan's skin.

In that stretched moment, something awakened within him. Not the rage of his father's Bloodfist lineage nor the calculated discipline of his mother's Stormshield blood, but something deeper. The amulet that hung around his neck suddenly warmed against his skin. The runes etched into its surface, symbols he'd always believed were merely clan markings, now pulsed with arcane energy that seemed to respond to his racing heartbeat.

Decklan flexed his wrists against the bindings, and the ropes unraveled just enough for his fingers to touch. The moment they connected, a concussive wave of energy erupted from his body, throwing Reyn backward into the circle of chanting priests.

"Impossible," Vexxa Darkseer hissed, her ritual mask cracking down the center.

"How—" Reyn snarled, scrambling to her feet, clutching her obsidian blade.

Before she could finish, a blinding flash erupted not from Decklan, but from where Kyra stood bound by ritual cords.

The restraints around her disintegrated into dust. Her body straightened as though gravity had loosened its hold, rising several inches above the ground. The plain traveling clothes she wore began to shimmer, transforming into flowing silver-white robes that caught the light of the three aligned moons overhead.

"It is time," she said, her voice resonating with power that sent ripples through the remaining ritual energies.

Vexxa Darkseer fell to her knees, recognition dawning on her face. "Light-spawn," she whispered, but then her eyes widened further. "No... not just a servant... you are..."

"I am Viviana, the Life Weaver," she announced, her form now radiating light that pushed back the shadows cast by the ritual. "I walk among mortals rarely, but your mother's prayers reached me, Decklan Stormshield."

The gathered warriors of both clans fell back, many dropping to their knees or prostrating themselves. Even Snarlgar looked stricken with awe.

Viviana moved toward the altar where Decklan lay bound. With each step, flowers bloomed in the trampled earth beneath her feet. "Your mother did not ask for your victory in battle," she continued, her voice somehow both intimate and vast. "She asked for your wholeness. For you to find peace within the warring halves of your soul."

Viviana reached the altar, her luminous fingers hovering over the blood-marked bindings that held Decklan. The ropes unraveled at her touch, slithering away like frightened serpents.

"No!" Reyn screamed, lunging forward with the dagger still clutched in her hand. "The prophecy must be fulfilled!"

Viviana did not turn. She simply raised her palm, and Reyn froze mid-stride as though encased in invisible amber.

"The prophecy speaks of choice, not destiny," Viviana said, her gaze never leaving Decklan's face. "It always has."

Decklan sat up slowly, his body aching from the ritual cuts. Blood still seeped from the symbols carved into his skin, but the pain had dulled to a distant throb. Something inside him had changed. The constant war between his orcish strength and human caution had quieted.

"Why?" he asked, his voice hoarse. "Why me? Why now?"

Viviana smiled, and it was like sunrise breaking over mountain peaks. "Your divided blood is not a curse but a blessing, a bridge between worlds that could heal instead of destroy. Such gifts appear when they are most needed, and it is needed."

She gestured toward the gathered warriors, the prisoners still bound at the edge of the clearing, and finally to Grom and Krella who watched with stunned expressions.

"For too long, these lands have been divided by hatred and fear. The prophecy speaks of one who could either unite the peoples or ensure their mutual destruction. The choice was always yours to make."

Vexxa had regained some of her composure, though she remained kneeling. "The ritual cannot be stopped," she hissed. "The energies have been gathered. The sacrifice must be completed."

"She speaks truth," Viviana said, turning to Decklan. "The power gathered here must find release. I am not allowed to directly interfere with another deity's sacred ritual once it had begun, the balance forbids it. But I can offer you a choice."

She extended her hand, palm up. Above it materialized a small sphere of light, pulsing with gentle radiance. "This power can flow through you, Decklan Stormshield. I offer you my blessing, but only if you will abandon the path of vengeance and embrace a new calling."

The dark vortex above the altar intensified, spinning faster as it sensed its intended sacrifice slipping away. Reyn's face contorted with fury as she fought against Viviana's restraint.

"You must decide now," Viviana continued. "The energies Reyn has gathered cannot be contained much longer. They will find release one way or another."

Her star-filled eyes captured Decklan's gaze. "Will you continue to destroy, or will you heal? Will you divide, or will you unite?"

Decklan looked at Grom, his blood-brother who had returned despite their differences. At Krella, who had followed him into impossible danger. At the warriors of different clans watching with a mixture of fear and wonder.

The weight of his father's shield emblem hung against his chest. Not a weapon, but a tool of protection. Not a symbol of division, but one of unity, combining elements of both his bloodlines in a single design.

In that moment, with the three moons aligned perfectly overhead, Decklan understood. Every struggle, every conflict between his dual natures had been preparing him for this choice. The prophecy hadn't chosen him because he was divided. It had chosen him because he could be whole.

"I am Decklan Stormshield," he said, his voice growing stronger with each word. "Son of Kargoth and Skye. I am of two worlds, and I choose to heal both."

He reached out and placed his palm against Viviana's, accepting the sphere of light. It melted into his skin, spreading warmth through his veins.

"I renounce vengeance," Decklan continued, the words coming to him as though he had always known them. "I accept this calling to be a bridge between divided peoples."

As he spoke, the shield emblem at his chest began to glow with the same silvery radiance as Viviana's form. The light spread outward, washing over the ritual symbols carved into his flesh. Where it touched, blood ceased flowing, wounds sealed, leaving behind silver traceries like delicate scars.

"The bargain is struck," Viviana said, her voice resonating across the clearing. "You have chosen to be a bridge rather than a breaker, a healer rather than a destroyer."

The dark vortex above the altar began to writhe violently, its energies seeking direction. Reyn, still frozen in Viviana's grip, screamed incoherently as she witnessed her ritual being transformed.

"The power must be channeled," Viviana instructed, her form beginning to fade. "I have given you the means, but the act must be yours. Take what was meant for destruction and turn it toward healing."

Decklan stood, feeling strength flowing through him unlike anything he had known before. The constant battle between his orcish and human natures had ceased. Not because either side had won, but because they had finally merged into something greater.

"What do I do?" he asked, as the vortex began to collapse inward.

Viviana's form was now translucent, stars visible through her outline. "Trust your whole self," she said, echoing Kargoth's final words. "The shield's purpose is not to divide, but to protect. That is your true inheritance."

With those words, her presence dissolved into motes of silver light that drifted upward toward the three aligned moons.

Reyn broke free from the fading restraint and lunged at Decklan with her obsidian dagger. "You cannot change what was written in blood!" she shrieked.

Decklan didn't reach for a weapon. Instead, he raised his hands, palms outward, and spoke a single word in a language he had never consciously learned, part invocation, part ancient command.

"Harmony."

The shield emblem at his chest flared with blinding light, and Decklan felt the ritual energies respond to his call. What had been gathered for destruction now awaited his direction.

In that moment, suspended between the aligned moons above and the blood-soaked ground below, Decklan Stormshield made his choice.

And the world changed forever.

Chapter Thirty-Eight

HEALER'S TOUCH

O nce again time seemed to slow as power surged through Decklan's body. The silver light from Viviana, from Kyra, pulsed through him, igniting something that had always been there, dormant within his blood. The shield emblem at his chest blazed, throwing shadows across the ritual ground as if the sun itself had descended among them.

"No!" Reyn screamed, her voice cracking with desperation. "The ritual is mine to control!"

But it wasn't. The corrupted magic she had gathered swirled above them, a vortex of dark energy that now responded to Decklan's will rather than hers. He felt it, every tendril, every current, as if it were an extension of himself.

"This ends now," Decklan said, his voice resonating with power not his own.

The dark energy recoiled from his light, backwashing across the ritual grounds toward those who had summoned it. Vexxa staggered backward, her carefully constructed magical web collapsing around her. Dark tendrils lashed her body, punishment for the control she had failed to maintain.

"What are you doing?" she shrieked, raising her hands in a desperate attempt to redirect the energy. "You don't understand what forces you're playing with!"

But Decklan did understand now. Not through knowledge, but through instinct, through the perfect unity of his dual nature.

He stood in front of the altar, his body no longer his own, yet more fully his than it had ever been. His hands glowed with radiant silver light, not the searing power of destruction but the gentle warmth of healing.

Grom remained bound nearby, eyes wide with wonder and fear. Decklan approached him, touched the ropes that held him, and watched them unravel at his touch.

"What... what happened to you?" Grom whispered.

Decklan looked down at his own hands, now traced with silvery lines where Vexxa's ritual cuts had been. "I stopped fighting myself."

Around them, chaos erupted as Blackhand and Bloodfist warriors witnessed the transformation. Some drew weapons, others fell to their knees in superstitious awe. The power emanating from Decklan was unlike anything they had ever witnessed, neither the cunning schemes of Nyxthera, nor the cold precision of Gallant, but something altogether different.

"Kill him!" Reyn ordered, her voice shrill with panic. "Kill the half-blood before he completes his transformation!"

Warriors hesitated, weapons half-drawn. In their hesitation, Decklan moved to Krella's side, touching her bonds which fell away like autumn leaves. The silver traceries on his skin pulsed with each heartbeat, casting rippling patterns across the ritual grounds.

"Are you still you?" Krella asked softly, rubbing her wrists.

"More than I've ever been," Decklan replied.

Snarlgar Zoggorn, massive frame tensed for battle, pushed through the crowd of uncertain warriors. "I don't fear gods or magic," he growled, raising his battle axe. "I've killed half-breeds before."

He charged forward, but three of his own Bloodfist warriors stepped between him and Decklan.

"Stand aside!" Snarlgar roared.

"No, Chieftain," said one, a scarred veteran. "I saw my brother's wounds heal beneath his touch. This is no ordinary magic."

Decklan turned to face Reyn, who stood trembling beside the altar, the obsidian dagger still clutched in her white-knuckled grip. The dark energy she had gathered now circled her like a shroud, feeding on her fear and hatred.

"The prophecy speaks truth," Decklan said, his voice carrying across the suddenly silent gathering. "Divided blood will determine our future. I choose unity."

He extended his hand toward her, not threatening, but offering.

"Your clan slaughtered mine generations ago," Reyn spat. "Your father preached peace while preparing for war. Unity is a lie told by the weak to save themselves from the strong."

"Then why do you tremble?" Decklan asked quietly. "I will not fight you."

"Then die without a fight!" Reyn screamed, unleashing what remained of her ritual power in a single devastating blast of darkness.

The energy crashed against Decklan's light, but instead of breaking through, it swirled around him like water around a stone. Then, inexorably, it began flowing back toward Reyn. Her own darkness, reflected and amplified.

"No!" she cried, attempting to break the connection. But she had bound herself too deeply to the ritual's power. The darkness rushed back into her, a tide of her own making returning to its source.

Reyn collapsed to her knees, then fell forward onto the ritual ground. The obsidian dagger slipped from her fingers, its edge dulled and cracked where it had struck Decklan's shield of light. She lay still, breathing but unconscious, consumed by the very darkness she had tried to wield.

Silence fell across the ritual grounds. Hundreds of Blackhand and Bloodfist warriors stood motionless, weapons lowered, eyes fixed on Decklan. In the distance, a wolf howled, once, twice, three times, echoing the alignment of the moons overhead.

Vexxa backed away, blood streaming from her nose and ears, the price of attempting to control forces beyond her mastery. "This changes nothing," she hissed. "The prophecy is not yet complete."

Before anyone could stop her, she threw down a pouch that burst into thick, acrid smoke, and slipped away into the darkness.

Decklan stood at the center of the ritual grounds, silver light still radiating from his skin, illuminating the faces of warriors who moments ago had been his enemies. The remnants of Reyn's dark power still swirled above the altar, unstable and dangerous.

"The ritual energy," Grom said urgently. "It has to go somewhere."

Decklan nodded. He approached the altar where he had nearly been sacrificed and placed both hands upon it. The stone was cold beneath his fingers, stained with the blood of previous victims. But where his hands touched, the stains began to fade, replaced by a soft silver glow that spread outward.

He closed his eyes and felt for the chaotic energy that still hovered above. Unlike Reyn, he didn't attempt to control it through force or binding. Instead, he offered it direction, a channel toward healing rather than destruction.

"Come," he whispered, not to the energy but to the wounded all around him.

Warriors approached hesitantly. First the wounded Shieldbearers who had been held captive, then a few brave Blackhand fighters with injuries from the confusion of battle. Decklan touched each one, and where his fingers met flesh, wounds closed, pain eased, and the silver traceries on his own skin pulsed brighter.

A Bloodfist warrior with a deep gash across his chest gasped as the wound sealed beneath Decklan's palm. "How is this possible?"

"The divided blood," murmured an elder Blackhand warrior. "The prophecy speaks of one who would bridge worlds."

"Or break them," Snarlgar growled, though he made no move to interfere.

As dawn approached, the dark energy dissipated completely, channeled into healing dozens of wounded from all three clans. Exhaustion hit Decklan suddenly, nearly bringing him to his knees. The silver light faded from his skin, though the traceries remained, faint lines marking where Vexxa's ritual cuts had been.

CHAPTER THIRTY-NINE

PRICE OF PEACE

The night's horrors receded into shadow as the first rays of light touched the ritual grounds, now transformed from a place of sacrifice to one of healing. Throughout the clearing, Blackhand and Bloodfist warriors who had been enemies only hours before now knelt alongside Shieldbearers, their weapons laid aside.

Decklan moved among the wounded, his hands still trailing faint wisps of silver light. The traceries etched into his skin by Vexxa's ritual knife now gleamed like molten silver, a permanent reminder of his transformation. With each person he touched, regardless of clan or blood, their wounds began to close, and the darkness of Vexxa's blood magic dissipated.

"I don't understand," a wounded Bloodfist warrior whispered as the black veins receded from his arm. "Why would you help me? We came to kill your people."

Decklan smiled faintly. "Because that's the point of being a bridge, you connect what was divided."

Nearby, former enemies carried water to the wounded, applied bandages, or simply sat in stunned silence. The air hummed with whispers of "the prophecy," "divided blood," and "Viviana's chosen." Some warriors openly wept at the healing touch that saved them when they'd come bearing weapons of war.

Grom approached, his own wounds bandaged, fatigue etched in the circles beneath his eyes. For a long moment, they simply looked at each other, the weight of all that had happened creating a chasm that words struggled to cross.

"My father was wrong," Grom finally said, his voice thick. "I was wrong."

Decklan shook his head. "We all were. We thought strength meant choosing one path. The real strength was in embracing both."

"You knew," Grom's lips curved in a reluctant smile. "Somehow, you knew."

"I didn't. I just finally stopped fighting against myself." Decklan gripped his blood-brother's forearm. "The same blood flows through us, Grom. Different streams, same river."

Grom returned the grip. "The rivers converge again, brother." His eyes flickered to the silver traceries on Decklan's skin. "Though you travel a different current now."

A cry from across the clearing drew Decklan's attention. Krella was attempting to stand, her face pale but determined. The wound from Snarlgar's blade still troubled her, though the worst of Vexxa's blood magic had been purged. Decklan hurried to her side.

"You should be resting," he said, supporting her weight as she swayed.

Krella's eyes held a mixture of pride and grief as she studied him. "I had to see it for myself. The warrior has become something more." She touched one of the silver markings on his forearm. "This power... it's not temporary, is it?"

"No," Decklan admitted. "Viviana's gift remains. But it comes with a price."

Before she could respond, a commotion rippled through the gathered warriors. Skye appeared at the edge of the clearing, leading a group of Moongazers and human representatives from Riverstone. Her eyes found Decklan immediately, widening at the sight of his transformed appearance.

She rushed forward, embracing him tightly. "My son," she whispered, her voice breaking. "I always knew your path would be unique." She pulled back, studying the silver traceries with knowing eyes. "Viviana's mark. She answered my prayers."

"Your prayers?" Decklan asked.

"Not for victory or power," Skye explained, wiping tears from her cheeks. "For wholeness. For you to find peace in being both orc and human, not torn between halves. I have been praying to her since you were born."

Decklan nodded, understanding now. "The shield was never the strength," he murmured, repeating his father's final message. "It was what the shield protected that mattered."

As morning fully arrived, clan leaders from the Blackhand, Bloodfist, and remaining Shieldbearers gathered. Even Snarlgar Zoggorn, chastened by the night's events, stood among them, his usual swagger replaced by cautious reverence.

"The son of Kargoth Stormshield," Snarlgar spoke, his voice unusually subdued. "Our warriors witnessed what happened here. They say Viviana herself appeared." His eyes lingered on the silver traceries that now marked Decklan's skin. "The prophecy spoke true."

Elder Varkus stepped forward, his weathered face showing both wonder and concern. "The Shieldbearer clan needs leadership, Decklan. With your father gone and our camp destroyed, the people look to you. They say the divided blood has proven its worth." Several Shieldbearer warriors nodded in agreement.

A representative from the Blackhand clan, one of their few remaining elders, moved to stand beside Snarlgar. "We have followed false promises long enough. Reyn Nightshade manipulated us all, turned clan against clan for her dark purposes." He gestured toward Decklan. "The prophecy speaks of one who would unite, not divide. Perhaps it is time for a council of all clans, led by one who understands both sides."

Murmurs of agreement rippled through the gathered warriors. Decklan felt the weight of their expectations settling on his shoulders alongside Viviana's gift. He looked at his mother, at Grom, at Krella, and finally at his father's shield emblem hanging from his neck.

"I cannot be your Chieftain," he said finally, his voice carrying across the clearing.

Shock registered on many faces, but Decklan continued before they could protest.

"My path now serves all peoples, not just one clan. Viviana has marked me as her priest, a healer between worlds." He touched the silver traceries on his arm. "These bind me to a different duty. But I agree that a council should be formed, representatives from all clans working together rather than against each other."

Decklan turned toward Krella, who watched him with understanding dawning in her eyes. "The Shieldbearers need a leader who embodies strength and wisdom. Someone who understands protection is our first duty." He extended his hand. "The clan would follow you, Krella Bloodfury."

A hush fell over the gathering. Krella's eyes widened in surprise, then narrowed in comprehension. With a steadying breath, she reached out and clasped Decklan's forearm in the traditional Shieldbearer gesture of respect.

"You would place the clan in the hands of a child?" challenged an older warrior from the back of the group.

"I would place it in the hands of the most capable warrior I know," Decklan replied without hesitation. "One who understands that true strength comes from protecting others, not dominating them."

Elder Varkus studied Krella with weathered eyes, then nodded slowly. "Kargoth would approve. She fought alongside him many times." He turned to the gathered Shieldbearers, but before he could speak further, Elder Nar'gul stepped forward from the crowd.

"The succession cannot be decided by mere words," Nar'gul declared, his voice carrying across the clearing. "Our traditions demand the trials. If Krella would lead, she must prove herself as Decklan did."

Murmurs rippled through the assembly. Grom raised his voice, "Nar'gul speaks truly. The Trials of Succession, strength, wisdom, and vision, have been our way since the First Clans."

"The girl has proven herself in battle," called a scarred warrior from the back, "but tradition is the bedrock of our people."

Krella straightened, her eyes flashing with determination. "I will complete the trials, as is proper. Any who wish to challenge my right to lead may face me there."

Two warriors, Thulsa Blackfist and the Nar'gul, stepped forward, their expressions resolute. "We would test ourselves against you," Thulsa announced.

Elder Varkus raised his hands for silence. "So be it. When the wounded are tended and the dead honored, the trials will commence. The shield of endurance and the pedestals of choice await those who would lead the Shieldbearers."

One by one, the warriors struck their weapons against their shields in agreement, the sound echoing through the trees like thunder. Even Snarlgar gave a grudging nod of respect, a calculating gleam in his eyes.

As the council continued discussing the formation of an alliance between the clans and the logistics of the upcoming trials, Decklan stepped away. His body ached with fatigue, the silver traceries on his skin pulsing with each heartbeat. He found a quiet spot at the edge of the clearing and sank down against a tree trunk, closing his eyes.

Soft footsteps approached. Decklan didn't need to open his eyes to know it was Krella.

"You could have taken leadership," she said quietly, lowering herself beside him. "They would have followed you anywhere after what they witnessed."

Decklan opened his eyes, watching the dappled sunlight play through the leaves overhead. "It wouldn't have been right. A leader belongs to their people. I..." he touched the silver markings on his arm, "I belong to something else now."

"To Viviana," Krella said, not quite a question.

"To the space between worlds," Decklan corrected. "To the bridges that need building."

They sat in silence for a moment, shoulders not quite touching. The distance between them seemed both infinitesimal and vast.

"I loved you," Krella said finally, her voice steady despite the past tense that hung between them like a blade. "Perhaps I still do. But our paths now lead in different directions, don't they?"

Decklan turned to face her, the silver traceries on his skin catching the morning light. "Your destiny is to lead the Shieldbearers. To rebuild what was broken. Mine is to heal the divisions between peoples."

"A chieftain and a healer," Krella said with a sad smile. "Not the future I imagined for us."

"No," Decklan agreed softly. "But perhaps the future our people needed."

Krella reached out, her calloused fingers tracing one of the silver lines on his forearm. "These marks... they're not just symbols, are they? They've changed you."

"They've completed me," Decklan corrected gently. "What I fought against for so long, being both human and orc, is now my greatest strength." He placed his hand over hers. "I don't regret what might have been between us, Krella. I only regret that I didn't understand sooner what I was meant to be."

"A bridge," she whispered, echoing his earlier words.

"Yes." He squeezed her hand once before releasing it. "The clans will need strong leadership in the days ahead. Reyn's manipulation left deep wounds that won't heal quickly."

"And Reyn herself?" Krella asked, her warrior's instinct surfacing. "She escaped in the confusion."

"With Vexxa," Decklan nodded grimly. "Their work isn't finished. The darkness they served still hungers."

They fell silent, watching the activity in the clearing as former enemies worked together to tend the wounded. The impossible had become reality overnight, orcish clans that had warred for generations now breaking bread together, sharing water, binding each other's wounds.

CHAPTER FORTY

BRIDGE BETWEEN WORLDS

T he Sun stretched its golden fingers across the valley where the Shieldbearer camp once stood. Where blood had soaked the earth just a month
before, now stood pavilions of varied designs, the angular tents of the Shieldbearers beside the curved shelters of the Moongazers and the practical wooden
structures of the human settlements. The scent of ceremonial herbs mingled
with cooking fires as members of all three peoples moved among each other
with cautious but growing ease.

At the center of this unprecedented gathering, a circular stone platform had
been constructed, incorporating elements from each culture. Shieldbearer clan
symbols were carved into the eastern face, Moongazer runes adorned the west,
and human craftsmanship formed the northern edge. The southern portion
remained deliberately blank, a space for what was yet to come.

Decklan stood alone in a small tent, fingers tracing the silver markings that
now permanently adorned his skin where Vexxa's ritual blade had cut him.
They no longer pained him, instead pulsing gently with a barely perceptible
light that strengthened whenever he channeled his healing abilities.

He adjusted the robes he now wore. The deep blue fabric was cut in the
practical style of Shieldbearers, but embroidered with the silver thread of

Moongazer craftsmanship. Around his neck hung the emblem from his father's broken shield, now set into a medallion of polished wood from the forests that separated their territories.

"It still feels strange," he admitted to his mother as she entered the tent. Skye's smile was gentle as she approached, her fingers adjusting the ceremonial sash at his shoulder.

"Change always does," she replied. "Your father would be proud of what you've become."

"Not a chieftain," Decklan said with a hint of his old doubt.

"Something more," she corrected him. "Kargoth understood this at the end—that leadership takes many forms. The Shieldbearer name was never about warfare, but protection. You've found a different way to shield our people."

He nodded, grasping the staff beside him. Unlike a warrior's spear, it was topped with an intricate carving that blended the geometric patterns and flowing lines of Moongazer artistry. Embedded at its crown was a crystal that caught the morning light, refracting it into the colors of all three moons.

"It's time," came Grom's voice from outside the tent. His friend, his blood-brother, had recovered from his wounds, though he still moved with a slight favoring of his right side.

"I'll see you from the circle," Skye said, kissing his forehead before departing.

Grom entered, his expression more solemn than Decklan had ever seen it. The ritual scars decorating his face had been joined by new markings, signs of the ordeals he had survived.

"Strange to see you in robes instead of armor," Grom said, his familiar half-smile finally emerging.

"Strange to wear them," Decklan admitted. "How does Krella fare?"

"Nervous. Though she'd cut out my tongue if I told anyone." His expression softened. "She's a good choice for chieftain. Strong enough to fight, wise enough to know when not to."

Decklan nodded. "And your father?"

Grom's face tightened momentarily. "Recovering. The elders have stripped him of the shaman's mantle. He accepts this as justice." He paused. "He asks to speak with you, after."

"I will," Decklan promised.

A drum began to beat outside—three distinct rhythms intertwined. The call to gathering.

"They're waiting," Grom said.

"I know." Decklan took a deep breath. "It's not easy to let go of what you thought you were meant to be."

"Perhaps you were meant for this all along," Grom replied. "The prophecy chose you for a reason."

Together they stepped from the tent into sunlight. The gathered crowd parted before them, Shieldbearers, Moongazers, and humans from Riverstone and other settlements standing side by side, some still with visible tension, others with burgeoning curiosity.

As they approached the stone circle, Decklan saw the leaders already assembled. Elder Varkus stood as representative of the Shieldbearer elders, his weathered face bearing new scars from the final defense of their camp. Beside him stood Harran of Riverstone, his once-suspicious eyes now thoughtful as they met Decklan's. Lyara, Skye's Moongazer cousin, completed the trio, her silver-streaked hair adorned with symbols of all three moons.

Krella waited at the circle's edge, dressed in the ceremonial armor of a Shieldbearer chieftain. The sight of her sent a familiar warmth through Decklan's chest, tempered by the knowledge of the paths that now separated them. She stood straight-backed and proud, but her eyes softened momentarily when they met his.

"It begins," Varkus announced as Decklan stepped onto the stone platform.

The gathered people fell silent. In that moment, looking out at the three peoples, his peoples, Decklan felt the weight of the past month. The battles fought, the blood spilled, the discoveries made. He thought of his father's final words: "Trust your whole self." Not his orcish half, not his human half, but the entirety of who he was.

"I stand before you," Decklan began, his voice carrying across the gathering, "not as I once was. Many of you knew me as Kargoth's son, heir to the Shieldbearer clan. Others knew me as the half-blood of prophecy." He paused, meeting the eyes of those who had once used such terms as insults. "Both were true, yet neither was complete."

He placed his staff at the center of the circle, where it stood upright of its own accord, the crystal at its top catching sunlight and casting prismatic reflections across the gathering.

"For generations, our peoples have lived divided, by mountains, by rivers, by old hatreds and fresh wounds. I too lived divided, always seeing myself as half of one world or half of another, never whole." The silver traceries on his skin pulsed gently. "It took loss to learn that I am not diminished by my mixed blood, but made stronger by it. Just as all of us are stronger together than we are apart."

Decklan gestured to the leaders standing at the circle's edge.

"Today we formalize what began in blood but will continue in peace. A Council of Three Peoples, where each voice carries equal weight. Where we govern not by conquest or subjugation, but by consensus and mutual respect."

Murmurs rippled through the crowd. Some nodded in approval, while others shifted uncomfortably. Change, even necessary change, never came easily.

"Krella Bloodfury," Decklan called, extending his hand. "Step forward."

She moved with warrior's grace into the circle, her chin lifted proudly. Their eyes met, a lifetime of shared memories passing between them in that glance.

"The Shieldbearer Clan requires a leader who understands that true strength lies not in domination but in protection. Who sees clearly that we are strongest when defending what matters most." His voice softened slightly. "I have seen you stand against overwhelming odds to protect your people. I have witnessed your courage and your wisdom."

"I, Decklan Stormshield, son of Kargoth, formally renounce my claim to leadership of the Shieldbearer Clan and recognize Krella Bloodfury as rightful Chieftain."

From a wooden box brought forward by Elder Varkus, Decklan withdrew a newly forged chieftain's shield. Unlike the traditional Shieldbearer shield, this one incorporated subtle elements that reflected their new alliance—the shield's rim etched with patterns that evoked both human craftsmanship and Moongazer symbolism.

He offered the shield, Krella closing her fingers around it.

"May you bear this shield in honor, as my father would have wished for the one who leads our people."

Krella's eyes shimmered with emotion, but her voice remained strong. "I accept this burden and this honor. The Shieldbearers will stand as protectors, not conquerors." She raised the shield high. "Let all witness!"

The Shieldbearers among the crowd pounded their fists against their chests in acknowledgment, the sound like distant thunder.

Elder Varkus stepped forward. "The council of elders recognizes Krella Bloodfury as Chieftain." He turned to Decklan. "And what of you, son of Kargoth? What path does the half-blood of prophecy follow?"

Decklan took a deep breath, his silver traceries gleaming in the morning light. "The path I was born to walk." He retrieved his staff from the center of the circle, feeling its weight, not as burden, but as purpose.

"Viviana the Life Weaver has marked me as her own." He gestured to the silver lines across his skin. "The warrior I was has died so that the healer I am meant to be can live. I will serve not one people but all, bridging the divides between us."

Whispers swept through the crowd. Some of the older warriors frowned, while several Moongazer elders nodded in approval. From the human contingent came uncertain murmurs.

"I have been called to undertake a sacred pilgrimage," Decklan announced, his voice resonating with newfound purpose as the silver traceries on his skin pulsed with gentle light. "Viviana has shown me a path that winds through the territories of all our peoples, a journey of healing and reconciliation."

He turned slowly, meeting the eyes of each faction gathered before him.

"To the Shieldbearers, I shall bring back the wisdom of how strength and protection can serve harmony rather than dominance, as my father ultimately discovered."

"To the Moongazers, I will return with knowledge of the healing arts, to strengthen your warriors in ways beyond blade and shield."

"To the humans of Riverstone and beyond, I promise to forge a deeper understanding between worlds that have for too long viewed each other with suspicion and fear."

Decklan touched the silver markings that traced across his forearms, their glow intensifying beneath his fingers. "This is Viviana's charge to me, not to build walls or claim territory, but to walk between realms as her emissary. Where I pass, healing will follow. What once was divided may find wholeness again."

Decklan raised his staff, and the crystal at its apex caught the light, casting a three-colored glow across the stone circle, amber like Calanthir, silver like Harmony, and a deep purple like Morvak, the three moons that had aligned during the ritual.

"The prophecy spoke of divided blood that would either unite or destroy. I have made my choice." His voice carried conviction now, resonating with a power that seemed to come not just from him but through him. "I choose unity. I choose healing. I choose to be the bridge, not the breaker."

Elder Lyara of the Moongazers stepped forward. "The wisdom of Viviana flows through you now. We recognize you as her chosen, neither Shieldbearer nor Moongazer alone, but something new."

Harran of Riverstone spoke next. "The humans of the eastern territories acknowledge your role as mediator between our peoples. May your sanctuary stand as testament to what we can build together."

Krella raised her voice, strong and clear. "The Shieldbearer Clan honors your sacrifice, Decklan Stormshield. Where you lead in healing, we will follow in protection." She paused, her eyes meeting his with unspoken emotion. "Your father's shield was broken, but its purpose lives on in both of us."

A murmur of approval spread through the gathering, though Decklan noted pockets of resistance—warriors who clutched their weapons tighter, elders whose expressions remained skeptical. Peace would not come in a single day.

"Let the Council of Three meet for the first time," Elder Varkus announced. "Let the boundaries of our new alliance be decided in wisdom, not in blood."

As the formal ceremony transitioned to the council meeting, Decklan stepped back. This part was not for him. He was no longer a leader of the Shieldbearers but something different. Something new.

Grom approached, clasping his arm in the warrior's greeting that had been part of their lives since childhood. "So you're to be a healer now," he said, his tone light but his eyes serious. "Strange paths we walk, blood-brother."

"All the stranger for walking them together," Decklan replied.

"Not so together anymore," Grom said, glancing toward Krella who now sat in council with the other leaders. "She's asked me to serve as her second."

Decklan felt a swell of pride. "She chose well. There's no one I'd rather see guarding her back."

An awkward silence fell between them, filled with unspoken words. Finally, Grom spoke. "Will you visit? The camp won't be the same without you challenging me to sparring matches."

"I'll visit," Decklan promised. "Though I suspect my sparring days are behind me."

Grom snorted. "A healer who can't defend himself won't last long in these territories. Besides," his eyes twinkled with familiar mischief, "I still owe you a broken nose from that tournament."

Decklan laughed, feeling the weight of the past weeks lighten. Some things would change, but not everything.

As the day progressed, the council deliberated while Decklan moved among the gathered peoples. No longer constrained by the boundaries of clan or race, he spoke with Shieldbearers, Moongazers, and humans alike. Some approached with reverence, others with curiosity, a few with lingering suspicion. To each, he offered the same quiet attention.

By late afternoon, the council emerged from their deliberations. Boundaries had been redrawn, hunting territories established, and trade agreements formalized. The details would take weeks to implement fully, but the foundation was laid.

As twilight approached, Decklan sought out Gar'zul. The former shaman sat alone at the edge of the gathering, his once-proud shoulders now slumped beneath a simple robe stripped of shamanic symbols.

"You wished to speak with me," Decklan said, settling beside him.

Gar'zul nodded, his eyes fixed on the distant mountains. "I would offer excuses, but they would change nothing. I feared what the prophecy meant. I feared change." He turned weathered hands palms-up. "In trying to prevent destruction, I invited it."

"My father's death was not your intention," Decklan said quietly.

"Yet it came by my hand." Gar'zul's voice cracked. "I betrayed my chieftain, my clan... my son."

Decklan studied the man who had once loomed so large in his childhood. "The council has stripped you of your position, not your knowledge. There will be a place for you in what we build."

"I deserve exile," Gar'zul whispered.

"Perhaps," Decklan agreed. "But healing requires all voices, even those who once chose wrongly." He touched the silver traceries on his arm. "Especially those."

Later, as the three moons rose in their separate paths across the night sky, Decklan found Krella standing alone on the bluff that overlooked the valley. She had removed the ceremonial armor, now dressed in the simple leathers of a Shieldbearer warrior, though the chieftain's emblem still adorned her shoulder.

"Chieftain Bloodfury," Decklan said softly as he approached, a hint of playfulness in his tone.

Krella turned, her silhouette strong against the moonlight. "Healer Stormshield," she replied with the same mixture of formality and familiarity.

They stood in silence for a moment, watching as the three moons cast their different lights across the valley. Below, the fires of the gathered peoples twinkled like earthbound stars.

"I never thanked you," Decklan said finally. "For believing in me when I couldn't believe in myself."

"You would have done the same for me," Krella answered simply.

"Would I?" Decklan mused. "I was so lost in what I thought I should be, I couldn't see what was in front of me."

The silver traceries on his skin caught the moonlight, glimmering faintly. Krella reached out, her fingers hovering just above them before gently tracing one of the lines that curved along his forearm.

"Do they hurt?" she asked, her voice softer than he'd ever heard it.

"No," Decklan said. "Not anymore." He caught her hand before she could withdraw it, holding it against his skin where the warm pulse of Viviana's magic glowed beneath.

For a moment, they stood frozen in the intimate gesture, the space between them electric with unspoken words. The moons cast their triple shadows across the valley below, merging and separating like the paths of their lives.

"You could have been chieftain, you know," Krella finally whispered, her eyes meeting his. "After what you did at the ritual site, even the most traditional warriors would have followed you."

Decklan shook his head, taking a half-step closer. "I found my purpose, Krella. Just as you found yours." His free hand rose to her face, fingers brushing the ceremonial mark of leadership that now adorned her cheek. "But there's something I haven't found the courage to say, even when facing death itself."

Her breath caught, eyes widening slightly.

"I love you," he said simply. "I think I always have. Through every sparring match, every argument, every time you pushed me to be better than I was."

"Decklan..." she began, voice uncharacteristically unsteady.

Krella's warrior composure broke into a fierce smile. "You always did talk too much," she said, and pulled him toward her. Their lips met with the passion of years of restraint finally broken, gentle yet hungry, familiar yet new. The silver traceries on Decklan's skin flared briefly, casting them both in ethereal light beneath the three watching moons.

When they finally parted, Krella's eyes shimmered with emotions rarely revealed. "I love you too," she said, "stubborn half-bl—" She stopped herself with a smile. "Stubborn healer. Now I worry about you since Reyn and Vexxa are still out there. The prophecy may not be finished."

"You're right," Decklan acknowledged, his gaze drawn to the dark moon Morvak hanging low on the horizon. "This peace we've built is fragile. Reyn won't abandon her ambitions so easily."

Krella's eyes met his, concern etched in her features. "We'll need to be vigilant. The Bloodfist clan still follows Snarlgar, and there are those among all our peoples who resist this new alliance."

"Which is why what we build must be stronger than what divides us," Decklan said. He reached up to touch the shield emblem at his neck. "My father understood this at the end, I think. That the greatest shield isn't forged of metal, but of bonds between people."

"Are you going to speak in riddles now that you're a healer?" Krella asked, the hint of a smile playing at her lips.

"Only on ceremonial occasions," Decklan promised, returning her smile. "The rest of the time, I'll be the same stubborn half-blood you've always known."

"Not half," Krella corrected him, her voice softening. "Whole. Just... differently whole than the rest of us."

The silence between them grew weighted with things unsaid, paths diverging yet somehow still connected. And as the last of the embers faded, they knew that the true work had just begun, a labor of unity and healing that would define their future.

EPILOGUE: THE WANDERER'S PATH

T wilight settled over the rolling hills as Decklan made his camp beneath an ancient oak. His first day as a wandering healer had been quiet, a blessing after the chaos of recent weeks. He'd walked the boundary between Shieldbearer and human lands, familiarizing himself with paths that hadn't been freely traveled in generations.

After arranging a small circle of stones, he kindled a modest fire, then settled his father's shield emblem before him. The silver traceries on his skin caught the firelight, glimmering like moonlit streams across his bronze flesh.

"Father," he whispered to the darkness, "I hope I've made you proud."

When the fire burned down to embers, Decklan knelt on the soft earth. He closed his eyes and began the meditative breathing his mother had taught him years ago, combining it with the rhythmic chanting of Shieldbearer prayer. The dual traditions no longer felt at odds within him; they flowed together as naturally as two streams joining to form a river.

"Viviana," he whispered, "guide my path."

The world around him gradually faded, the chirping insects, the rustling leaves, the cool night air, all dissolved into stillness. When Decklan opened his eyes, he knelt in an inch of crystalline water that stretched endlessly in all directions, reflecting a star-filled sky above. Before him stood Viviana, radiant and ethereal, her form shifting between solid and translucent like morning mist.

"You have embraced your purpose, Divided Blood," she said, her voice like distant chimes. "But your journey has only begun."

Decklan bowed his head. "I will serve as you guide me."

"The prophecy of the half-blood is bigger than just uniting the orcs," Viviana whispered, her words sending ripples across the water's surface. "The divisions between peoples run deeper than you yet know."

She moved closer, her light illuminating the silver traceries on his skin, making them pulse with gentle power.

"Your first mission is to bring healing to the people of Lunara and lead others to worship me," she continued. "Many have forgotten the way of balance between the forces of light and darkness."

The water beneath Decklan rippled outward from where he knelt, carrying images of suffering people, human, orc, dwarf, and elf, ravaged by wounds that seemed to fester with the same darkness he'd seen in Vexxa's magic.

"Pray each morning as the sun rises," Viviana instructed. "I will grant you a small number of miracles that will grow with your devotion. These gifts will not be as powerful as what you channeled during the ritual, but they will strengthen as your connection to me deepens."

She reached forward, her fingertips brushing his forehead. The silver traceries on his skin illuminated briefly, then settled into a steady, subtle glow.

"You must also continue to learn traditional healing methods," she said, her voice growing fainter. "The herbs, the bandages, the splints, these are the foundations upon which greater healing is built. Magic without wisdom is as dangerous as a blade without restraint."

Decklan felt the water growing shallower beneath his knees, the vision beginning to fade.

"There are others like you, Divided Blood, bridges between worlds. You will find them, or they will find you, when the time comes."

"I vow my life to your service," Decklan said, the words emerging from some place deeper than thought. "To heal rather than harm, to unite rather than divide."

As the vision dissolved around him, Viviana's final words echoed across the fading waters: "Remember, Decklan Stormshield, the shield's true strength lies not in what it keeps out, but in what it protects within."

Decklan opened his eyes to find himself back beneath the ancient oak, the fire now reduced to glowing coals. But something had changed. The shield emblem resting before him shimmered with a faint silver light, and when he touched it, he felt a warmth that seemed to flow into his fingertips and spread throughout his body.

In the distance, a wolf howled at the three moons, still unusually close in the night sky despite having passed their perfect alignment. Their light cast three distinct shadows behind each tree and stone, a reminder that the world remained in a time of transition.

AFTERWORD

Thank you for reading *Burden of Blood*. This book has been a long time coming, a seed planted in my mind way back in the early 1990s. It all began during high school, playing Dungeons & Dragons with my brothers, Luke and Joe, and our friend, Steve Carey. That's when the character of Decklan first started to take shape in my imagination.

In 2020, the pandemic offered an unexpected opportunity. I managed to get some family members interested in playing Dungeons & Dragons online, and I began to meticulously write down all the lore and adventures I'd envisioned over three decades of thinking about Dungeons and Dragons campaigns. Though that particular game didn't fully materialize, all that world-building wasn't in vain. I've taken everything I created for that adventure, and it will serve as the foundation for my upcoming book series. *Burden of Blood* is, in essence, my high school character's origin story. Now, the real adventure can truly begin.

This book is my first foray into publishing, and I've poured a lot of myself into it. As a self-published author, every error you might find is solely my own, and I welcome any feedback you're willing to share to help me grow as a writer.

I sincerely hope *Burden of Blood* has provided a clear explanation of how a half-orc, raised within a clan dedicated to gods of war, ultimately found his path as a healing priest.

I'm incredibly grateful to my wife, Lisa, for providing me with the space and encouragement to be creative. And to everyone who showed interest in playing

Dungeons & Dragons with me, even if we never completed a campaign—thank you.

Finally, a heartfelt thank you to you, the reader, for embarking on this journey with Decklan. I am excited to introduce you to more of the world of Lunara and all of the interesting characters and places in it. I'll be posting updates and insights on my TikTok at @author-zach. You can also discover more about the intricate world of Lunara at lunarasaga.com.

www.ingramcontent.com/pod-product-compliance
Lightning Source LLC
Chambersburg PA
CBHW020125120726
47903CB00007B/2107